Justine Elyot's kinky take on erotica has been widely anthologised in *Black Lace*'s themed collections and in the most popular online sites.

She lives by the sea.

Praise for Justine Elyot

'If you are looking for strings-free erotica, and not for deep romance, *On Demand* is just the book . . . Indulgent and titillating, *On Demand* is like a tonic for your imagination. The writing is witty, the personal and sexual quirks of the characters entertaining'
Lara Kairos

'Did I mention that every chapter is highly charged with eroticism, BDSM, D/s, and almost every fantasy you can imagine? If you don't get turned on by at least one of these fantasies, there is no hope for you'
Manic Readers

'. . . a rip-roaring, rollercoaster ride of sexual indulgence; eloquently written, at times shocking, and always entertaining'
Ms Love's Books

Also by Justine Elyot:

On Demand

Justine Elyot

Seven Scarlet Tales

BLACK
LACE

1 3 5 7 9 10 8 6 4 2

First published in 2013 by Black Lace, an imprint of Ebury Publishing
A Random House Group Company

The Random House Group Limited Reg. No. 954009

Addresses for companies within the Random House Group can be
found at: www.randomhouse.co.uk

A CIP catalogue record for this book is
available from the British Library

The Random House Group Limited supports The Forest Stewardship
Council® (FSC®), the leading international forest certification
organisation. Our books carrying the FSC label are printed on FSC®
certified paper. FSC is the only forest certification scheme supported by
the leading environmental organisations, including Greenpeace.
Our paper procurement policy can be found at:
www.randomhouse.co.uk/environment

Printed and bound by CPI Group (UK) Ltd, Croydon, CR0 4YY

ISBN 9780352347305

For everyone who understands.

Practical Criticism

'All right, Miss Vanessi. You asked for it and you're going to get it.'

Leo couldn't fail me now, and he was encouragingly forceful when he grabbed my wrist and dragged me to the bench, stage-right. I'd told him over and over, 'Do it for real. Don't hold back. Put your arm into it.'

At first rehearsals, he'd been reluctant, laughing and abandoning the endeavour halfway through, when he could even be persuaded to lay a hand on me.

'I can't do this, Callie. It's not as if you really slap my face or anything in the bit before. It just seems . . . wrong. Assault, like.'

'It's not assault if I ask you to do it,' I said, upright again in the middle of the hall while the rest of the company watched us, agog. 'I have a reason for this. I think it'll win us the contest. Trust me.'

Leo didn't understand how smacking my bum on stage was going to win us the Amateur All-Comers trophy, and neither did anyone else, but it wasn't their place to question the actor-director, and so they didn't.

'God, Petruchio's such a bastard,' drawled my Bianca the day Leo finally got his act together and gave me more than a limp-wristed hand-flap on the seat of my jeans.

'We're not playing this for PC points,' I reminded her. 'The whole premise is dodgy as fuck from the outset. Taming a shrew, for God's sake. And why a shrew, anyway? Shrews are cute.'

Bianca, whose real name was Louise, laughed.

'I know. They'd make good pets. It's just hard to feel comfortable with it. Basically, he's an emotional abuser.'

I sighed.

'I know. But let's just concentrate on getting the musical numbers together, shall we? Then we can write a sequel in which Petruchio gets a good kick in the nads.'

'Soprano solo, nice.'

That was the fourth or fifth rehearsal. Leo had taken hold of me around my waist and bent me over his lap.

'No, that was like a guy stepping up to waltz with his lady love,' I said. 'I'm going to fight you. You have to use force.'

Leo looked as if he might burst into tears.

'I feel like such a twat, though,' he said.

'Welcome to acting.'

He huffed and puffed for a bit but his next attempt was so much better.

I looked at the little row of fingermarks on my upper arm that night in bed and pushed my thumb tip into the bruises. The tiny nag of pain was piquant and sweet, reminding me of the transient glow Leo's hand had brought to my bottom.

I brought out again my application details for the competition, with the fulsome foreword by the judge and patron. Peregrine Sands had the sort of face that mocked you, even in repose. Take a look at yourself, you despicable creature, it seemed to say. Don't insult me with your scrutiny until you can smoke a cigarette as contemptuously as I can.

'Say what you like,' I whispered to his curling lip. 'You are going to give me this prize. Because I know about you.'

The weeks passed, subsumed in rehearsal and publicity and fine-tuning. Leo's hand got harder and harder, and he learned to leave his liberal conscience in the dressing room.

When the night of the performance came, Louise and I shared a nip of Dutch courage in front of the lightbulb-mirror, lacing each other's stays good and tight.

'I couldn't do what you're doing,' she said.

'What? Play this role? Direct this show?'

'No, I mean . . . that scene.'

'What, the spanking scene?'

'Yes. In front of everyone, on stage. Don't you find it embarrassing?'

'Not really. It's acting, isn't it?'

I kept my tone brisk and light, and changed the subject immediately afterwards. But secretly her words had given me a between-the-legs thrill. She was embarrassed for me. She, and everyone else, thought that I was being publicly humiliated.

Well, guess why we're doing *Kiss Me, Kate* and not *Mary Poppins* . . .

I stood in the wings watching the first number, 'Another Op'nin', Another Show', trying my level best to work out where Peregrine Sands might be sitting. He was here, wasn't he? Supposing he was delayed, or ill, and hadn't turned up? All my careful calculations would come to nothing.

But I saw him at last, midway through the third row, his suit sharp, his legs crossed, a notebook balanced on his knee. Nothing could be gleaned from his face, which was impassive, but his fingers occasionally tapped at the velvet arm rest, in rhythm with the number.

He was here. It was going to work. I could stop worrying and throw myself into the performance until, much more quickly than I expected, *that scene* came up.

Leo looked good in tights. He had powerful thighs and the kind of full, shapely calves that were so fashionable in eras past. We sparred all over the stage, verbally at first, and then I took my faux-swings at him until he spoke the fateful words. I had been asking for it, and I was going to get it.

I twirled out of his way but he caught my arm in the exact iron-clamp grip that I'd been goading him towards all these weeks and dragged me across to the bench. When I turned my feet inward, so he had to haul me bodily, he didn't let up the pressure but played his part with utter conviction. If I got hurt, it was my own fault. I'd told him so often that he'd finally internalised it.

I let my fists fly and my feet scissor-kick when he yanked me over his lap on the bench. He did everything I'd taught him. He took my wrists in one hand and twisted them into the small of my back. He clamped my ankles between his. He got me helpless and restrained and then he raised his arm and brought his palm down flat and hard on the seat of my skirts.

I was wearing petticoats so it didn't hurt particularly, even though he was giving it his all, but the sound was fantastic, echoing out into the auditorium like gunshots. I overacted the outrage and pain, trying to remember what a normal person would do in this situation. I had to work hard to disguise my enjoyment, though.

While he whaled away on my behind and the safety curtain rolled slowly down, I was feeling the smart, and I couldn't help looking out towards Peregrine Sands, to see if his expression had broken its stern mould, while I gasped and struggled under Leo's hand. It hadn't, but that didn't necessarily mean anything.

I probably shouldn't have looked at him.

Perhaps that was a mistake.

The curtain fell and Leo held his hands to his chest and muttered, 'You OK, Cal?'

'That was bloody brilliant,' I said, crawling forward off his lap. 'The business. Thank you for keeping it real, darling.'

'It's so weird, though,' he said, helping me to my feet. 'I keep worrying that I might get arrested, or something.'

I tapped his cheek, smiling into his anxious brown eyes.

'You can't get arrested for acting,' I said.

'Yes, you can.'

'Don't worry.'

At the after-party, I longed for Sands to show his face, but he didn't. I questioned everyone I knew in the audience about his reactions and any remarks he might have made, but apparently he'd sat in silence, spoken to nobody and left as soon as the curtain fell.

I got a bit drunk and flirted with Leo.

'You're not one of nature's doms, then?' I said.

'One of what?'

'Oh, never mind. What's this?'

The theatre manager had appeared at my elbow.

'This was handed in at the stage door for you.'

It was an envelope. I opened it to find a postcard. The picture on the front was a rather artistically framed shot of a man's hand closed around the top of a riding crop. On the back, in jagged black ink, was written: 'You, Ms Reddish, are a very bad girl. Your come-uppance awaits.'

'What's it say?' Leo peered over my shoulder, but I had dropped it straight away into my handbag.

'Nothing. I'm just going to the ladies'.'

I stood against the cubicle wall with my heart pounding. Who was it from?

Every cell of me wanted it to be Peregrine Sands. But the chances were that it was just some perv in the audience who'd come for the spanking scene alone.

It was a nice picture, but I should disregard it. *Kiss Me, Kate* was bound to throw up a few oddballs. And I was the oddest of them all, probably.

I took the postcard from my bag three weeks later at the awards ceremony and perused it under the table while the others necked back champagne and star-spotted.

We had performed our number from the show, and now we had to sit through all the others, waiting for the results to be announced.

Peregrine, I understood, did not like to be seen at this event until he stepped forward to confer triumph or disaster, but he had to be somewhere backstage. Perhaps he was watching us all from some spyhole. I adjusted my figure-hugging, sequinned evening gown, just in case.

I thought about the gamble I had taken and my reasons for doing so.

I knew about Peregrine Sands.

I knew because a friend of mine called Emma, a professional actress, had a little sideline when she was 'resting'.

'It's not prostitution,' she told me. 'It's just a little bit of role-play.'

'So they don't get to have sex with you?'

'Well . . .' Her eyes shifted off to the left. 'You can if you *want* to. But you don't *have* to. And if you want to have sex, and the person isn't paying, then it isn't prostitution, right?'

'Right. So. Tell me about this place again. The Geisha Garden.'

'We're not really geishas, obviously. None of us is Japanese. We just kneel on this mat in this Japanesey-looking nightclub, wearing not very much, and pour tea and stuff.'

'For men.'

'Yeah. We just, sort of, serve them. And they can ask us to do anything they like and we have to do it. Like we have to get into different poses, do a little dance or whatever. And, if they can afford it and they fancy it, they can pick one of us to . . . spank.'

'They pay to spank you?'

'They pay the manager. It's a hundred quid for five minutes. They can pay extra if they want to use implements.'

'What if it's too much? Too painful?'

'You can take time out, or ask them to continue with another girl.'

'Wow.'

'We all want to get chosen for the spanking. Because we get to go off shift as soon as it's over. If you're the first girl chosen, in theory you get paid a six-hour rate for twenty minutes' work. Not bad.'

'But there's no sex?'

'There's a strict no-touching rule. Except for the spanking. If they want sex afterwards, they can put a note with their phone number in your stocking top. It's up to you to call them, and meet up outside the club.'

'Have you ever done that?'

'Now and again.'

'Wow.'

This had made my imagination click wide open. I wanted to see it for myself, rather badly.

'Do you ever get women customers?'

'Hardly ever. Nearly all men. Quite wealthy men, because it's expensive and the girls are all gorgeous.'

'And you all serve one man at a time?'

'They get to take a look at us all, see us in action, if you like, when they come in. The punter chooses his favourite for the spanking. If he can afford it. Otherwise, he just pays for drinks until he gets bored or runs out of cash.'

'So is it all businessmen from out of town?'

'Mainly. There are some regular customers. Some are friends of Allyson – the manager. If you swear, cross your heart and hope to die, not to tell a soul, I could give you a couple of names.'

We started whispering, even though we were alone in my flat.

'Peregrine Sands,' she said.

'The critic?'

'Yeah, him.'

This was interesting news. Peregrine Sands, the man for whom the phrase 'coruscating wit' seemed to have been invented. The man all those called by the dramatic muse feared and courted in equal measure. The man who could shut your play in a day or power you to your thousandth performance.

Oh yes. Interesting news indeed.

'And does he . . . pay?' I asked, delicately.

'I don't think he's ever met any of the girls outside the club. But he likes what goes on inside it. He likes it very much.'

'I guess he'd give it a rave review.'

'Hell, yes, honey, five stars.'

I had just placed my entry for the competition. Initially, I'd been considering something modish and stark, but now my choice seemed clear. I'd go retro. Spanktastically so.

Still, there was no guarantee that my cunning plan would pay off. Certain of Peregrine Sands' switches might be tripped by a good old spanking scene, but I didn't know that his critical faculties would follow suit, and we had some stiff competition out there.

I watched the stiff competition parade across the stage in sequence, including Denny and Roger and our guys singing 'Brush Up Your Shakespeare'. I had chosen not to perform tonight.

Finally, the last spangle-clad butt waggled offstage and we all waited, breath bated, for the master of ceremonies to make his grand entrance.

I could never quite decide whether or not I fancied him. He was attractive in a pale, wasted sort of way. There was a languor about him that I think he affected in order to disguise his venomous core.

He took to the stage, commanding it without doing anything at all – an enviable talent – and stood at the lectern, waiting for pin-drop hush before launching into a lecture.

His words of appreciation on the subject of am-dram were pithy and scintillating and I felt quite touched that he didn't save his best lines for the professionals and give us some of his second-rate stuff.

A couple of times, he glanced towards me, eyes flashing like silver blades, piercing my abdomen and spreading a pool of warmth inside.

By the time he made the announcement, I had decided. I did fancy him. Quite a lot. I especially fancied his voice, which was clipped and authoritative, in the manner of a

1950s Movietone News broadcast. It pleased me that people still talked like that. It pleased me even more to imagine him calling me a very bad girl in those tones.

He didn't call me a very bad girl, though. He called me a winner.

We had won.

The applause caught me by surprise and for a moment I couldn't stand up, my knees seeming to have deserted my legs.

I went up to the stage and stood in his orbit, accepting the statuette and the envelope containing a cheque for ten thousand pounds to put towards our drama club funds. I shook his hand and thanked him profusely and made a silly speech full of names and the word 'lovely', but I didn't once look him full in the face.

Then I was back at my table and he wasn't there any more.

It had worked. My plan had worked. And I supposed that was that.

Until I looked inside the envelope.

There was more than a cheque in there.

There was a postcard, the twin of the one that had been delivered to my dressing room after the performance.

And in the same handwriting was written a message:

'Come-uppance time, Ms Reddish. If you want my honest critique of your performance, meet me in the prop room in one hour.'

'What's that?' Leo tried to peek over my shoulder but I returned the card swiftly to the envelope.

'Nothing, just a compliment slip.'

'You're blushing. You never blush. What is it?'

'Nothing, I'm just flushed with success. That's all.'

He laughed and put his big hand on my knee.

'Want to celebrate somewhere more private later?' he whispered.

'Leo!'

I was astonished. I had no idea the big lummox of a boy was remotely interested. He was handsome in a fresh-faced farmboy kind of way and a lot of the girls – and some of the boys – were after him, but we had started to assume that he was in the closet.

'Sorry. Sorry. That was inappropriate,' he said, withdrawing his hand as if I'd stung him. 'Too much champagne. Forget it.'

'Hey, it's OK,' I soothed. 'No harm done. I just didn't know you cared, that's all. Thanks. I'm, uh, flattered.'

'God,' he groaned. 'Flattered. That's the ego-killer, right there.'

'Oh, for pity's sake, don't sulk. Just dust yourself off like a big boy.'

'You don't have to patronise me, Callie. I am a grown man.'

'Some might say overgrown.'

He looked at me with eyes like a hurt cow, then turned back to his champagne glass. Somewhere in the bubbles, the word 'bitch' might have been uttered.

I didn't have time for rejected drama queens, though. I had my meeting with Peregrine Sands to plan. There was no question of my not going. I had to see him and find out what he had to say. And do.

'To be honest,' I said, rising to my feet and addressing the table, 'I'm bushed. I think I'm going to leave early, and let the victory feeling sink in, before I end up too drunk to remember.'

There were protests, and entreaties to stay, but I brushed

them off and left the room, intent on slipping into the backstage area.

It was easy enough. I found the ladies' toilets and lurked in there, perfecting my maquillage while I ran through fifty mental scenarios of what might happen next.

Was I going to get spanked? Was I? Really? And by Peregrine Sands?

According to Emma, he was a master of the art. She had had the privilege of baring her bottom to his learned palm, and the lesson imparted had been unforgettable. Or so she said – she was prone to exaggeration, like most of us.

I contemplated being late. If I wasn't already due an appointment under his hand, I certainly would be then. On the other . . . hand, I didn't want to overegg the pudding. I had a feeling Peregrine Sands didn't wait for anyone.

The props store was located in the lowest basement room of the theatre, and it took me a little while to find the right combination of staircases and doors, so it was just as well I hadn't lingered too long over my lipstick.

When I pushed at the door, I tried to make as little noise as possible. I wanted to get my bearings before I got his attention.

The room, which was large and low-ceilinged, was in darkness. I could make out the shapes of huge backdrops used in past productions. Forests, by the look of them, and the turrets of a castle. Looming less, but still just about visible, were all kinds of strange-shaped objects and furnishings, plus a pony trap, minus the pony.

A little unnerved, I thought he must have changed his mind, and I considered turning back.

'Hello,' I said.

With an accompanying click, light flooded the room,

causing me to blink and look wildly around. I still couldn't see anyone.

'Mr Sands? Sir?'

That was a flash of inspiration, it seemed, for he stepped out from inside a large wardrobe, instantly made flesh.

I bit my lip to stop myself from grinning. This was utter madness, but I was desperate to know what was going to happen next.

'You used the magic invocation,' he said. He crooked his finger at me, beckoning. 'Come here.'

My sequinned gown swept through the dust.

When I was about a foot away from him, he put out a hand to stop me.

'I want to look at you,' he said.

This suited me, because I wanted to look at him.

Up close, he looked younger than he did on television and in the papers, but at the same time he had more wrinkles, at the corners of his eyes and mouth. This was a good sign – he must smile more than one ever noticed. Or perhaps it was just the legendary chain-smoking.

He wasn't smoking now, though. He was thinner in real life, too. He was of the type you might call 'elegantly wasted'; beautifully dressed with ruthlessly neat hair and bright, shrewd blue eyes.

Those same bright, shrewd blue eyes bore into me while I stood, chin up, looking as bold as I dared, waiting for the next thing.

His fingers brushed my shoulders. They were tinder-dry and I could see the yellow smoker's tinge on the inside of his left index finger. They left a trail of delicious sparks behind them, moving slowly across my exposed collarbone, then up the centre of my neck, to the soft underside of my chin.

He prodded it higher, straining the back of my neck, making me look directly up at him.

'Caroline Reddish,' he intoned.

'My friends call me Callie.'

'I'm not your friend.' He smiled, a thing of cruelty and sex. It made me smile back.

'I know,' I said, my voice as smoky as I could make it.

'Why did you come here?'

'Because you asked me to.'

'No. Why did you come here?'

I swallowed, which wasn't easy with my head tilted so far back.

'I wanted to see what would happen.'

'What were you hoping for?'

'You, well, you offered a, uh, a critique, which I would be very grateful to hear, from the lips of our greatest living theatre critic.'

He laughed, or rather made a 'ha' sound at that, and removed his finger from my chin, and tapped my cheek instead.

'You're a little slyboots, aren't you?' he said. 'I like that. I like to deal with those kinds of tendencies. But first, I have another question for you. Why did you choose to perform *Kiss Me, Kate*?'

'Oh. Well, it's a classic, isn't it? And it plays to all my company's strengths – musical numbers, comedy, drama . . .' I trailed off. He had a look on his face that showed quite clearly that he wasn't buying this line.

'There are plenty of shows that do that,' he said. 'I think you had another, more specific, reason. And I'm going to worm it out of you, believe me, my girl. So you might as well tell me now.'

'I just thought you might like it.' I was speaking in a

shamed whisper for some reason. I felt guilty, a kid caught scrumping apples in the meadow.

'Yes. You thought I might like it. And why did you think that? Have I ever, in any of my columns, expressed the slightest enthusiasm for this kind of thing?'

Well, no, he hadn't. His columns tended to favour the hard-hitting, depth-plumbing type of thing. Light musical comedy was rarely mentioned.

'Well . . . We did win,' I said. 'So I must have got the right idea, from somewhere.'

'Someone,' he pressed.

I couldn't look at him. I turned my face away but he cupped it in his hand and twisted it firmly back.

'OK,' I said. 'I might have heard a rumour.'

He merely flashed his eyes at me, inviting me to go on.

'About you and your, uh, your tastes. Certain specialist tastes. And it made me think of *Kiss Me, Kate*.'

'Delicately put. I need the provenance of this rumour now, please.'

'I don't want to get anyone into trouble.'

'You can name the establishment rather than the employee. I just need confirmation.'

'Oh God. People are going to get into trouble, aren't they?'

'Only people who deserve it, Caroline. People who deserve trouble will get it.'

'I'm sorry, I'm not prepared to say.'

'Sorry, are you?' He looked supremely irritated for a moment, then he took a breath and seemed to change tack. 'Well, we can come back to this. You didn't come here to be investigated, did you?'

'Um, no.'

'You came here, knowing my tastes, having received two provocative messages from me. Certain conclusions have been drawn, Caroline. Am I wrong to draw them?'

I looked around me while I sought a mental escape route. The brightly painted sets lent a surreal air to the situation, as if we were characters in a pantomime. Perhaps we were.

'Not wrong, maybe,' I said.

I looked back at him.

'Are you going to spank me?'

His smile was more guarded this time.

'I think that's what you came here for, isn't it? At least . . .' His long, thin finger drew the outline of my ear. 'I hope so. Of course, it's entirely possible that you only came here to compromise me . . .'

'No,' I said, trying not to sound too 'actor-doing-sincerity'. I always found genuine emotion hard to express since theatre school. 'No, I wouldn't do that. I'm an admirer of yours. I always have been. And there's no more to it than that. Nobody knows I'm here, and I wouldn't tell a soul, I swear.'

'Not even Emma Frayne?'

'Not even her. Oh!'

She was busted, then. Oh well, it couldn't be helped.

'That's good,' he said, giving my earlobe a little tweak. 'Because I set a lot of store by discretion. I wouldn't normally go about things this way. But when I saw you in that scene, oh, Caroline, you convinced me. He was really spanking you, wasn't he? That bronzed, muscular Adonis whose lap you decorated so well. He wasn't holding back, was he?'

'No,' I admitted, my cheeks heating up.

'And that was too perfect,' he said. 'I loathe musical theatre and yet I sat through this performance keeping a tight grip on myself, knowing what to expect and expecting disappointment. A hand that skimmed away just at the point of impact while somebody slapped the bench behind you. You can't imagine how it affected me when I realised you were really being spanked. Because, you know, you can't act a spanking. If it isn't real, it isn't convincing. The faces and the body language are always overacted. I've seen too many pathetic magazine shoots to be taken in any more.'

'It was real, all right. I made Leo do it. He didn't really want to.'

'I think he did. But one must put up the weak protest, for fear of being seen as a monster.'

'Really?'

'Really. Turn around.'

I hesitated then presented him with my rear view. The dress was backless, plunging down to my coccyx in a way that drew attention to the tight, sparkly silk around my hips and bottom.

I gasped when Sands put his hand on the curve of my arse and moulded his palm to its shape.

'Who could resist this?' he said, and his voice was directly in my ear. 'No straight man alive.'

The way he held his hand there was so possessive and so natural that I knew I had gone beyond turning back. A ripple had gone all the way through me, upwards, outwards, downwards, inwards. And most particularly, cuntwards.

I had been excited from the start, but now my wetness was undeniable. My nipples were protruding out from the midnight blue silk and my breath was short and laboured. My body was telling him to do it. Do whatever he wanted. My mind could not summon up the effort to argue with it.

'Did you get hard?' I asked him. 'When you watched me?'

'Of course I bloody did, you little minx.' He pushed his body forwards into mine. He was hard now. I could feel the outline of his erection just under the cheeks of my arse. 'I had to put my programme over my lap. It was fucking inconvenient. I know there are rumours about me, and people would have been watching for my reaction. And you knew that. And believe me, you're going to pay for it.'

'I know I've been bad,' I said, shutting my eyes in rapture. 'I know I've misbehaved.'

'He gave it to you hard, didn't he?'

Sands' breath was hot in my ear, and his lips brushed the tender skin behind it, kissing then nipping.

'Leo? Petruchio. Yes, yes, he did.'

'How did it feel?'

'Even with the petticoats, it stung. He left red marks on my bum. I looked at them in the dressing room afterwards.'

'Mm, I bet you did. Did it turn you on?'

'Yes. I rubbed them. Then I rubbed myself. Lower down.'

'You dirty little bitch.'

'Mmm.' I pushed myself back against him, wriggling my hips.

He took off his jacket and threw it over a wooden painted cloud.

'I think I'd better get the deed done before I end up bending you over and fucking you senseless, Ms Reddish, what do you think?'

'Either way,' I moaned, butting my head into the hollow of his neck.

'That'll do, Miss Sex Mad,' he said primly with a preliminary smack to my bottom. 'Now let's determine the sentence. I want you to take off your dress and stand on that chair over there.'

'Take off my dress?'

'Yes,' he said, so calmly that I started to do it immediately.

The tight-fitting silk with its non-existent back had meant I couldn't wear a bra, so when I pushed the shoulder straps down my arms, my breasts were soon bared to his inspection. He didn't flinch, just watched with avid greed.

'Your nipples are hard,' he said, folding his arms.

I didn't really have an answer for that.

My beautiful sparkly sequins slid to the none-too-clean floor. I didn't stop to consider my nakedness until I'd picked up the gown and folded it neatly on a table. But, that done, I could no longer ignore my sheer stockings, my tiny thong or my bare backside. All of them were on show to Peregrine Sands.

I climbed on to the chair and stood, feeling three times more exposed, on its seat.

'Are you going to review me?' I asked.

'None of your impertinence, madam,' he said. 'But yes. I'm going to give you a review. A long, painful and scathing critique, which will be given not in words but in actions.'

Oh dear. I was for it now.

'Now then,' he said, coming to stand in front of me. His eyes were directly in line with my crotch; what a happy coincidence. 'I need you to give me your own honest assessment of your performance. And I don't mean your performance on stage. I mean the little subterfuge that led you into this position.'

Not sure what he wanted me to say, I shook my head.

'Well, uh, I think it worked out pretty well,' I said. Strange words to speak, when standing naked on a chair, with a man who meant to spank me hard glaring into my pubic region. I'd stand by them, all the same.

'No, that's not what I mean. Of course your little scheme was successful. You won the award and you're about to get your personal prize. I want you to list all the bad things you've done, Ms Reddish, en route to this ignominious position.'

'Oh, I see. Well. I suppose I was a bit sly. Crafty. I used some insider knowledge to nobble the jury. The jury being you. And I—I used dishonest means to get my way.'

'Yes, that about sums it up. Dishonest means to get your way. Is getting your way very important to you, Ms Reddish?'

'Yes. I suppose it is.'

He put a hand on my thigh and patted it. I nearly fell off the chair.

'I understand. I'm the same. I like to get my way. Which of us is about to get it now, I wonder?'

'Maybe both.'

He smiled at that, quite a tender little smile.

'I hope you're right. Spread those feet a little wider. Put your hands behind your back.'

He inspected my parted pussy lips at close quarters, dipping his head so close that his breath warmed the moistened slit. He held me upright – just as well, because I might have collapsed otherwise – with his hands on my inner thighs.

'Wet,' he murmured. 'What a very bad creature you must be. Do you always get this wet when you're about to be spanked?'

'I don't know,' I whispered.

He looked up sharply.

'How can you not know?'

'I've never done it before. Apart from, you know, on stage.'

He took a step back, frowning.

'Turn around,' he said.

I presented my rear view.

'No marks,' he said. 'Your Petruchio can't have tamed you very much. He's left the better part of the job to me. Do you think you can be tamed, Ms Reddish?'

'I doubt it,' I said, suddenly defiant. I wanted the conflict, the tension. I wanted to reprise my stage role and have him overpower me until I had to submit.

'Oh, you doubt it, do you? There's a challenge if ever I heard one. Very well. Kneel down now.'

I did it. The seat of the chair was uncomfortable on my knees but it was good to be able to cling to the back rung.

'This is for your friend Emma,' he said, laconically, 'though I'll be giving her the message in person, as well, make no mistake.'

His hand was at once sharper and harder than Leo's. I think he had it held in a particular way, the palm open but the fingers tight. It was more painful than Leo's fumbling lunges.

I yelped and almost tipped the chair forward, but he put a hand on my shoulder and carried on.

What was this like? Was it what I had expected? It hurt more than I thought it would, the peppery sting spreading across my cheeks. Peregrine never left me a moment to process each stroke, but laid them on quickly, until I was gasping and wriggling around. I held on to the chair, though, my knuckles whitening as the heat built.

'And here's something else for being a little schemer.'

If possible, he began to smack even harder. I was uncomfortable now, itching between my legs and sore above them. I felt my skin tighten under the onslaught. I waggled my feet and jerked out a plea to stop. I didn't want him to stop. I just needed to catch a breath.

'You've bitten off more than you can chew,' he said

dispassionately, holding fire. 'It's not unusual. I've often rendezvoused with girls who promised more than they could deliver. Get your dress on and run along now.'

'No.' My voice ground against my lungs, low and hoarse. 'I can take it. Just not used to it.'

'Are you sure? Because what I just gave you was only a warm-up. You'll find you can bear a bit more, perhaps, now that you're good and hot.'

'I can. I'm sure I can. Give me more.'

'I'm going to try you with my belt. Don't panic. I'll start gently and build up.'

The sound of it, sliding sweetly through the loops, did nothing to stem the flow of juices in my pussy. I squirmed with anticipatory dread.

'This is for your barefaced cheek, madam,' he said.

It was no more than a little flick at first, a localised dart of sting, almost a caress after his mean, hard hand. I sighed with the unexpected pleasure of it and pushed out my bottom for more.

'Yes, you like this, don't you?' he purred.

The next stroke was harder and made a gorgeous splat sound against my skin. I felt the stripe sizzle into a welt. I hoped it would leave a mark.

I hoped my whole bum would be one swollen mass of red stripes when he came to throw down his belt and grab my hips and enter me from behind. But I was getting ahead of myself.

First I needed to live through this whipping. Breathe through it, clench through it, survive it.

The strokes came harder and faster. At first I was almost wild with the relentless pain, but before I could jump away or beg for mercy, something happened, and the heat became sweet instead of fierce.

'You deserve this, don't you?'

'Yes, oh yes. I deserve it.'

I wasn't sure if I was falling into some kind of delirium, but I was convinced I could take this forever. The glow possessing my bottom cheeks was moving inside my body, lighting it up from crown to sole until I felt as if I were made of neon. Horny neon.

I shimmied my hips and pushed my bum out further. He could do his worst. I was never going to be taken to my limit. I didn't seem to have one.

But, of course, I did really, and he found it in the end.

'Please,' I gasped, when the soreness was huge in its magnitude and my skin stretched over my rounded cheeks so tightly I thought it might tear.

'Aha. You've had enough. Well, that was very good, for a beginner.'

I let my shoulders sag, searching for breath. Now he had finished with his belt, I noticed the ache in my knees and I unglued them, one by one, from the seat.

I was trembling. I hadn't realised I was trembling.

'Have you learned your lesson?' he asked.

I nodded.

'Which is?'

Ah, now he was asking. I wasn't sure what the lesson was supposed to be. All I felt I'd really learned was that I enjoyed being whipped with a leather belt.

'I should respect you,' I decided upon.

He liked that a lot.

'Yes,' he said, a smile in his voice. 'You certainly should. Has any other profound epiphany stricken you while you were being struck, as it were?'

'Just that . . .' I floundered for coherent speech. 'I need this.'

'You need it? You have a taste for it?'

'Yes, yes. A taste. That was so different from the way Leo did it. You had so much more purpose. You weren't afraid.'

'You liked it, I can tell. It's very obvious.'

In the air between my thighs, I felt a disturbance – his hand, so close to my lips, which I now understood were slick and juicy.

'Touch me,' I whispered.

His fingers were light and yet firm, somehow, stroking up and down the slit.

'This is part of you, Ms Reddish. This need is in you and you can't ever rid yourself of it.'

'I know,' I moaned, rocking back and forth to encourage his deeper touch.

'But who will be there when you need to be soundly thrashed? Who is going to administer the medicine? I'm a busy man.'

He was: very busy. Especially his fingers.

'I'm happy to oblige when our diaries allow, but I can't always be on hand. With my hand.'

His aforementioned hand was doing sterling work. He rubbed my clit and filled my cunt with fingers that were still warm from their sharp contact with my bottom.

I was writhing like a serpent now, greedy for his masterful manipulations.

'You need someone,' he mused. 'I think I know who, too. Are you close?'

'Who-oo-oo?' I wailed, so very near to that melting moment.

'This young man I see watching us from the doorway,' he said.

I was coming and yet I wasn't coming, trying to stop

myself, unable to stop myself. I jerked upright and yanked my head towards the doorway, my face a rictus of unwanted orgasm.

Leo stood there, looking, frankly, rather terrified.

I gabbled senselessly, still impaled on the elegant digits of Mr Peregrine Sands, notorious theatre critic of the *Universal*. Leo could see exactly where they were, and he could see me, kneeling on a chair with my bottom bright scarlet and swollen with welts, naked and ashamed.

Dear God, what a moment. I still masturbate over it now.

I hid my head in my arms and sobbed out the remnants of my climax.

Sands pulled out his fingers and smacked me smartly on the rump.

'You can't hide, you know,' he said.

Presumably he then turned to Leo and addressed him.

'Well, don't just stand there, man. Come in. Your leading lady has a proposition for you.'

'I don't,' I muttered, but I made no move to stop the scenario from unfolding.

'Me? What's happening here?' Leo's voice was thick, syrupy. He was turned on.

'I hardly think it could be much clearer,' said Sands, dryly. 'Your Katharina here is paying the price for some shrewish behaviour, in a manner Petruchio would approve. You do approve, don't you?'

Leo said nothing for a while, but I surmised that he must have nodded, because Sands said, 'Good.'

'You'll see a more detailed review of the performance in the *Universal* next week,' he continued, 'but I wanted to give you a small, and more focused, critique of your spanking style, if you'd care to hear it.'

'Uh, carry on, by all means.'

'It was rough and ready but with a certain crude effectiveness,' said Sands. 'However, you need to develop more finesse, particularly with your pacing. You also need to take care that you target the fleshier, lower portion of the buttocks rather than aiming too high. Don't go in all guns blazing. You need to take a more considered approach. I'd give you three stars.'

'Three. Thanks.' Leo sounded as bemused as I felt.

'You can improve. A little practice will take you to the required level of expertise. If you like, I can tutor you.'

'Excuse me.' This was enough now. I held myself upright and twisted my neck to glare at them both. 'I am physically present, you know. I am here. And it sounds as if you're making deals that might need my approval.'

'Ms Reddish,' said Sands, coldly. 'You yourself have stated that you need to be spanked. I'm facilitating this for you. I don't think the tone is quite called for.'

'I don't know what to say,' said Leo.

'Don't you want this?' Sands was waspish.

'I do. If she does.'

The ball was in my court. And my court was hot, and so over singles games. I wanted doubles now. Well, of a sort. Obviously I'd be unpartnered.

'What you're saying,' I said slowly, 'is that I can count on either of you for a bit of hanky-spanky fun whenever I fancy it? Is that what you're saying?'

'Precisely. And young Petruchio here has said that he's amenable if you are.'

'M'name's Leo,' he mumbled uncomfortably.

'A lion among men,' said Peregrine. 'Lions shouldn't cower. Come over here and I'll give you a lesson.'

I looked sharply around at Sands. Did he mean to spank me again? The glow was fading now and my bottom didn't hurt much at all, but there was a residual tenderness that might not take kindly to more of the same.

'She's still a little pink from my attentions,' said Sands. 'Both disciplinary and otherwise. But I think she's ready for more.'

'Isn't that for me to say?'

He ignored me.

'She has a sturdy bottom, capable of absorbing a hard session, though you'll need to build up her endurance. I recommend starting with your hand only and moving up to implements when you can't achieve the desired level of discomfort in the same time. Come here and put your hand on her.'

Leo's hand was bigger, brawnier and rougher than Sands' but it felt electric on my cooling flesh. Whatever my mind thought, my body was happy to have him there.

'You must remember to keep the strokes low. Don't go above this imaginary line.'

Sands' finger traced a delicate path across the broadest section of my bum.

'I wish we could draw it on,' said Leo, with a nervous laugh.

'Well, perhaps in the early stages you could.'

'Excuse me,' I said. 'I'm not walking around with magic marker all over my arse.'

'Excuse me,' said Sands, 'nobody asked your opinion.'

I made to rise up, and he back-pedalled.

'But no doubt you can make your own arrangements between yourselves.'

I relaxed again, wanting to know what was going to happen next.

'I hope you're going to behave yourself now, Ms Reddish. You are a very lucky girl. Two men want to address themselves to your rear. Not many women get this opportunity, you know.'

'My night just gets luckier and luckier,' I said.

'Now, then, Leo. Let's see what you're made of.'

Leo's hand landed, not particularly hard and rather clumsily, across the crack of my arse.

'No, stick to the cheeks,' advised Sands. 'You can alternate or you can focus on one at a time. Focusing on one and excluding the other makes for a remarkably uncomfortable experience for your submissive, actually. I only do it when I'm feeling especially cruel.'

Leo began to rain spanks, first on my right cheek and then my left.

'Harder,' said Sands. 'She won't break.'

As Leo grew in confidence, I found myself respecting him anew. He wasn't holding back now, and I liked it. Both liked and hated it, if I'm honest, but that tension was the thing that drove me wild and I wanted to keep it going.

Sands interspersed little nuggets of advice with the strokes.

'Not so high. Yes, you can really see the colour start to deepen now. If you want to go down to the thighs, that's fine. I think the inner thighs and more delicate areas are for the more advanced spanker. Perhaps another time.'

I gasped for breath, sweat prickling on my brow and making me itch. Leo had reawakened every iota of the sting from Sands' previous work. Now it was flaring rapidly through me, relighting the fire between my legs, which seemed to have forgotten all about the relief Sands' fingers had afforded.

I moaned and began to plead.

Leo stopped.

'Is that enough?'

I didn't know if he was asking me or Sands.

We both replied simultaneously.

I said, 'For a start.'

Sands said, 'What do you think?'

Leo pondered for a moment.

'That's a great colour,' he said, then more awkwardly, 'Callie, are you OK?'

'I've forgotten what OK is,' I said. 'I can't even answer. I'm a long way outside anything I thought would ever happen.'

'Follow your desires,' said Sands. 'Don't look to any preconceived schema of what's right or acceptable. You won't find one. This is about doing what you feel. What do you want now?'

'I want your attention. Both of you. On me. On my body.'

'You're a greedy girl, aren't you?' said Sands. 'You deserved that spanking. But I'm sure it can be arranged. Very well. Stand up and take off the rest of your clothes.'

I nearly fell off the chair, but I made it to my feet somehow and looked anxiously over to the door.

'Shouldn't we think about locking that?'

'Why?' said Sands. 'If anyone bothers to come down here – which they won't, having no business to – they'll just see what's what, won't they?'

'What do you mean?'

He stepped closer and whispered into my ear.

'They'll see a very badly behaved young woman behaving very badly, won't they? And getting her just desserts. Getting her dirty, greedy, filthy desserts, on her knees in the dust. Two men going at her. And a sore, bright red bum. I don't think they'll get the wrong idea, will they?'

'No,' I whispered back.

'No,' he reiterated. 'So undress. Or perhaps you'd like Leo here to help you?'

'I'm fine.'

In a kind of trance, I began removing the rest of my clothes. First my stockings, and then my thong. I was shimmering, glittering, glowing.

I looked down at my breasts, noting the swollen state of my nipples. Somebody needed to touch them. Now.

I walked up to Leo and cupped them in invitation.

He understood, and put the pad of one thick finger to my stiff red bud.

I looked over at Sands. This was all about him watching me, for some reason. Watching me and grading me, dispassionately. Something about that turned me on more than I could express.

I imagined his review in my head as events unfolded.

Caroline Reddish was an adequately whorish little piece, bringing flashes of submissive brilliance to her role. The moment when she begged her lover to pinch her nipples is a case in point.

I sucked in my breath, feeling the burn of pain as Leo, with a stunned look on his face, closed his finger and thumb tight.

'Yes,' I whispered, looking again at Sands. 'Hurt me. I need it.'

'Get on your knees and suck him,' said Sands abruptly.

A frustrated director – I knew it!

I obeyed swiftly, wishing the floor wasn't quite so grimy, but then I thought it was fitting and I should get my knees dirty.

'I want to see that slutty mouth wrapped right around his cock,' said Sands.

Leo stood there, motionless, while I unbuttoned his fancy trousers then guided the elastic of his boxers over the swollen cockhead they concealed. I'd always thought he'd be a big boy, and I was on the money, it seemed.

The oral sex scene in the first act gave Ms Reddish an opportunity to use that greedy mouth of hers to stimulating effect. Leo Bradley played strong and silent to the hilt, but the simmering tension beneath was apparent to all.

He jerked his hips forward, eager to get my lips on him. I sucked him down, enjoying the warm bulk when it filled my cheeks and lay on my tongue.

'She's done that before,' commented Sands. 'She's an experienced cocksucker, I'd say.'

Reddish demonstrated ample technique in the art of fellatio, but Bradley didn't allow himself to be bested, taking his co-star by the hair and roughly fucking her face.

He stopped when I began to gag.

'You all right, Cal?'

'She's fine,' said Sands, laconically. 'She likes it rough. Don't you?'

I nodded, mouth still full, but it seemed my performance was destined to be cut short anyway.

'So how are we going to play this, Leo?' Sands wondered aloud. 'She wants fucking, that much is plain. I don't suppose you've double-topped before, have you?'

'Um . . .'

'No, I thought not. Well, what if I direct you and then take her myself afterwards. Would that satisfy all of us? No, don't take his cock out of your mouth, Reddish. You can stay on your knees. I know *you're* going to be satisfied, that much is a given.'

I waited for Leo's verdict, hoping it wouldn't be long in coming. My jaw was starting to ache.

'Direct me?'

'Yes,' said Sands with a trace of impatience. 'You can take direction, can't you?'

I chuckled, the sound coming out like a snuffle around Leo's stiff shaft.

'I suppose.'

'This is one production I'm rather keen to see. Believe me, it beats the dreary Rattigan revival I'm supposed to be reviewing tomorrow. Take your prick out of her mouth now and let her stand up.'

I gave him one last lascivious lick for the road and stumbled to my feet. My knees were ashy grey.

'Sit yourself down on that sofa there, Leo, and have her straddle you. I'd like to watch her little red behind riding to and fro. Little red riding whore.' He laughed at his own joke.

Leo, beyond questioning any of this, shucked off his trousers and boxers and went to sit on the dusty sofa, some kind of chaise longue affair used in an Oscar Wilde comedy perhaps.

I looked over my shoulder at Sands, who offered me a grim nod.

But the star of the show, undoubtedly, is Ms Reddish's rosy, highly spankable arse. I shall hope to see a great deal more of it in the future.

I put my hands on Leo's shoulders and positioned my knees on the buttoned velvet, either side of his thighs.

'You might need one of these.'

Sands prowled up behind me and pressed a foil square into Leo's hand.

A condom.

And now this seemed real, at last, where it had been dreamlike before.

Leo fumbled with the condom while I swayed my hips, putting on a show for Sands.

Once it was on, Sands clapped his hands.

'Now. Fuck her. Hard.'

Leo gripped my hips and jolted me downwards over his cock. Although I was wet and tingling with need, I wasn't quite prepared for the speed of the coupling and I yelped.

'Got you,' he snarled. 'Now you're exactly where you should be.'

'Steady on,' I muttered. 'And don't go thinking this means we're an item. It doesn't.'

He settled straight away into a punishing rhythm. I was in a good position to control some of the movement, but he was just so damn strong that in the end I had to give in and go with it. And besides, that was what Sands was telling us to do.

'Keep at her, man. Don't show her any mercy. Just a good, hard fuck. It's what she wants; you know that.'

Leo pumped and grunted, grunted and pumped. The friction was incredible, building up inside me, spreading heat all over my body. I bent down and pressed my breasts into his upper body, still in its dinner jacket and white tie.

'You just wanted somebody to smack your arse,' gasped Leo. 'Well, I can do that. I'll do it any time you like. And then I'll fuck your pussy raw.'

'Get hold of her bum cheeks,' instructed Sands. I don't know whether he'd heard Leo's words, but I suspected he had. 'That's it. A good handful of those lovely hot buns. Spread them wide for me. I want to see what's between them at the same time as I can see your cock going up inside her.'

'You're a filthy pervert,' I sighed. Just the way I'd always imagined him.

'Yes, I am, and that's why you came here.'

I knew what he was looking at. I knew that that shrewd, piercing, intelligent attention was directed not at the finest drama of our generation, nor at some unfortunate show doomed to close at the end of the week because of his damning notice. No, the gaze of the UK's finest theatre critic was aimed squarely at my exposed anus. I hoped it wasn't a two-star affair or worse.

But I needn't have feared. It didn't seem that I was going to ruin this production in the final scene.

'I bet you've been touched there before,' he said.

My ears were rushing with the force and energy of the fucking, together with Leo's astonished grunts and my own chaotic breath, but I caught the gist all right.

'Yeah,' I gasped, clinging to Leo's shoulders and grinding.

'Often?'

'Enough.'

'Leo, put your finger up her arse.'

I thought about screaming, Don't you dare, but Leo moved a swift fingertip to the target and it was pressed right up against me before I could think.

And when I thought, the only thing that came to mind was: That's so good, so dirty, so wrong, but so good, with Sands watching.

So instead of tighten up or push myself away, I relaxed into the intrusion, letting my cheeks splay and my hips shimmy, trying to match the probing of his finger with that of his cock.

'No, no, lubricate first,' tutted Sands. 'Get some of her juices. I'm sure she isn't short of them.'

I wasn't, it was true, but neither did I want Leo to interrupt what he was doing. I'd had lovers do this very thing at the crucial moment and, while a cock might need a bit of easing in, a finger was not a problem. As long as I could keep from tightening up.

'Just do it,' I muttered to Leo.

'What? Don't?'

'Don't take your finger away. Push it in.'

'Oh, I say!' exclaimed Sands, genuinely impressed.

I had triumphed!

Ms Reddish seals a wonderful performance with a daring anal insertion, performed without prior rehearsal. This breathtaking finale was a testament to the implicit trust between the director and her co-star.

Oh! Bloody hell! Was that what it was?

Had I been hot for Leo, all this time, without knowing it? And did we work so well together that, not to put too fine a point on it, life was now able to mimic art?

These were, as Sands might put it, profound epiphanies to be experiencing with a man's thick, fat finger up one's back passage. I blanked them and surrendered to the moment, gathering in all the sensory data and embracing it tightly. The feeling of occupation inside my bottom, while Leo's finger wriggled and explored, was right at the forefront of everything, inescapably rude. Then there was the pleasure his thrusts and my grinds were building inside me, heading towards zenith. The knowledge that I was being watched as Leo did all this to me – a pair of beady eyes on my scarlet bottom cheeks. A low voice, just out of my earshot, uttering phrases I longed to hear. Was Sands commentating the fuck? Would he type it up in précis and file copy just in time for Monday's edition?

I almost hoped he would.

Then everything happened at once, the words, the watching, the thrust, the grind, the heat, the shame, the headlong helplessness of orgasm.

Sands stopped talking while I sang as lustily as I'd ever performed on the musical stage. Leo's solemn bull-like bass-baritone joined me in a duet.

Harmony.

I laid my forehead on Leo's shoulder, eyes stinging, bones melting.

A round of applause rang out from behind me.

'Excellent. Absolutely excellent. Not perfect, but the potential . . . Well, shall we say I'm looking forward to the next production?'

I didn't want to respond. I wasn't even sure I could move. I lay in this position on top of Leo until he patted my back and shifted, retracting his cock.

'Are you OK?' he whispered, kissing me under my ear.

'Uhhh,' was all I could manage.

'I'd say that shrew was well and truly tamed, wouldn't you, Leo?'

The endorphins tried to hold me back but they didn't quite succeed.

'I beg your pardon?' I snapped, giving him daggers.

'Don't fuss,' he said, laconically. 'Just my little joke.'

'I could take offence at that,' I said.

'Well, then I withdraw it, because that would never do. I want to see a lot more of this dynamic you seem to have with your colleague here. And you have the best new bottom I've discovered in a long time.'

I wasn't sure I should feel flattered, really, but I did.

Leo and I read the review in bed, two days later.

'*Winners' laurels were deservedly bestowed upon the Falstowe Light Opera Company, who managed something of a coup – a production of* Kiss Me, Kate *that offered a fresh and untried approach to the am-dram staple. I hope to see a great deal more of Caroline Reddish, who directed herself in the dual roles of Miss Vanessi and Katharina. If she happens to be playing opposite her theatrical nemesis, Leo Bradley, then so much the better. This is a pairing made in thespian heaven.'*

'Thespian heaven, eh?' I put aside the newspaper and settled down in Leo's arms, looking up at his big, smiling face.

'He talks a lot of bull, doesn't he?'

'But he's the great Peregrine Sands. How can you say that?'

'Do you think he spanks all the people he gives good reviews to?'

'You know, I think maybe he does. Wouldn't that be interesting to know?'

The bedside phone rang and I picked it up.

'Oh, Mr Sands. We were just talking about you. Why, yes, I think drinks at the Geisha Garden would be just lovely. Shall I bring Leo? And Emma can make up a foursome. I look forward to it. Ciao.'

Tea and Ceremony

The Geisha Garden owed very little to traditional Japanese culture, and a great deal to the fact that its owner had been offered a job lot of silk, patterned wallpaper and screens, after an ambitious teriyaki restaurant in the area had gone bankrupt.

In the past, it had been one of Soho's most notorious clip joints, offering a cloudy cider-like beverage it called 'champagne' for a hundred pounds a bottle. 'Offering' is not perhaps the right phrase. 'Forcing upon one with menaces' might be.

When the owner – at least, the man named on the deeds – had been imprisoned, a new 'owner' had appeared on the scene. In fact, the premises had not changed hands at all, both landlords being in the pay of the same Mr Big, but as far as the local police were concerned, the slate was clean and a fresh start could be made.

The fresh start had an ersatz flavour of the Kyoto tea gardens, and sold exactly the same cloudy cider-like beverage under the name of 'sake'.

But there was more to the Geisha Garden than buying a

pretty girl an overpriced drink. In fact, hardly anybody ever bought the sake any more, so no looming toughs in tuxedos had to enforce the purchase. Because now there was a new game in town, and those that liked to play were both welcome and wealthy.

Emma Frayne wasn't sure exactly how Japanese jasmine-scented joss sticks were – surely they were more an Indian thing? – but she lit a few nonetheless, and left them to smoulder, before heading upstairs to change out of her urban-friendly jeans and plaid shirt combo.

In the small, sweaty room with its plasterboard walls and fly-spotted mirrors, she found three of her fellow employees, all in various stages of undress.

'Em!' exclaimed the tallest, a rangy girl in Marks and Sparks matching underwear and nothing else. 'How did you get on with the drama llama last night?'

'Mr Sands?'

Emma's reply was to unbutton her jeans and lower them slowly over her backside, waggling it in her friend's face. The impressed gasps this won her made her smile through the residual pain.

'Oh my God, he used the cane! He actually used the cane. Wow. Can I touch them?'

'Be my guest.'

Emma stood patiently with her back to the room while each of the three women in turn ran their fingertips along the dozen scored welts that crossed her bottom. She hadn't put knickers on and had wondered about the jeans – her baggiest-arsed, most comfortable pair – but a skirt without knickers seemed out of the question on the windy Northern Line she had to use to get here.

All the same, it was a relief to drop them. It was also a

relief that their boss, Allyson, insisted on neat, square-cut fingernails for all Geisha Girls, otherwise this curious inspection of her cane stripes would have been much worse.

They traced the marks like lines of latitude on a map. The Tropic of Cancer crossed the central swell of her buttocks, the longest of the lines, while the equator sat a couple of inches lower, at the low curve that men liked to grab and squeeze. The Tropic of Capricorn lay stingingly and unforgivingly at the very top of her thighs.

'Jeez, these must hurt,' said one of the other girls. 'I hope nobody ever pays to cane me. I think it would kill me.'

'Surely you've told Allyson you won't do the cane?' said Emma, in surprise. 'It is allowed, you know.'

'Oh, you know.' The girl sighed, and retreated to pull on a stocking. 'I was worried she might not hire me if I started dictating terms. I need this job or I'll have to drop out.'

'Yeah, but you like it, right? You applied when you saw the ad on Fetlife? So you're into all this?'

'Yes, yes, I am, I've done it with boyfriends but . . .' The girl's lower lip trembled, and Emma stepped out of her jeans and put an arm around her.

'It's normal to be nervous, your first night,' she whispered. 'But you're perfectly safe. Allyson has cameras in the private booths – she'll know in a second if a girl's being pushed past her limits.'

'Are you sure?'

'Of course I'm sure. She banned the only bloke who ever tried it on with me, for life. But every single other customer has always respected me and gone no further than I've wanted him to. I promise you.'

'I know. I know you're right. And I trust Allyson.'

'There. Come on, get your dress off. I'm really sorry – I

know Al told me when she introduced you, but I've forgotten your name.'

'It's Poppy.'

'That's right! So pretty. The red flower. Could be appropriate.'

They giggled, and Poppy unzipped her shift dress with a little more alacrity. Ridiculously, she'd been nervous of getting naked in front of the other girls.

How pathetic can you get? she thought. You've just taken a job that involves baring your bum for paying gentlemen, and you're scared of something you did countless times in the showers at school. Get a grip, Popster.

Shimmying out of her dress, she listened vaguely to Emma's colourful account of her painful appointment with Mr Sands.

She learned, as she unclipped her bra, that this was a punishment for divulging his identity to a third party.

She distracted herself, on lowering her knickers, from the fact that her neatly trimmed pubic triangle was visible to all by laughing at the reproduced dialogue – Sands' wit, Emma's cheek, all ending with the Geisha Girl in a bent-over posture with her hands clasping her ankles.

'You know the sound the cane makes when they swish it through the air?' said Emma insouciantly.

The other two geishas murmured recognition, suddenly sober, not laughing any more.

Poppy's skin broke into goose pimples. Probably the cold, she thought. Being naked.

She picked up the absurd costume she had been given. No Japanese geisha had ever worn such a thing, she was sure. It might be made of flame-red satin with silver and gold embroidered flowers all over, but it barely skimmed her thighs. She wrapped it around her body, trying hard to make it cover her generous breasts, but it was a stretch at best.

She attempted to cover her little pants of frustration and effort by disguising them as laughs when Emma's story headed towards its high climax. She had a way of telling the tale that made it sound like a fun adventure, but Poppy still feared that length of rattan more than she could say.

'I swear, I thought I'd taken drugs,' Emma said. 'My head had left the planet. I was, like, floating. It wasn't until Drama said, "I will have your attention, young lady"—'

There was a burst of laughter, this being, apparently, a well-known catchphrase of the client in question.

Poppy picked up the wide black sash, modelled on the obi, but far less complicated to put on. No fancy bows to be tied, just a pad of velcro at the back. Looking into the mirror, she frowned at her cleavage, but at least the sash held the gown in place, preventing the threatened nipple-spillage. The hem was still hair-raising though. It would probably raise something completely other than hair when she wore it down in the club.

She would have to be careful with the sleeves, too, which hung heavily from her wrist. There would be endless opportunities to drag them in candle flames or knock glasses from tables with them. Poppy, never the most co-ordinated person, was going to have to keep herself on alert.

Emma, having finished her story, was accepting the tributes of her friends as she changed into her own scandalous version of geisha attire.

'I can't believe you said that to him.'

'He's got a soft spot for you, or he'd complain to Al.'

'Oh, Sands wouldn't say anything,' said Emma airily. 'He

wouldn't ever do anything to threaten his special relationship with my arse.'

'Did he try anything after? Extras?'

'Nah, says he's got a new girlfriend.'

There was a collective 'ooh'.

Poppy tied the matching red satin scarf around her neck and began to pull on a pair of fishnet hold-ups.

What was she going to do if somebody wanted extras?

A fifth girl popped her head around the door, one of the bartenders.

'Is Poppy here? Al wants a word.'

'Oh. Just a minute.' Poppy squeezed her feet into black, patent-leather, high-heeled Mary Janes and tottered after the messenger.

'You forgot something.'

She turned back to Emma, who held out her fan.

'Oh. Yeah. Thanks.'

It was a difficult journey along narrow corridors and up and down rickety stairs, but eventually they found Allyson's office. The messenger left Poppy there after knocking on the door.

'Come in.'

Allyson looked just as forbidding as she had during Poppy's interview. Her dark hair was scraped severely back and she wore a charcoal trouser suit with a wine-coloured shirt underneath. The tough image was probably necessary, Poppy reflected, when you ran a Soho sex club with an entitled clientele, but there was no need to project it at her.

She almost collapsed with relief when Allyson took off her spectacles and smiled.

'Hi, Poppy, great to see you again,' she said, waving at

an unoccupied chair. 'You look fantastic. Our gents will be falling over themselves to be served by you.'

'Oh, thanks.' Poppy subsided into the chair, grimacing down at the way her hem rode even higher up her thigh.

'I just wanted to give you a few words of encouragement before you go out there. Remember, nobody can make you do anything you don't want. If a gentleman wants to close the screens, make sure you negotiate what you are prepared to let him do first. I know it's hard, for a shy girl like you to speak plainly about this kind of thing, but you have to ask him if he wants straight spanking, strap or paddle – or all three – before he shuts those doors.'

'What if he wants the cane?' she whispered, thinking of Emma, while her mind rebelled against the idea of calmly discussing her forthcoming spanking with a paying stranger. If her mind rebelled, though, her sex did not, feeling quite deliciously wet and squirmy between her thighs at the thought.

'Novices never take the cane,' said Allyson. 'A man who wants to deliver a caning will know to ask for one of our experienced girls. Emma, Lizzie or Frances. Those are the names to give him if he tries it on with you.'

'OK.' Surely Emma couldn't take another caning tonight! Poppy's eyes bulged at the prospect.

'Remember,' Allyson continued, more gently, 'you must always act your part. Respectful, submissive, meek. Speak when spoken to, laugh at his jokes. You'll get to know the different customers – because it's a fetish club, we get a high volume of returning customers and not so many new faces. This is a big advantage. The girls will tell you all about everyone, so mention who you've been with afterwards and you'll get chapter and verse on their little quirks and idiosyncrasies.' She smiled at Poppy, who had tensed up again without realising it. 'You're going to do very well here, Poppy. You're exactly the type so many of our gentlemen go for. Shy and sweet, with a gorgeous little figure. Hell, I'd hire you myself.'

Poppy blushed, fit to singe her hairline, and looked everywhere but at her new boss. What a thing to say!

'Er, thank you,' she said with a nervous laugh.

'Don't mention it. One last thing – extras. I expect the other girls have mentioned this?'

'Sort of.'

'Nothing can take place in the club. We aren't a brothel. But if you want to take your relationship with a customer outside, you're welcome. I know some of the girls make a bit of money on the side from, well, call a spade a spade, prostitution. That's up to you. But keep it clean and keep it discreet. OK?'

'Oh, I wouldn't!'

'Fine. You'd better go and do your make-up then. Your shift starts soon. Best of luck – I know we'll be proud of you, Poppy. Ask Emma how to use your fan.'

It was only then that Poppy realised she had been snapping her fan open and shut throughout the conversation. She put it to her lips, which she had pursed in a kind of facial apology, and muttered her thanks before fleeing for the dressing room.

Oh, where was it?

By the time she found it, she had only ten minutes in which to apply dead white face paint, complicated sweeps of black eyeliner and enough deep red gloss to make her lips look lacquered.

She hurried with the other girls into the main club area, in time to see a barman dropping supermarket-brand tea bags into delicate little teapots with birds and gardens painted on to the china.

'Here's your station,' said Emma, showing her to a small square space, bordered on three sides by sliding paper-walled doors. She was to kneel on a large futon-style floor covering, with her hands pressed together as if in prayer, until a man decided to join her for tea. It could be anyone's pretend version of Japan, but for the shiny leather strap and the oval-ended wooden paddle laid out beside her.

What if nobody wants to join me?

What if somebody does?

At first, everything went so slowly. In the early part of the night there were few customers, and those that came in weren't interested in Poppy.

A small group of businessmen, different nationalities, joined Emma in her booth, but there appeared to be no spanking, only drinking.

She stood up periodically, when nobody could see her, to stretch her legs, looking out into the large, dim room with its ornamental fountain playing endlessly in the centre.

The entrance of another customer sent her quickly back to her knees, but he wanted Lizzie, and asked for her by name.

Within ten minutes, Poppy heard the sound of the screens being drawn close and then the lively percussion of hand on bare flesh, rhythmically repetitive, accompanied by breathless little mewls of dismay from Lizzie.

Once this was over, the screens re-opened, and she saw Lizzie leave the club in the company of her visitor. She remembered the rule that having taken your spanking you were then free to leave. The clients weren't generally keen on pre-reddened bottoms. Canings were especially expensive, because the marks took so long to fade, and could put a girl out of commission for a few days.

Clearly, Emma was an exception to this rule. Perhaps she just really loved her work.

Poppy was musing inwardly on the logistics of having a kinky partner and keeping this job going – would they have to eschew all the slap and tickle in case it ruined her bottom for work? – when one of the doormen loomed over her, in company with a man.

'This is our new girl,' said the doorman.

'First day?'

The man's voice was foreign, maybe French. Poppy didn't dare look up at him. She had an idea that she was meant to keep her eyes cast down at all times.

'That's right. You haven't been here before?'

'No, I am on holiday here.' 'Oliday 'ere.

'Perhaps you should try one of the more experienced . . .'

'No, no, I like this one. Please, some tea.'

Poppy saw a pair of feet in the regulation black velvet slippers the clients were given, then bending legs in trousers as he came to sit, cross-legged, on the futon opposite her.

'I'll have the barman fetch it for you, sir,' said the doorman, leaving, apparently with some reluctance.

She saw his hands, folded, pale, no wedding ring, a slight yellowness on the right index finger. Smoker. Neat fingernails.

If he was on holiday, he obviously wasn't the slobbing-out-in-a-trackie type. He wore smart, crisp cotton trousers and jacket in a mid-beige colour with a white, open-necked shirt.

If she raised her eyes, she'd be able to see his face.

But did she dare raise her eyes?

There was a slightly awkward silence.

'Hallo,' said the man with a self-conscious catch, almost a laugh, but not quite. He moved his hands as if he meant to snap his fingers.

Was this permission to look up?

'Good evening, sir,' she faltered.

She did it. She looked up.

He was fortyish with kind, tired brown eyes and a sharp-featured, handsome face.

He smiled, a little ruefully, as if he expected Poppy to be judging him for his filthy, perverted tastes.

'So you are the new girl?'

'Yes, sir.'

'I am your first customer?'

'Yes, sir.'

The tea tray arrived, and Poppy was grateful for the distraction of pouring and tending to her visitor's tastes.

'I prefer coffee,' he confessed. 'In France we don't drink so much tea.'

'You're French?'

She wasn't supposed to ask questions of the clients, but it wasn't really a question, was it? Just a mirroring of his own admission.

He nodded, picking up his tea cup and sniffing at it with some suspicion. He put it back down again.

'I thought I will try the English vice,' he said. 'But it isn't so English, not really. We French have enjoyed such pleasures from long, long ago.'

'And the Marquis de Sade was French, after all,' said Poppy.

'Of course. And there is also *L'Histoire d'O*.'

Poppy smiled. She wanted to know more about him now.

But of course, she couldn't ask.

'I hope the tea is to your satisfaction,' she said.

'Not really,' he said. 'Why do you choose to work here?'

'I answered an advert on a BDSM website.'

'So it is your interest? Your fetish? A spanking?'

Poppy blushed the deep scarlet of her namesake, and nodded.

'OK. I like that,' he said. 'The girls here like their work. This feels better for me.'

'Did you think we might be prisoners?'

'It happens.' He gazed pensively into his cup. The tea looked revolting, Poppy realised with a pang. It was weak, and the splash of milk made it almost white.

'I suppose it does.'

Poppy felt that same little chill she'd experienced on entering the building for her interview. Sex work, with all the age-old implications of degradation and human trafficking it brought with it. She'd told this client she was willing, but how could he take her word for it? What kind of man did that make him?

He had, at least, asked the question.

'So you have done this in your real life? With your lover?'

'I, well, that's a personal question, but . . .'

'I'm sorry. Am I being . . . rude, is that the word?'

Poppy waved her hand, well out of her depth, and strained her eyes to see where the bouncers were.

'Not rude,' she whispered. 'But it's against the rules for us to talk about ourselves, while we're in the club. I'm sorry. It's meant to be for our safety.'

'Meant to be?'

'Well, they turn a blind eye to girls meeting clients, afterwards. But while we're here . . .'

Poppy made a palms-up gesture and lowered her eyes again.

'OK, I understand. So, you have poured me the tea. I don't really want to drink it. What happens now?'

Poppy wished she knew.

From another cubicle came distant slapping and ouching, which Pan-Pipe Moods XII, leaking from the stereo speakers, did little to drown.

'If you want a more experienced girl—,' she said, her throat closing up, eyes hot with pre-tears.

'Non, non, non, shh. You are good, don't worry. I am new, you are new. I just want to know if there is a . . . routine.'

'Oh.' Poppy smiled.

He looked so earnest, and a little anxious. Such sweetness was completely unexpected and had thrown her for a loop; she had been expecting cartoonish sadistic bastards in business suits.

'Well,' she mused, 'I suppose you have to act a little stern. Like maybe you think I've done something wrong. Or— Yeah! You don't like the way I made the tea. And you tell me off.'

'Tell you off?' He frowned.

'Rebuke me, uh, scold or—' She wagged her finger in pantomime show and he nodded with recognition.

'I know,' he said. 'Then I?'

'If you want.'

'I can try.' He took another sip of the tea, and pulled a face. 'This is not good.'

'I'm very sorry, sir.'

Poppy, much more comfortable now the pretence had begun, threw herself energetically into the role, staring at the floor and bowing her head.

'I come here for a nice cup of tea.' He said 'nice cup of tea' in a ridiculous parody of an English accent, which made Poppy squash a smile. 'But this is not nice at all. This is like hot water and mud.'

'Would Sir like me to make him another cup? I will try harder next time.'

'You can make me another cup. But first I will give you something to make you, to make you, oh, I don't know. I'm going to spank you.'

Poppy did her best frightened little squirm and sharp intake of breath.

'Yes, sir,' she breathed. 'I deserve it. I am sorry I displeased you.' Under her breath, she added, 'You need to shut the screens.'

He drew the shutters closed.

'Listen,' he said, once they were confined in their little private square. 'Is it permitted to ask your name?'

'Ichisumi,' said Poppy mechanically.

He sighed.

'OK. Well, I am Bruno. So I guess you could come here.'

He was kneeling back on his heels and he patted his thigh.

Poppy crawled slowly forwards on all fours, pushing the tea tray aside to clear her path. When she reached Bruno, she looked briefly up at him, then at his lap, making absolutely sure that that was what he was asking of her.

She had thought it would feel exciting and hot to drape herself, bottom up, over a strange man's thighs for a spanking but, now it came down to it, it was ludicrously like a drama role-play at school. It made her feel giggly and frisky, but not particularly sexy.

'You are very obedient,' commented Bruno. 'So.'

He tugged the hem of the tiny skirt, then lifted it. She

could almost hear his heartbeat and sense his Adam's apple bobbing as he swallowed. He shifted slightly underneath her. She pushed her bottom up, suddenly engulfed by those sensations she had found lacking seconds before.

She was ready to be spanked. Her first paid spanking. And the man was attractive and seemed, actually, quite nice. She must count herself lucky.

'OK, you are ready?' he whispered.

She nodded.

His hand fell, a moderate swipe, conferring the gentlest of stings to her bare bottom.

It was far removed from the walloping and grunting now reaching her ears from the next booth along. This was delicate, erotic rather than punishing. She relaxed her shoulders, looking forward to more.

'How often do you get spanked?' asked Bruno, trying a few more.

'Not often enough,' said Poppy, in a burst of honesty.

'Really? You are such a bad girl? You need a lot of spanking?'

'Yes, sir, oh yes.'

He was varying the tempo and the landing spots, covering her cheeks with perfect little firecrackers, just strong enough to send a longing message to her pussy. It was so nice, and such a long time since she'd been spanked so enjoyably; the doms she met from BDSM networking sites were always in such a rush to get to the whips and chains.

Bruno's happy-go-lucky technique took her back to her first time, before all the knowledge and the sophistication – an innocent time, she now thought.

She had wondered then why people ever thought spanking was a punishment. The top had been just as sweet and considerate as Bruno, almost afraid to hurt her, it seemed. She had ended in a warm, pink glow that had lasted through the rest of the afternoon's lovemaking.

'This is learning your lesson, yes?' Bruno said, adding a few lazy swats to the tops of her thighs.

'Yes, sir.'

He can see it all. He can see my bum, and see my pussy through that stupid gauzy thong thing. He must be able to see that it's wet.

'You don't make much noise, do you?'

Well, no. You aren't hitting very hard. I do want to sigh and moan with pleasure, but perhaps that would be bad form.

'I'm well trained, sir.'

'Well trained? You had to practise to take a spanking? Tell me about it.'

'Oh. Well.'

Damn, creative thinking isn't easy when your bottom is deliciously hot and tingly and your clit blooming like an obscene flower.

'Hmm?'

A harder smack shocked her into words.

'Oh! We geisha girls, we all go to a class, once a week.'

'Oh yes? Tell me about that.'

He stopped for a moment and rubbed her cheeks. When she didn't start straight away, he spanked her again, good and hard, so that she gasped.

'It's a class that teaches how to take a spanking. Ow! We are a group of twelve girls and we are only permitted to wear a tight T-shirt and a thong.'

'What is a thong?' He pronounced it 'song' and Poppy giggled.

'What I'm wearing – skimpy panties.'

'Skimpy? Oh, never mind. Go on.'

'We sit together on a long bench and our teacher makes us come to the front, one by one, and take a spanking from her.'

'Teacher is a woman?'

'Yes.' Poppy was imagining Allyson in the role. She thought she might appreciate it. 'The first lesson, she spanks us with her hand. You can imagine, her hand got quite tired and sore, so after the first three, she made us spank each other.'

'Yes? All you pretty girls spanked each other? Hmm.'

Poppy had known Bruno was getting hard for a while, but now she felt a particular prod into the soft flesh of her stomach. Oh dear. Perhaps this was ill-advised. Perhaps she shouldn't be driving the customers into a frenzy of lust with far-fetched tales of sapphic-themed spanking. But she'd started now, and she was honour-bound to finish.

'Yes, until our bottoms were bright red. Then she made us line up and took a photograph of us all. Of course, we didn't all take it well. Some of us needed more training than others, while others could go straight ahead to strapping class.'

'Strapping class?'

'Yes. I wasn't ready after one lesson, so I had to go to Allyson for extra classes. She spanked me a little longer and a little harder each time, until I was able to last, without crying, until I was beacon-red and burning hot.'

'You can take more than this, then?' He started to spank harder.

Poppy wondered why she could never stop her imagination running away with her. Sometimes it could be a curse.

'Yes, sir. A little,' she said through clenched teeth.

'And then you go to the . . . what class?'

'Strapping class. They use leather belts, and straps, and

tawses. A few more strokes each time. Then it's – ouch – paddles and, oh, ow, whips and canes and stuff, ow, ow, ow!'

'Now you feel it,' he said, with some satisfaction. 'And your, what, we call them *fesses*, are a beautiful red. I think, scarlet.'

Poppy could believe it, but she tried to maintain her submissive tone.

'Thank you, sir,' she said.

He stopped, rubbing her all over her rounded mounds again.

He sighed deeply.

'But I think I hurt you,' he said.

'I learned my lesson, sir.'

'And it is painful,' he said. His palm rested on her right cheek.

Poppy wriggled, very, very slightly.

She knew it was against the rules to solicit him for sex, or to try and invite a fingering but, oh Lord, she wished it were not.

'But you like it,' he whispered.

Two of his fingers fluttered idly near the wettest part of her gauzy thong. If they just moved, just touched, just . . . He removed his hand from her and she clamped her thighs together in an agony of frustration.

'So what now?' he asked.

'It's done,' said Poppy. 'You can take more tea if you want.'

'I don't.'

'Then you pay me the rate for a hand spanking and, er, that's it.'

'That's it.'

He pulled her skirt back down and lifted her from his lap. Poppy hardly dared look at him but, when she did, she saw a misty, affectionate expression on his face that gave her complicated feelings.

Don't get involved with the customers. Don't think of them as people.

She should take that advice. She should take the money, and nod a submissive farewell.

He put his hands on her upper arms and bent close to her. She could smell the sour tea on his breath and, beneath that, a hint of brandy.

'When do you leave?' he asked softly.

Here it came. The big decision. To accept an assignation outside the club or to walk away. She should say no. She lacked the experience and he could be the proverbial axe-murderer . . .

'I can leave now,' she said, the words spilling anyhow. 'I only have to take one client.'

'That's good. Listen. It is your choice. I will be in the pub on the corner, you know it?'

She nodded.

'For one hour. If you want, you can meet me. If not . . .' He shrugged, then put a fingertip to her cheek. 'If not, then thank you. OK?'

He took a wallet from his shirt pocket and handed her the spanking tariff in crisp twenty-pound notes.

'I wonder if your Queen knows what she is paying for,' he said, looking at Her Majesty's face on the final purple banknote.

Poppy's nerves dissolved and she smiled.

'Good evening, sir,' she said. 'And thank you for correcting me.'

It was the script. She had to say it.

'I hope you will.'

He opened the screens and left.

Poppy re-arranged the booth into perfect order then made the trip upstairs to Allyson's office, nodding at the security guards so that they would know she was clocking off for the night.

'My goodness.' Allyson greeted her with evident surprise, looking up from her computer screen. 'New girls are always popular, but you've broken the record, I think. We've hardly been open ten minutes.'

Poppy blushed and held out the wad of banknotes.

Allyson counted them carefully. 'There's fifty over,' she said. 'He must have liked you.'

'Oh, he was French. Perhaps he just didn't understand the exchange rate or something.'

'All the same, take your tip and your half of the fee. Well done, love. That's a good first night's work. Back tomorrow, I assume, since he only used his hand?'

'Oh, yes, that's fine. Same time tomorrow, then?'

Allyson smiled.

As Poppy turned to go, she stopped her.

'Poppy, did you enjoy yourself?'

Her face was tilted on one side, as if the answer mattered to her.

'Yes, it was cool,' mumbled Poppy, wanting nothing more, now, than to get out of this silly costume and meet Bruno in the pub.

'Would you mind showing me your bottom?'

'Oh! Er, all right.'

It seemed an outlandish request but then, considering this was a spanking club, perhaps Poppy was being over-sensitive. Allyson probably needed to make sure she hadn't been marked.

She turned around and lifted the brief satin skirt of her robe, exposing the newly-spanked cheeks.

'Lovely and pink,' commented Allyson. 'But you won't have bruises tomorrow. Perfect.' There was a long and pregnant pause. 'All right, you can go.'

Poppy's throat was dry and she needed a long drink of water before she slipped back into her dress. The dressing room, so shabby and prosaic, seemed to lower her mood and warn her against meeting Bruno.

He thought she was a prostitute. He expected sex. No matter how attractive and sweet he seemed, no matter how sexy his accent, this was what he was after. Wham, bam, *merci madame*.

However you looked at it, it wasn't romantic.

Poppy, back on the street, joined the teeming nightlife and hoped she could slip past the pub unnoticed. She wove a path through the gangs of men peering into peepshows, and past the windows filled with mannequins in rubber basques. It was so old-fashioned now, this sexscape, it almost seemed like a fabricated street in a heritage museum. Serious sex-seekers went online – all you found here was tourist curiosity.

Around the corner lay freedom and fashionable restaurants. She ducked as she passed the pub, hoping that a combination of busy streets and frosted glass windows would be her friend.

But she couldn't resist a quick look inside the open door on the way past.

Bad move.

He was there, at the bar, right in her line of vision, and he caught sight of her as she crept by.

'Allo!' he exclaimed, taking two steps forward.

She froze.

He looked so pleased to see her, and Poppy could never resist anyone's good opinion of her.

She changed course and went into the pub.

'I wasn't sure,' she said with an apologetic look.

'You would like a drink?'

'Oh, maybe a vodka and cranberry. Thanks.'

Squashed into a corner, their thighs touching, they clinked glasses and smiled, him radiantly, her nervously.

'Bruno,' she opened. 'I'm not a prostitute. If that's what you think. I just like you.'

'That's good. I am not going to pay you for sex,' he said.

'You aren't?'

'No. Maybe you can tell me your name now?'

There didn't seem any harm in it.

'Poppy.'

'Pop-py,' he said, seemingly finding it enchantingly novel. 'What is poppy?'

'A flower. Red. Like, um, the Somme, Flanders Fields, the First World War, remembrance . . .' The reference he was most likely to understand was the grimmest.

'Oh, *coquelicqot*,' he said, grinning. '*C'est joli*.'

'Yes, I remember looking it up in the French dictionary at school. I don't suppose anyone has that name in France? What a mouthful.'

'And it is Poppy's first day in the spanking club,' he said.

She looked around, dreading that they might be overheard. Everybody was engrossed in their own affairs, though, and she turned back to Bruno.

'Yes, as I said.'

'I just wondered. You know, you seem so . . . I did not expect a girl like you. I thought perhaps you were playing a part, the innocent. But this is really you?'

'I'm not so innocent. I knew what I was getting into. Please don't cast me in the role of victim. I'm not.'

'OK, no, I see that. You have a strength.' It took him about five minutes to mangle the word 'strength' and Poppy's brief fit of pique evaporated.

'Thanks,' she said.

'I am going to confess to you. I didn't think you would come. Or if you did, you would try to get me into a room upstairs, for a fuck.'

Poppy had nothing to say to this, but her wide eyes and open mouth must have said it for her.

'But it seems like you are not in that situation. You are a genuine employee, who goes to her home a free woman after she is spanked.'

'I told you. I'm not a prisoner.'

'You told me the truth, so now I will tell you. I am not really interested in spanking.'

'You . . . I thought—'

'OK, I like it now. But I never thought about it before, not much.'

'So, why . . . ?'

'I am here on a work visit. I am a police detective in Paris, I recently change my job and work on prostitution, drugs, that kind of thing.'

'This is a set-up?'

Poppy half-rose and looked wildly around her, expecting uniformed officers with handcuffs to emerge from all corners of the room.

Bruno put his hand on her forearm, drawing her back down.

'Calm,' he said. 'You are not in trouble. Not at all. Don't worry.'

Poppy sat back down, but she couldn't shake a strange sensation of being under arrest and bound to answer all interrogations.

'It's legal. I pay tax,' she said.

'OK, it's OK, I know. I don't say you are doing anything wrong. I am here for study. There are links between gangs in Paris and London. I am getting an idea of them, you know? A feel, you say.'

'Gangs? There's no criminal stuff going on at the club.'

Bruno gave her a long look.

'You believe that. But your whole club is a front for drugs and prostitution. It is used to launder money.'

'No!'

'Oh, Poppy, of course it is. My God. How old are you?'

'Nineteen.'

'Nineteen. I have a daughter, four years younger than you.'

'You're married?'

'Divorced. This job, you know.' He waved his hand, his face darkening.

'I'm sorry. So what were you doing in the club? Investigating? Are you trying to catch somebody?'

'No, not at all. Like I say, it is study. Research.'

'And you came to me just because you wanted to question me?'

'I'm afraid you think I am using you?' Bruno laughed. 'If a man wants to hit you or fuck you for money, that is fine, but if he wants to talk to you, that is very bad. You don't think this is strange, Poppy?'

'I don't know. It is a bit, I suppose,' she said, still feeling as if the cuffs were upon her.

'Who is in charge of the club?' he asked.

'I don't want to tell you, now.'

'I can find out very easily,' he said with a shrug.

'She's called Allyson. Allyson Bruce.'

'She hired you?'

'Yes.'

'And you really, absolutely truthfully, like working there?'

'The money's good. I'm a student, so I always need money. And it's not exactly hard work.'

'I would find it hard.'

'You aren't, you know, into that kind of thing.' Poppy looked away, flushed. She suddenly felt very old and it wasn't a good feeling.

'If you were my daughter . . .' he said.

'I'm not. It's my life. My decision.'

'I wish I could take you away from it.'

Poppy was trying to devise a coherent response to this when two people came and sat down at the table opposite them.

One was Emma from the club, the other a gentleman Poppy recognised as the theatre critic, Peregrine Sands.

'Poppy,' said Emma, glancing at Bruno with a trace of steel in her eye. 'Is this a friend of yours? Would you like to introduce us?'

'This is Bruno,' said Poppy, a sinking sensation of impending doom settling upon her stomach.

'Hello, Bruno. I'm Emma and this is Mr Sands. How do you two know each other, then?'

'We met in the club. It's OK,' blurted Poppy. 'I know it's allowed.'

'Yeah, it's allowed,' said Emma. 'But it's your first night, love. It's her first night,' she said again, for the benefit of Bruno. 'She's new. I'm not sure it's a good idea.'

'Bruno isn't a punt—' opened Poppy, but a kick on the ankle from Bruno silenced her.

'That is up to Poppy, I think,' he said, accepting a peanut from the packet Emma proffered. 'If she wants to be friendly to me, that is up to her.'

'You don't have to, Poppy,' said Emma. 'But if you're hell-bent on it, how about we make it a foursome?'

Sands coughed. 'Actually, Emma, I'm meeting Caroline for a late supper. I don't have to worry about marking *her*. But thank you for the rather titillating idea. Who needs theatre when one's life is so rich with dramatic colour?'

He rose and left.

'I'm sorry, Poppy,' said Emma, once he had gone. 'But I'm just looking out for you. If you go with him, I go with you.'

Bruno's posture was stiff and alert. Poppy wondered what he was plotting. Surely he wasn't going to take Emma up on her offer? Surely the thing for him to do now was to make an excuse and bow out?

'Perhaps you will like to come to my hotel for a drink?' he said at last.

'Good man,' said Emma with a nod. 'I won't charge you for me if you don't want me. If you like, I'll sit in the bathroom while you two get down to things. But I'm not letting Poppy go alone. If you do want a threesome, though, I'll have to charge you the market rate.'

In the cab on the way to Bruno's hotel, Poppy felt numb and bemused. Bruno sat beside her while Emma took the front seat. He put his hand on her thigh and whispered into her ear, 'Don't worry.' When he noticed Emma looking in the rear-view mirror, he turned the whisper into a nibble of Poppy's earlobe.

She whispered back, 'I'm scared. What are you doing?'

'Nothing you don't want. She is watching. I will have to kiss you. Do you mind?'

Poppy didn't. The nearness of him gave her butterflies and their lips were already so close, nearly touching. The warmth and scent of him were exotic somehow, deliciously different.

He put an arm around her and pulled her into his lips. They kissed for the rest of the journey while the taxi stopped and started, the gears squeaked, and Emma made desultory conversation with the driver.

Poppy felt her apprehension turn to excitement. It was like being in a spy drama, having to keep Emma in the dark about the true nature of their relationship. There was a spice of danger that didn't seem too real. Allyson was nice. The club was legitimate. Bruno had some funny ideas about it, but he didn't understand, that was all.

She let her body twist and turn against his, let him press closer and allowed his hand to wander up and down her leg, stroking the nylon along her inner thigh so that she tingled and trembled. She was as wet now as she had been after he spanked her. He must know that, if he wanted it, she wouldn't object too strenuously.

She moved her lips near his and tried to brush them, inviting a kiss, but he turned his head away.

'This is the place,' he said to the cabbie.

The three of them tipped out of the car, and streamed up the steps to the lobby of a mid-range hotel, close to the St Pancras Eurostar terminus.

'It is not a luxury place,' Bruno muttered, shepherding them into the lift, which he had to summon by means of a secure key card.

'Not exactly,' Emma agreed, frowning at herself in the elevator mirror, under the glare of a striplight.

'I've stayed in much worse,' said Poppy reassuringly. 'In Paris, funnily enough.'

'Oh, really? Where did you stay?'

'Near the Place de Clichy.'

Bruno laughed.

'*C'est logique*,' he said.

The lift arrived at his floor and they trooped along to his room, accessed once more by the key card.

'Well, here we are,' announced Emma, spreading her arms wide. 'Where do you want me?'

He didn't want her, Poppy thought, and he made it pretty obvious by the way he looked at her.

'You can help yourself to a drink from the minibar,' he said. 'Perhaps take it into the bathroom.'

'You want to get straight down to business, eh? Can't blame you. She's a pretty little peach, isn't she?'

She tickled Poppy beneath the chin. Poppy squealed and sat down on the edge of the bed, watching the hostility between the other two take its course.

'I would like some privacy,' said Bruno, opening the minibar for Emma.

She took a bottle of mineral water and swigged from it before retiring to the ensuite.

'Any funny business, Poppy, and you just need to shout, OK? I'm here for you. I'll take you home afterwards.'

'Thanks.'

Poppy watched the door shut behind her, then looked shyly up at Bruno.

'So, do you want to?'

'I told you, I don't pay for sex,' he said, his voice very low, almost a whisper. 'Here.'

He sat down beside her and spoke into her ear.

'I'm a policeman. I can't pay you for sex.'

'But,' she whispered back, 'do you want it?'

He looked astonished and he jerked back, reading her face intently.

'What? Are you offering?'

'Oh, I mean. It doesn't matter. But I thought you might want to.'

'Poppy, you don't have to fuck any man who asks you, you know.'

'I know. I know that.' Tears rushed forwards, threatening to spill.

'Do you?'

'Yes. Just because I let men spank me doesn't mean I give it up to anyone and everyone. Do you really think I would?'

'No. Not now. But in a few years, you know, maybe that will change.'

'I'm not planning to do this for years. Only until I get my degree and a good job.'

Bruno looked towards the bathroom door.

'She thinks we are going to fuck. And if we just sit here, all quiet, she will think it is strange.'

'So?' Poppy was confused. Now it sounded as if Bruno was going to shag her just to keep Emma off the scent. Wasn't that worse than doing it because they felt like it?

'We will play the role, as we did earlier. Do you mind if I take off my clothes?'

He didn't wait for Poppy's answer but stood and began unbuttoning his shirt straight away. Poppy watched in stunned fascination as her strange new companion's chest was revealed, buff and tanned above a classic six-pack abdomen.

'Perhaps if you just take off your dress,' he suggested. 'I don't ask for more.'

Poppy quickly wriggled out of it. Even though she wasn't showing him anything he hadn't already seen, she felt coy and embarrassed at letting him see her knickers.

'OK.' He had taken off his trousers and stood in just boxers, preening a little as if expecting her to gasp and faint. 'Are you OK? Let's get into bed.' He raised his voice, for Emma's benefit. 'I want to fuck that sweet little pussy, baby.'

Poppy covered her mouth with her hands, but he winked and pulled her under the duvet with him.

'I don't mean it,' he whispered. 'We just hold each other, yes, and make some noise. Make the mattress, what do you say?'

'Creak? Squeak?' Poppy bounced her bottom and heard the springs groan rewardingly.

'That's it,' he said, putting an arm around her. 'Lie down.'

Poppy was reminded of earlier in the evening, when she had thought the spanking felt too much like role-play to be sexy. How was it, then, that this blatant role-playing felt horribly, dangerously erotic? Something inside her was wrongly wired, she theorised, a blue strand where a red should be, and vice versa.

Lying pressed against Bruno, breathing him in, feeling his strength and hardness, made her want to wrap herself tight around him and open up her legs. He smelled of older-man authority and responsibility and it intoxicated her. Screw the bad boys, what could be sexier than a good man who wanted to do right by you?

'Hey,' he whispered, rolling over a little so that he held her down underneath him. 'You are playing this a bit too well, you know?'

His mouth was an inch from hers, his hair falling over his brow and tickling her. Their pelvises were in alignment. Only a double layer of cotton kept their genitals apart.

'Kiss me,' she begged, almost silently.

'You want me to?' He sounded amazed, and it turned her on even more.

She nodded. 'I like you.'

'I shouldn't.'

'Please.'

She raised her head a fraction, bringing their lips together. If he was reluctant, he didn't show it. He gave in to her, so easily and sweetly, as if it could only happen this one way.

How right it seemed. They shared a connection Poppy wasn't sure she'd experienced before. She gave herself up to him in rapt surrender, letting her body fall free. They rolled around all over the bed, rumpling the sheets, making the mattress sing. Emma was getting a good performance now.

He broke the kiss and she let out a laugh of delight.

'You like to be kissed?' he whispered, as if any answer were necessary.

'Love it,' she said out loud. 'Love it, love it, love it.'

'You need to talk for her.' He inclined his head towards the bathroom door. 'Some moans.' He raised his voice again, holding her tight. 'Oh yeah,' he said.

'Mmm,' she contributed, squirming in order to get some consolidation from the mattress.

'Say "Oh my God, it's so big!",' he suggested, and Poppy giggled at his outrageous male vanity.

'I'm not saying that!'

'Oh, do, why not?'

She rolled her eyes, then put her hand on the bulge in his boxers.

'Wow, this is nice,' she said, sincerely and aloud.

'Poppy!' He tried to remove her hand, but lamely, not

putting his full strength into the gesture. 'You are a bad girl, you know.'

'I do know. That's why you had to spank me, isn't it?'

'I can't. Please don't make me fuck you, Poppy. I can't.'

She let go of him, stung and embarrassed.

'I'm sorry. I didn't mean to, to, cross your personal boundaries.'

'Shh, Poppy, you know, I would love to. I would love to fuck you all night. But I can't. I really can't. Listen to me. I'm going to give you my number. If you need me for anything, just call me. If anything happens at the club, will you tell me?'

'What do you mean by "anything"?'

'Anything at all. To you, to another girl, to a client.'

'You want me to be your informant?'

'I will pay, of course.'

'You mean all of this was to get me to—'

'No, no. I know these people, these club people. I know their associates, I know what they do. I worry for you, Poppy. I need to know you are OK. Will you keep my number? Will you call me if you want a friend?'

She nodded, sobered by the seriousness of his tone.

'Good,' he said. 'I wish I could take you away from it, but . . .' He shrugged. 'It must be your decision.'

'Right.'

She watched while he reached for his wallet and took from it a business card, which he slipped inside her bra. Then he took out a condom packet.

For a second, she thought he must have changed his mind. But he took the condom out of the wrapper and then threw it into the wastepaper basket, along with the foil.

'For safety,' he said.

'What if Emma sees that the condom isn't used?'

'You think she will look so close? I don't. Come on. Let's get to it.'

They spent five minutes bucking and jerking around on the mattress, gasping and groaning for effect, until Poppy judged that the time was right to fake her orgasm and Bruno grunted in unison.

Oh, if only it could be real, she thought, lying back on the pillows while Bruno tried to make sure the bed looked rumpled enough. If only he could be her French cop boyfriend, about to make her some strong coffee and smoke a Gauloise after hours and hours of sex. Why could they not, just this once, break a rule?

'I wish we could,' she said, reclaiming her breath after all the hysterical huffing and puffing.

He stroked her forehead.

'So do I,' he said, looking down at her. 'Believe me. But not tonight, *petit coquelicqot*.'

'Now I'll be measuring up all the clients in the club against you. I think I'm in for a lot of disappointment.'

'You know you can call me any time.'

'Yes. Thanks.'

'OK, I think you have to go now. If you stay longer, I will have to take off your panties.' He shook his head. 'I can't stop myself.' He raised his voice and called, 'We are finished, you can come in.'

Poppy left the bed reluctantly and pulled her dress back on.

She couldn't quite trust herself to look at Emma at first, convinced that something in her face would give the game away.

But Emma's attention was on Bruno anyway, watching him lounge in the bed, mostly undressed, jabbing at buttons on his phone.

'I hope you didn't let him take pictures,' she said to Poppy.

'Oh, no, I didn't.'

'Good. If you showed up on a sex tube site Allyson wouldn't be amused.'

Bruno reached for his wallet again.

'Here,' he said, counting out a wad of notes and proffering them.

'Oh,' said Poppy. 'But . . .'

'Take it,' he hissed through clenched teeth. 'Now.'

'Thanks.' She put the money in her jeans pocket without counting it.

'Is it all there, love?' Emma prompted her. 'I hope you agreed the price up front.'

'Yeah, I trust him.'

Emma laughed. 'You really are green, aren't you? Never mind. We'll soon sort you out. Ready to go?'

Poppy slipped on her ballerina pumps and grabbed her jacket from the bedside chair.

'I guess. Well, goodbye then.'

They were turning to leave, Poppy with some regret that Bruno hadn't offered her so much as a farewell kiss, when the door began to bang and a man started shouting in rapid French.

'*Putain*, he is drunk, ignore him,' said Bruno, running to the door and admitting a blotchy-faced middle-aged man, who stank of beer and red wine.

Emma and Poppy were in the corridor, the sounds of an altercation between Bruno and the drunkard floating behind them, before either of them spoke.

Emma pressed the lift button.

'Did you know he was a cop?'

Poppy felt her stomach twist.

'What? How do you know?'

'I speak French. They're clearly both cops, it was obvious from the conversation they were having. You did know, didn't you, Poppy?'

'I . . .' She couldn't lie. The elevator mirror showed her cheeks a bright, unhappy scarlet.

'What did you tell him?'

The lift door opened and Emma marched, holding Poppy by the wrist, out on to the street.

'*What* did you *tell* him?'

'Nothing, nothing. He just wanted to know if I'd taken the job willingly, and I said yes. Honestly, that was all.'

Poppy was disgusted with herself at the tears leaking from her eyes, but it had been a weird evening and she couldn't seem to stop them.

'Shh, all right, don't make a scene. Come on.'

The pair of them sat down on the hotel steps, Emma wincing slightly, obviously still affected by the previous day's episode with the cane.

'He fucked you and he paid you for the fuck,' mused Emma. 'He could get into trouble for that. Now I wish you had got some photos.'

'He isn't out to make trouble, I swear. He's on some kind of research trip.'

Emma shook her head. 'Where did you come from, girl? Did they shake you out of a tree?'

Poppy rubbed her eyes, trying to blot out the tears.

'I'll get the sack, won't I?'

'No, no, you'll be all right. I'll take care of it. I'll cover for you. But you have to tell me *exactly* what you told him. Did he ask about the club?'

'Only about whether the girls did it of their own free will. Oh, and he asked about Allyson.'

Emma inhaled sharply. 'He knew Allyson was in charge?'

'No, he wanted to know who was in charge.'

'And you told him? Shit. She won't like that.'

Poppy started to cry again.

'I've told you, I'll cover for you,' said Emma, testily. 'I'll say we shagged him as a duo and it was my idea.'

'But then you'll lose your job.'

'Oh, no, I won't lose my job. Me and Allyson, let's just say we have an understanding.'

Poppy didn't understand what Emma meant, but she was too tired to protest further, and fell gratefully into the cab Emma hailed, ready to erase the night.

Poppy checked her phone after her nine o'clock lecture and saw that she had a missed call from the club.

She phoned back and was treated to a terse, 'Poppy, get to the club, quick as you can,' from Allyson.

'I have to go to the library,' she began to protest, but Allyson cut her off.

'Now.'

'I'll be half an hour.'

'Good.'

She clicked off without a goodbye. Poppy had to sit on the wall and catch her breath. Trouble. What had Emma said? Had she kept her word and covered for her?

She thought of calling Bruno and telling him that his secret was out, but she had an irrational fear, now, that perhaps the club's owners were having her phone tapped, and she didn't dare.

By the time she arrived at the seedy little alley where the side door was hidden, Poppy's legs would hardly carry her.

One of the bouncers responded to her faint-hearted

knocking, and took her upstairs without a word, clearly expecting her.

Inside the office, Allyson sat on her side of the desk, reading the newspaper, it seemed. Poppy didn't see Emma at first until suddenly she noticed her, standing in shadows with her nose in the corner. She was wearing a pair of leather hotpants and a corset, pretty odd attire for this time of the morning, Poppy thought.

Allyson put down her paper and glared.

Poppy cowered.

'One day on the job and already you're here in front of me,' said Allyson with a sigh. 'Please don't tell me I've made a mistake, Poppy. I don't like mistakes.'

'I didn't mean any— I'm sorry.'

'All right. Sit down. Emma's told me all about last night.'

'Has she?'

'Yes, and it was very good of her to come and help you out with your first punter. Pity he turned out to be the wrong sort. I can forgive you, in your inexperience, for not realising sooner, but Emma should really know better.'

'She was only trying to help me.' Poppy whispered.

'I appreciate that, but she was indiscreet and she has to be punished. And you, my dear, can take a lesson from witnessing her punishment. And, for future reference, you don't tell anyone anything about this place. Got that? You can lie, you can evade, you can tell them what you like, as long as it isn't the truth. I thought one of the other girls would have made that clear, but they obviously had their eye off the ball last night.'

Allyson got up and leant over the desk, taking Poppy's chin between her finger and thumb.

'You do understand me, don't you?'

Poppy nodded, a restricted little shiver of a nod.

'Right. Now watch and learn what happens to silly girls who can't keep their mouths shut.'

Allyson opened her desk drawer, and shunted everything that lay on the surface down into it, until only the polished veneer remained. Then she took out a rolled-up padded mat, which she laid out flat on the desktop.

'Here, slut,' she said, patting it, and Emma came out of her corner and climbed up on to the mat on all fours. While Allyson and Poppy watched, she laid her head down against the padding and pushed out her backside. The leather shorts were so brief that they exposed a large portion of her bottom, the edges of the cane welts peeking out, now a purplish pink colour.

'You've been disgracing yourself this week,' said Allyson softly, running a frighteningly manicured magenta nail along one of the welts. 'Mr Sands had to cane you for saying too much, and now you're in the same position again, only two days later. I think we should keep you in a ball gag, my dear, don't you?'

'If you wish, ma'am.'

'Yes, I do wish.'

She opened the lower drawer again and took out a length of black elastic with a bright red rubber ball in the middle of it. Poppy watched, half-enthralled and half-horrified, as Allyson tied it around Emma's head, pushing the ball between her teeth.

'You can wear that for work tonight and your customer will know you've been a naughty blabbermouth. And I hope he'll spank you all the harder for it.'

Emma said nothing. Well, how could she?

Allyson returned to her rear and reached underneath to

loosen the leather hotpants. When she pulled them down over Emma's bum, Poppy saw that she was naked underneath. Her pale bottom wore nothing but the silvery purple streaks left by the cane.

'Hmm, how are these feeling, I wonder?' Allyson asked, squeezing and pinching the welts with cruel satisfaction. Emma couldn't answer verbally, but she twisted this way and that, gasping through her gag. Presumably they still hurt, then. Poppy grimaced in sympathy.

'Yes, I see that face, madam,' said Allyson, turning her attention to the younger girl. 'You don't want to be in this position, do you? So make sure you're careful in future because, believe me, I wouldn't think twice about pulling down your knickers and giving you the hiding of a lifetime. In fact, it would be a pleasure. So think on that. Right. What am I going for today?'

Allyson stepped back, chin in hand, contemplating Emma's vulnerable backside.

'Got to make it hurt, of course. And I know this girl, Poppy, I know what she can take. She loves to be whipped, so I've got to take her past that and make it count. What would you recommend, love? Hmm?'

'Me? You're asking me?'

'That's right, sweetheart. You heard me. So?'

Allyson folded her arms, waiting.

Poppy could not, for the life of her, imagine how she would punish somebody. The thought had never even occurred to her. And when it was somebody who was taking the rap for her own silly mistake?

'I don't know.'

'Tell you what, I'll get a few bits and pieces out and you can choose.'

Allyson opened the drawer for a third time, grabbed a handful of items and dropped them with a clatter over the desk in front of Emma's head.

Stealing forward, Poppy inspected a multi-stranded flogger, a spoon-shaped wooden paddle, a heavy strap with a handle and a purple fibreglass cane.

'While you're making up your mind . . .' said Allyson, and Poppy almost jumped out of her skin, as a loud crack reverberated around the room, closely followed by a volley of repeats. Allyson had begun smacking Emma's thighs with her hand, and Poppy jumped back as Emma began to twitch and breathe heavily through the gag.

Poppy saw that she had better hurry up if she was not going to prolong Emma's suffering unnecessarily. Without thinking more, she snatched up the paddle and held it out to Allyson, who stopped smacking and smiled.

'Ooh, you little bitch,' she said. 'This one really hurts.'

'Look,' blurted Poppy, 'this isn't fair. I wish you'd punish me instead. It was my fault.'

Allyson put down the paddle and laughed, long and low. She reached out and stroked Poppy's hair from her face, making Poppy tremble.

'What a little sweetie,' she said. 'What a brave girl. So you think you deserve a paddling too, do you?'

'It wasn't Emma's fault,' whispered Poppy, electrified by the situation. Her head was light with fear, and yet a huge exhilaration welled inside her. She had stepped off the edge of a cliff.

'Was it your fault, Poppy?'

Poppy nodded.

'Do you want Auntie Allyson to punish you for it?'

She didn't know how to answer. She knew she didn't want

Emma taking what was hers by right but, on the other hand, she was hardly desperate to give Allyson license to do what she wanted with her. God knew what that might involve.

'I don't think it's fair on Emma,' she quavered. 'If she takes all the blame.'

'You're a good girl,' said Allyson. 'What a good girl you are. Now just sit back down, sweetie, and watch. I know you don't want Emma taking all the blame, but she's the experienced one here and she must be punished, long and hard. That's it. Sit tight. And learn.'

Allyson gripped the paddle by its rubber-coated handle and tapped it a few times against Emma's bottom. Emma moaned in a kind of pre-emptive despair, as if knowing how she was going to feel. She probably did, thought Poppy.

'Now then, Emma, you're going to get properly paddled on your bare bum, and Poppy is going to watch every single second of it. So make sure you behave yourself and keep nice and still, or you'll get extras with the lexan cane.'

Poppy cried out at the first stroke, even though Emma did not.

Allyson glanced over at her. 'Sympathetic, eh? What are you like when they actually touch you? Don't answer that. I'd like to find out for myself.'

Poppy pressed her lips together then, determined to draw no more attention to herself. She watched dully as Allyson plied the paddle, over and over, with hard, fast splats, to Emma's already punished bottom. She saw how Emma screwed up her face and chewed on the rubber gag, how she clenched her fists and stiffened her back and tried not to react. She was so strong. Poppy was sure she couldn't have taken half of what Emma did without leaping up and clutching her buttocks.

'Plenty of hard swats: got to drive the lesson home,'

muttered Allyson, single-minded at her work. 'Come here, Poppy, and look at how red her arse is now.'

Poppy obliged, and was duly impressed at the angry crimson flush covering Emma's rounded cheeks down to mid-thigh. The cane welts were swelling up in the midst of the redness, darker than they had been before.

It must be agony, thought Poppy, and she rubbed her thighs together a little, feeling the dampness at their apex.

'What do you think? Has she had enough?'

'Yes, yes, I think so,' said Poppy.

'You're soft-hearted, aren't you, love? You couldn't do my job. When you're in charge of a gaff like this, with sly little sluts like Emma on your books, you have to be tough. It's dog-eat-dog, this game.'

'Oh. Is it?' Poppy, way out of her depth, simply nodded sympathetically.

'You have to understand that girls like Emma need to be reined in. They need reminding. Hard. And often.' Allyson accompanied these words with driving swats that flattened Emma's red buttocks. 'You'll notice that she hasn't even yelled out yet.'

'I know. I would have.'

Allyson turned and smiled indulgently.

'Would you? Yeah, I'll bet. So look, Poppy, I'm going to offer you a choice here.'

'A choice?' Poppy swallowed. Something in Allyson's eyes was too rapt, too rapacious, for comfort.

'Yeah.'

Allyson put down the paddle and picked up the purple cane. She held it out to Poppy.

'You can give Emma six with this, and you'll have to make it hard. Or you can take them yourself.'

Oh God, oh God. If she'd picked any other implement, the choice would have been clear and easy. She'd have stood in for Emma like a shot. But the cane . . .

She looked again at Emma's bottom. She wanted to touch it, to feel the evidence of her suffering, so that she could make a properly informed choice. She wanted to ask Emma what she thought. But of course, Emma was in no state to express an opinion.

So she took the cane and ran her fingers along it. Then she bent it. It was made of some indestructible, shatter-proof material that would fall like a thin brand on the skin.

She couldn't use it on Emma. She couldn't use it on anyone.

'I can't cane Emma,' she said quietly. 'I can't, when it's me who . . .'

Allyson nodded.

'Brave girl,' she said, and she rubbed her shoulder with awkward approbation. 'And I think you need this. If you're going to be one of us.'

Poppy raised her eyes to Allyson. That hard face, that professional-bitch attitude. Did she want to be one of them? She wasn't sure about that, but she did want to bend to Allyson's will, to feel the punishment she had earned. Allyson was strong, and strong people made her feel safe, no matter what dodgy business they might be tangled up in.

'Everything'll be all right, love, once you've got your stripes,' Allyson said.

She smacked Emma's bum loudly.

'Down you get,' she ordered.

Emma clambered stiffly off the desk and stood on the carpet, head down, looking as if she wanted to hide the ball gag from sight. Her leather hotpants were still around her ankles.

'Get in the corner, slut, now.'

Emma shuffled to the corner she had occupied before, and stayed there.

Poppy couldn't have told anything from her face. She didn't look distraught, nor did she look happy. She was a perfect blank. Had she learned that? Did Allyson insist upon it?

'Right, Poppy, let's have your jeans off.'

She put the cane down on the desk and Poppy's heart began to lurch chaotically in her ribcage. She looked at the door, one eye on escape, but she knew there was none.

Why not, though?

Surely she could just say, 'Sorry, but I'll pass,' and leave. Nothing was stopping her. It would mean losing the job, but at this stage, the job was low on her list of priorities, a long way after survival and sex.

Poppy unzipped and dropped her jeans, then realised that she would have difficulty pulling them over her boots.

'It's OK,' said Allyson. 'You can leave them like that.'

She pointed at the chair Poppy had been sitting on.

'Bend over it, hands gripping the sides of the seat, bum up.'

Poppy obeyed, feeling the cotton of her knickers stretch over her rump.

Allyson walked up behind her and caressed her bottom cheeks, sending furious, itchy heat to her pussy.

'Miss Sensible-Knickers,' she teased. 'Pack of seven, was it?'

'Yes,' she whispered.

'Yes, what?'

'Yes, ma'am?' Was that what Emma had called her?

'Good. Fast learner. Let's see what you learn from this. Hold tight.'

At least Allyson wasn't going to make her take her knickers down, thought Poppy. They might give her a tiny bit of protection.

But when the cane swished down and bit into her, she realised how misguided this assumption had been.

She leapt to her feet, clutching her behind, wailing in pain and confusion.

'Hurts, doesn't it?' said Allyson, with steely satisfaction. 'Five more. Back down now.'

'I can't,' pleaded Poppy.

'No? Then you know what you have to do. Emma!'

'No! No, I'll try.'

Even as she bent back down, Poppy wondered if she'd gone mad. That first stroke had been purest agony. Five more couldn't possibly be tolerated.

She didn't take them well.

She jumped up each time, and even made for the door at one point, but something kept bringing her back, something kept her bent over the chair, waiting for another bar of exquisite pain to be laid across her bottom.

Marks of war. Marks of shame. Marks of pride.

It felt like a rite of passage.

'That's five. One more, sweetheart. You're doing well. I didn't take more than three, my first time. And Em screamed the place down, didn't you, darling? Oh, sorry, I forgot. Anyway. Speaking of Emma – come out of the corner, love. I want you to give the sixth stroke.'

Emma wouldn't hurt her. Emma was her friend.

'And I think we'll take down her knickers, just for this last one. Ooh, look.'

Allyson pulled the garment free of Poppy's bum, exposing the marks to view.

Emma made a garbled sound that Poppy interpreted as 'very nice'.

'I haven't lost the touch, have I?' said Allyson with satisfaction. 'So neat. Right. All yours, Em. And make it a good one.'

The final slice cut into Poppy's bottom. She screamed and jumped up, grabbing great handfuls of flesh. Surely there must be blood?

But no. Allyson and Emma were laughing.

'She's a screamer,' said Allyson. 'I'll have to put that in her notes. Some of the gents love a screamer.'

Poppy was trembling all over, but she scarcely realised it until Emma took her into her arms and hugged her tight.

'Well done, love,' said Allyson. 'Well done. You're on our side. You're one of us. I think you've earned a reward. I'll slip a little something extra in your pay packet this week.'

The other two women fussed and made much of Poppy so enthusiastically that, before long, she forgot the shock and pain, regardless of the continuing throb of her welts. Besides, they were starting to feel different now, a kind of afterglow.

She relaxed into their attentions, breathing in their complementary perfumes, snuggling against their softnesses, until she was drowning in a new sensuality.

'Now you just go to the corner, love,' whispered Allyson, 'and watch the show.'

The corner? Poppy allowed Allyson to steer her over to the spot so lately vacated by Emma, but she was allowed to face into the room from her vantage point, and she saw what followed through a kind of haze.

She saw the ball gag removed from her friend's mouth and then Emma was on her knees in front of Allyson's desk chair, her face up inside Allyson's tight skirt while lapping, snuffling noises emitted from within.

Allyson's complexion went from too-much-sunbed to flushed, her eyes from watchful to blank, as Emma worked away with loving patience.

'That's it, slut, that's it,' she panted and then there was one quick outward kick of Allyson's legs and a pained whimper before her body crumpled inwards, depleted by orgasm.

Emma's head bobbed back up, her chin shiny with Allyson's juices, her face impishly bright.

'You gorgeous little bitch,' muttered Allyson, her neck lolling on the chair back. 'Get those shorts back on and take Poppy for a coffee. Go on. Get out of my sight.'

Poppy watched Emma pull the tight hotpants over her still-crimson flesh with some difficulty. They hadn't been the greatest choice of outfit, she thought, but perhaps Allyson had ordered her to wear them.

It was only then that she realised she ought to be engaged in the same struggle with her knickers and jeans. The thought of anything rubbing or making frictive contact with her cane marks made her want to suck breath in through her teeth, but she made a sterling effort, holding the knicker elastic out as far as it would stretch before bringing it gently to rest above the danger zone. The added heat on her bottom wasn't exactly welcome, but the jeans would be the true test.

She gritted her teeth through the ordeal, hating the process of zipping them back up for the way it brought the rough denim into contact with the burning stripes. The rest of the day promised much in the way of discomfort.

'It'll be a reminder to you,' said Allyson, as if reading her thoughts. 'Stay away from the punters until you're ready for that kind of thing. You're too green for it, whether Emma or one of the other girls is with you or not.'

Poppy nodded.

'What shall I do about work?' she asked hesitantly. 'I'm on the roster for tonight, but . . .'

'Come in,' said Allyson. 'Lots of our gents like to spank a girl with cane marks. Gives them more of the "naughty girl" feel, if you know what I mean. You'll be popular.'

'Oh.' She heard this with some dismay. Getting spanked while she felt this tender and sore wasn't exactly a delightful prospect.

'Lesson learned?'

'Yes, ma'am.'

'Good.'

She went to hold the door open for them, but before they left, she grabbed hold of Emma and pulled her into a passionate snog.

'Mmm, the taste of me.' Allyson held Emma's head against her bosom for a moment, then let her go.

Around the corner, in an Italian coffee place, the girls elected to stand at the counter, rather than sit to drink their cappuccinos.

'Are you OK?' asked Emma. 'Ally's a bit full-on but she's protective of her girls. She'd stand up for you if it came down to it. She's been brilliant with loads of the girls. Paid Sharlie's court costs when she had to fight an eviction, sorted out private healthcare when Lia thought she had cancer, all sorts. She's great like that.'

'Are you in love with her?'

'Nah, I wouldn't say I was in love with her, but I do fancy her rotten. She's fucking hardcore, that girl. I like a bit of both, so I wouldn't commit, but yeah. I like her. You're going to stay, aren't you?'

Emma looked anxious and she reached over and put her hand on Poppy's.

'I tried to keep you out of it. I thought Ally would be happy to take it out on me alone. But she is what she is. Are you traumatised?'

'No,' said Poppy. 'I think my bum is. But I'm not.'

Emma grinned. 'Our arses go through a lot in this game. We should get them steel-plated or something.'

And do the same for our hearts, thought Poppy, thinking of Bruno.

She put her hand in her pocket and stroked the slim outline of her mobile phone.

Which way should she jump?

Two Tops One Crop

The brochure hadn't lied. The cottage was as isolated and rustic as promised, with an Aga in the kitchen, a log fire in the living room and a septic tank out in the back yard.

Standing on the front step, Lucy looked out over a vista of purple and green, doing all that rolling hill stuff, with white dots that must be sheep spaced here and there. Behind and above it all, a sky like the bruises she often found on her bum the morning after a good session: dark, violet and grey, fading to yellow.

A storm was a-coming.

Oh yes.

She took her mobile from her pocket and saw, for the eighteenth time, that there was no signal for her network here. Perhaps she'd have to climb to the top of that hill if she wanted to make sure her companions weren't tailgating on the M4 or hopelessly lost in some nexus of unpronounceable villages with names that began with 'Ll'.

She should go inside, make a brew, enjoy the peace and quiet while it lasted, because once Rob and Richard were here, there would be precious little of it.

Richard and Rob had been 'TopoftheCrops' and 'ChiefWhip76' when she'd first got to know them. She opened her laptop and left it to boot up while she sorted out a cup of tea. The mobile signal might be non-existent, but the broadband connection was surprisingly good. If she logged on to MasterMe.com, she might find a message or two on there.

But there was nothing except the usual chancers, ignoring the fact that she'd set her status as 'taken'. No, she wasn't interested in a piercing party in Newark and neither did she want to meet a man who looked like the Incredible Hulk for 'kinky fun'.

She was quite happy as things stood, thank you.

Or at least, she'd thought she was. But if that was true, would she have agreed to this weekend away *à trois*?

For ten months, she'd seen Richard one week and Rob the next, both knowing about the other, everything as civilised and happy as can be. She'd ricocheted between the two of them like a ping-pong ball between paddles – not an inapt simile, given their joint love of the wooden bat. A love her bottom did not share.

And then things had started to change, slowly and subtly at first. Richard started to ask about Rob. Rob wanted to see her more often. Their activities in bed, after the spankings, grew more adventurous and filthier.

'Does Rob do this to you?'

'Has Richard ever touched you here?'

'Bet Rob hasn't got a set of these?'

'Fuck Richard, this arse is mine, oh fuck, yes, ohh, yes.'

Somehow, a discussion of what the other man did with Lucy became an integral part of their sexual dynamic, a spicy sauce without which the main dish seemed blandly lacking.

Then the rivalry grew and developed. Lucy spent more

time with both of them and, as the gaps between rendezvous narrowed, it became less easy to turn up without marks on her bottom or a lovebite on her breast.

Each man tried to outdo the other, sending her to his rival with a neater set of cane stripes, or a prettier cluster of needleprick bruises, or a sorer pair of nipples than the other.

Lucy became accustomed to the initial inspection when her lovers arrived at her flat. Almost before they were through the door they would order her to strip, or show them her bottom, and she would spend some time being thoroughly examined for signs of the Other.

Two Wednesdays beforehand, she had waited for Rob after work, dressed in the short wine-red skater dress she knew he liked, no knickers underneath, sheer stockings and suspenders her only concession to lingerie. As she always did before he called, she had laid out her collection of straps and paddles and the rest on the bed ready, but instead of sitting demurely on the sofa, she paced up and down, looking periodically out to the street for signs of him.

Sitting down wasn't an option, because Richard had birched her three days earlier, and it hadn't stopped stinging like buggery. Speaking of which, he'd been more than usually enthusiastic in his commandeering of her arse afterwards and she felt the rawness of it still.

Rob was going to have to take it easy tonight, and he wouldn't be best pleased.

She watched him turn the corner of the street and cross towards her building, the collar of his tan leather jacket turned up against the blustering wind. He was long and lean and fine-featured where Richard was squarer, darker and more rugged, but she still couldn't acknowledge a preference. Either one would do. Either or both.

Besides, she was tired of comparing and contrasting. Rob more sensitive, Richard playing the brute with such effective menace. Rob funnier, Richard cleverer. Rob younger and more open-minded, Richard with his wealth of experience.

Rob rang the bell and she buzzed him up, then headed for the fridge and the bottle of chablis, readying it on the coffee table with the big fishbowl glasses.

That was another one – Rob white, Richard red. Like the chess pieces in *Through The Looking Glass*. The red king and the white king. And she was Alice. It certainly felt as if everything was topsy-turvy back-to-front often enough in her life.

Rob called her from the hallway and she went to greet him, putting her arms about his neck and pressing herself against the deliciously cold leather of his jacket for a taste of his deliciously warm lips.

'Mmm,' he said, patting her bottom. She tried not to wince or clench. 'My favourite dress.'

He was barely through the door, still wearing his coat, but it didn't stop him from sliding a hand beneath the flippy skirt and seeking Lucy's grazed cheeks.

He felt the birch marks straight away, his stroking fingers chafing her skin.

'What's he done *now*?' he exclaimed, stepping back. 'Turn around, lift up your skirt. How the hell did he do that? What was it, some kind of whip?'

Lucy, facing away from her interlocuter, patiently held her skirt up for him to get the best view of her welted bottom.

'Birch,' she said.

'Birch? This is the middle of London. Where did he find a fucking birch rod?'

'We drove out to the countryside, Sunday afternoon.'

'So now he's taking you out and about?' Rob huffed. 'I'm going to have to up my game. He's taking the piss now.'

'Rob, calm down. Come and have a glass of wine. How was your day? How have you been this week?'

His face was still pale and his eyes overcast when he took his place on the sofa for their traditional inhibition-loosener.

'I'm good, thanks, fine. I missed you. I wish you'd come out with me, to the movies or something. Have you seen the James Bond? We could go this weekend.'

'Maybe.'

She smiled, too brightly. Things were getting out of hand. She poured the glasses of wine, hovering over the coffee table.

'Maybe, maybe.' He raised the glass to his lips and took a gulp, then shrugged off his jacket and dumped it over the arm of the sofa. 'Sit down.'

His voice had lost the grumpy, whiny edge. He was in role, quicker than a fingerclick.

'It hurts,' she said apologetically.

'Sit. Down. And then you can tell me exactly what Richard did to you.'

Lucy had to plump up a cushion and place herself slowly and gingerly atop it. Work had been hell these last three days. She was a PE teacher, so at least she didn't have to do much sitting, but the running up and down the hockey pitch, even in her loosest tracksuit trousers, had still been a mite uncomfortable.

'Alcohol's an analgesic, isn't it?' she said ruefully, taking a big mouthful of wine.

'You'd better hope so, because you're going to need a bucket of it by the time I'm finished with you.'

Rob put down his glass and folded his arms.

'So? I'm waiting.'

'I wasn't planning on seeing him on Sunday. We were meant to have a date Friday night, but he got stuck at this conference, and couldn't make it back to town in time.'

Rob mock-pouted. 'Shame,' he said.

'But then he showed up in church! I turned around to offer the sign of peace and there he was! I nearly screamed. He's never said anything about being religious.'

'Money's his religion, isn't it? Fucking accountant.'

'Stop it. He's not an accountant.'

'Accountant, banker, whatevs.'

'Do you want to hear this story?'

'Do you want to use that tone with me?'

Hard stare.

She swallowed.

'No, sir,' she said softly and he smiled for the first time.

'Go on, then. What happened next?'

'We left together at the end of the service, and he offered to drive us out to the country, for a nice pub lunch somewhere. Well, I didn't have anything planned, apart from marking my year 11 coursework folders, so I took him up on it.'

'I hope you got your marking done, young lady.'

'I did, sir, don't worry. But I had to do it standing up.'

He snorted.

'No doubt. Where did he take you? No, hang on, first of all, what car does he drive?'

'Oh, I don't know about cars. A Mercedes, I think. Silver, quiet as a mouse.'

'Fucking stiff. If I had his wedge, I'd drive a Bugatti Veyron.'

'Good for you, sir. Anyway, um, he took me to some place near the river, near Maidenhead. Very nice. Lovely food, bottle of wine I'd have to take out a second mortgage to afford.'

Rob sniffed. 'I'll take you down Harvester for a carvery and half a lager top, if you like. Can't compete with that, though.'

'Sir,' she said gently, always finding it judicious to open with an honorific if it seemed she might be overreaching herself. 'With respect, it's not a competition. I don't want you to compete with him. You aren't him. I like that you aren't him. And I like that he isn't you.'

He put his head to one side, a little sheepish at being caught out in his jealousy.

'I just worry that he might dazzle you, you know. Lure you away from me.'

'He won't. I'm not like that.'

'I know. So, anyway. You ate the food and drank the wine and somehow your arse got covered in stripes. How did that happen?'

'After the meal, he drove us to Virginia Water. We went for a walk along the shores of the lake.'

'Sounds very romantic.'

'It wasn't really. You know, not self-consciously. I mean, we weren't trying to be romantic. Just friends enjoying an afternoon together. But then we got into this quiet part of the wood, and nobody else seemed to be about, and he took out a Swiss Army knife.'

'As one does, during a romantic woodland walk.' Rob grinned. 'Bit unnerving.'

'Well, yes, a bit. But he handed it to me and pointed at a tree and said, "Cut me some switches".' She laughed despite herself at her impersonation of Richard's deep, Northern tones.

Rob laughed with her. 'If I ever hear him talk for real . . . I bet he sounds nothing like that.'

'He does, though! Like Sean Bean, but a bit posher. And then he said, "Supple as you can, please." So I guess the tree was a birch, but I don't know much about trees.'

'Trees, cars. What *do* you know about?'

'I can name you every Olympic and Paralympic sport if you like.'

'Thanks but no thanks.'

'Anyway, yes, the tree was a birch. I know weeping willows and oaks and conker trees.'

'Horse chestnuts.'

'Yeah, those. But birches just look like a lot of other ones really, don't they. Anyway, it wasn't really a tree, more a kind of bush.'

'A shrub.'

'I suppose. I cut some bits off it. Richard wanted about six. I felt really guilty and I kept thinking that some official royal gardener might catch us, and have us arrested for defacing Her Majesty's trees or something, and we'd end up in the Tower. But nothing like that happened.'

'Richard would have paid them off. He's probably good mates with Prince Charles or something.'

'I don't think so. After I cut the little branchy things, I gave them to Richard and he made me go and stand with my arms around a tree trunk.'

Rob's jaw dropped. 'He didn't whip you in the open air, did he? The fucker. I want to do that! I've been waiting for the summer. The bastard.'

'He didn't do it properly. Said the switches needed trimming first and besides, I was dressed for church in a corduroy skirt, so it wasn't going to hurt as much as he likes it to. And I was very antsy about Sunday strollers happening upon us.'

'And did they?'

'No, luckily. Richard just gave me a swipe across the seat of my skirt with each wand, to test them. The cord deadened the sound a bit, but it was still bloody painful. I was kind of dreading what might happen next.'

'What did happen next?'

'We came back here.'

'You never go to his place, do you?'

'He has a teenage son.'

'Oh, right. I didn't know that.'

'Why would you? He doesn't know you live in a shared house in Acton, either.'

'I need to get my own place. I've got enough for a deposit on a flat saved. I'm going to make an appointment with the bank next week.'

'Let's not descend into mortgage chat, eh? This isn't a dinner party.'

'Oh, I'm going to enjoy thrashing you today. You're in one of your moods.'

Lucy cast down her eyes at once.

'Sorry for disrespecting you, sir,' she said, as ingratiatingly as she could.

He chuckled. 'Too late,' he said, patting her thigh. 'You're going to wish you hadn't let his Lordship go to town on your bum. Bad move, Luce. Anyway, go on. You came back here.'

'Yes, we came back here and Richard made me strip to my underwear, then he sat me at the kitchen table with his knife and the birch rods, and made me cut off all the rough, sticky-out bits that might break the skin. Then I had to kind of whittle it.'

'Really? Whittling? Woodland crafts?' Rob chortled. 'Amazing, the skills you can pick up in the course of a corporal punishment fetish.'

'Yes. Then I had to tie them all together with tape, until they were in a big bunch. Well, you've seen them before, I'm sure.'

'Not in real life.'

'I'll show you it later. Richard makes me keep them soaking in a bucket of salted water. Stops them drying out, apparently.'

'Really? And how do you explain a bucket of birch rods in your bathroom to visitors?'

'I don't have visitors, apart from you and Richard.'

'Just as well.' He smiled, but then he seemed to look at her more closely, a flicker of concern in his cheery blue eyes. 'You sounded lonely just then.'

'I'm not lonely. I'm fine. Anyway.' Lucy wanted to hurry the conversation off this track. 'Back to last Sunday. Where was I?'

'In the kitchen.'

'Uh, oh yeah. So, well, he birched me, basically.'

'Lucy! You can't just leave it like that. I need details. How many? What position? How did it feel? I need to know if it's something I should be seriously considering.'

He put his slender fingers under her chin and tilted it, forcing her eyes up to meet his. His smile always looked so kind, Lucy thought, and yet he was capable of remorseless severity.

'I had to take down my knickers and bend over the kitchen table,' said Lucy, her voice quietening now. She still found having to vocalise her experiences difficult and embarrassing. She knew that was why both Richard and Rob always insisted on it, too. Well, partly. That, and the wisdom of knowing your opposition.

'Legs together or apart?'

'Together, this time. I was scared of a rod whipping somewhere it shouldn't. Since it was my first time, Richard allowed it. Next time he's going to make me stand with my feet hip-width apart, he says. I should trust his aim. I suppose it is pretty good, in general.'

'So's mine.'

'Yes, my dear sir, so is yours.' She gave him a cheeky smile, enjoying his little chinks of insecurity when they appeared. 'I got twelve. I didn't think I'd make it through. The first two or three didn't really feel that bad, just a bit warm and stingy, but it soon got very painful.'

'Did you yell?'

'Yes, I did, I'm afraid. And I very nearly cried.'

'Seriously? You? You only cry when I'm hideously cruel to you.'

'I know. It really hurts though. It feels as if it's getting under your skin. Reminded me of those stories of martyrs being flayed alive. When I looked at myself in the mirror, afterwards, I was quite surprised to see that there wasn't any blood. Though there were these little red pinpoints, where I hadn't whittled quite as thoroughly as I should have done.'

'They're still there. It must have looked incredible, just after he finished.'

'It did. A lattice of long red lines, all cross-hatched and raised, all over my skin.'

'Fuck. My mouth's watering. I'm going to have to do that one day. Show me the rods.'

She took him through to the bathroom where they lay,

looking perfectly innocuous, like those arrangements of spray-painted twigs in vases, in a corner by the shower.

Rob picked them up, shaking the excess drops of water into the bath, and swished them through the air a few times, practising his forehand then his backhand.

'This is lovely,' he said, reverently. 'I'm going to be obsessed with the birch now. Show me your arse again.'

Lucy bent obediently over the sink and lifted her skirt.

Rob put down the rods and cupped her cheeks in his hands, tracing the leftover welts with his thumbs as if reading braille.

'And it's still so sore,' he said, in a soothing, tutting voice. 'I know what you need.'

He reached up to the bathroom cabinet and took out a bottle.

Lucy gasped.

'Oh, no.'

'It's good for you,' sang Rob. 'A little iodine on your wounds works wonders.'

Lucy clutched the sides of the basin as the fire, only half-doused anyway, roared back into full flame at her rear.

'Ohh,' she moaned. 'Noooo!'

Rob continued to dab an iodine-soaked cotton wool ball over her bottom, joining little points of scorching pain up like a dot-to-dot puzzle until conflagration was achieved.

'We don't want any nasty infections, do we?' said Rob, tossing the cotton wool in the bin and stepping back. 'You've gone darker red again. Stand up and take off the dress.'

Lucy obeyed, shifting from her left foot to her right in an attempt to distract herself from the sting. When she was naked, except for stockings and suspender belt, she put her hands by her sides, as he liked her to, and looked down at the floor.

Later on, after a sound slippering and an exhausting session of rear entry sex, Lucy lay with her head on Rob's chest and her bottom off the mattress, cooling in the breeze from the open bedroom window.

She luxuriated in the throb, and the pleasant fatigue of her limbs, breathing in Rob's scent of faded aftershave and fresh sweat, hearing his heart hammer in her ear.

'I think I want to meet your Richard,' said Rob suddenly.

Lucy raised her head, heavy eyelids flying open.

'You don't.'

He levelled a steady, serious gaze at her.

'I do. We should definitely meet.'

'Why?'

'Because we have so much in common. You, in particular.'

'What if I'm happy with the way things are. What if he is?'

'You aren't happy with the way things are, Lucy.'

'I am.'

'All right, then, you are. I'm not.'

She propped herself on an elbow, heart racing in dismay.

'Rob, I can't lose you. Please don't—'

'You're not going to lose me.'

'If you want me to choose between the two of you—'

'Lucy, calm down. Lie down. Come on.'

He snuggled her back into the crook of her arm, but she was still tense and taut with dread of what he might say next.

'I'm not saying you have to choose between us. And I'm not saying what you're doing is bad. I just think it could be better if we all knew each other, properly.'

Lucy lay silent for a while, staring at Rob's shoulder. Her cheek rose and fell in rhythm with his breathing. Was it such an outrageous idea?

.

The thought of sitting between the pair of them on some sofa in some bar made her sex heat up again, despite its recent exhaustive use. Caught between two lovers. Two doms. Twice the kink, double the fun. Could it ever be as simple as that?

She was sure she could never pick one over the other, if matters came to that head. Perhaps this might be a way of avoiding such a crisis? Or precipitating it?

It was dangerous, but alluring.

And Rob wanted it, and what Rob wanted, he generally got. It would probably save a lot of machinations and manipulations if she just gave in now.

'So, you want me to, like, introduce you to Richard?'

'Yeah. I think we should all spend some time together. It's been getting on for a year, Lucy. I want to take things a step further. Don't you?'

'I don't like making decisions.'

'I know you don't. So I'm making one for you. Talk to Richard. See what he thinks of the idea. And then perhaps we can get something off the ground.'

Lucy had tried to mention it to Richard, but somehow it had taken her three visits – and three painful punishments from Rob for her procrastination – to finally bring the subject up.

She expected him to reject the idea out of hand. He was a wealthy, busy man who slotted Lucy into one compartment of his life, never cross-contaminating it with the others. Richard's life was organised in ranks: job, family, social life, sex. The first three could overlap; the fourth, never.

Or so Lucy had always seen it.

So when he nodded and stroked his chin and said, 'Why not?' she was startled.

'I thought you'd hate the idea. I've been afraid of mentioning it.'

'You're not usually afraid of mentioning things. As these stripes on your bottom testify.'

He was kneeling between her legs while she lay on her back with her knees bent, spread and hovering near her ears. He was inserting a butt plug. It might not be the obvious moment to discuss arrangements for meeting up with your other dom, but Lucy didn't really understand the concept of there being a time and a place for everything.

'I'm sorry I said that, sir. It was rude of me.'

'Yes, it was.' He paused in the application of lubricant to her defenceless back passage. 'I won't hear any more allusions to grey hairs, thank you very much.'

'It was a joke.'

'A bad one.'

The plug went inside her without much finesse. Perhaps she should show more contrition, she thought, whimpering.

'There's something to remind you of your place,' said Richard sternly, twisting the plug without mercy. 'Now, tell me what Rob did with that dildo and the chilli flakes. He sounds highly imaginative. I'm surprised you dare suggest that we meet and compare notes.'

'It is stupid of me,' sighed Lucy. 'I see that now.'

Richard took hold of her hips and eased himself into her pussy, keeping her knees high and wide, his gym-flat stomach flexing in her line of vision . . .

And now she was here in this miles-from-anywhere cottage, perfectly alone, waiting for them both.

It had been Richard's suggestion that they meet on neutral territory, somewhere without distractions, where they could get to know each other in depth. He could afford to hire anywhere, but he didn't want to show off in front of Rob, which Lucy thought was rather sweet of him. There was a sensitivity that he kept hidden behind his layers of mannered strictness and prestige but, when it flashed a glint now and again, Lucy was deeply grateful for it. After all, Rob could be a bit chippy sometimes. So they had paid equal thirds for the rental cottage, and nobody could claim to be the biggest stakeholder in the experience.

It was raining sincerely, and Lucy had pulled the curtains against the gathering gloom when a flare of rounded light shone through the patterned calico. A car headlamp. She put down her mug and hurried to the front door, peering out of the porch, avoiding the heavy drips from the roof.

It wasn't Richard's Mercedes, but that wasn't really the right car to be driving around here, anyway. It was a large, expensive-looking Range Rover, powering through the mud on the drive until it came to a halt in the side yard. Luckily the resident chickens were all sheltering in the coops, so this didn't cause a problem.

Richard jumped out, dressed for the countryside in waxed jacket and waterproof trousers, and took his bags from the boot.

The rain flattened his dark hair and dripped off the end of his rather prominent nose, but he was smiling as he approached Lucy.

'You were expecting this weather?' she said, watching him pull off wellington boots and put them in a rack on the porch. His feet were cocooned in thick woollen socks. He had to duck to get through the front door, and he filled the tiny front room of the cottage like a giant, making all the furniture look miniature.

'Of course,' he said. 'It's Wales.' He looked around the room. 'Cosy,' he said with a laugh.

'I don't suppose it compares with your country estate, my Lord. I hope you didn't forget your shooting stick.'

'Don't cheek me, or it'll be a different kind of stick for you.'

He put down his bags, which occupied most of the floor.

'No sign of our friend yet?' he asked, peering through the open door to the kitchen.

'No, not yet. I hope he's OK. His car's more or less clapped-out. I did offer to give him a lift but he said he wanted to drive himself. In case he needed a quick getaway, I think. I'd try and phone him but there's no signal here.'

'No landline?'

'No. Look, you're soaked through. Take your coat off and I'll get a towel.'

Lucy ran up the wooden stairs to the big bedroom with its huge four-post bed. Not for the first time, she wondered about sleeping arrangements. There was only one other bedroom, more like a box room, tiny and narrow with a candlewick-covered single divan. They could, in theory, all fit into the four-poster, but would that be acceptable to all parties? Lucy rather hoped so.

Her phone bleeped and she took it out of her pocket, bemused.

It seemed that a weak signal was available in the upstairs rooms.

Rob had texted her.

'Punto wdnt start, abandoned at mway services, have caught train from Swindon. Can u pick up from rway station? Prob won't get there till 10/half past.'

'Oh dear,' said Lucy out loud.

'What's up?' shouted Richard from downstairs. The cottage was too small for secrets, apparently.

'Rob's having to take the train,' she called down. 'We'll have to get him from the station. But he's going to be at least another three hours.'

She texted him back, 'OK c u l8r xxx' and headed back down with the towel.

'Three hours?' Richard had shed his waterproofs and sat on the sofa in a chunky jumper and jeans. It seemed so wrong to see him out of his suits. Well, obviously she had seen him naked, too, but this casual, informal Richard was alien to her. 'What are we going to do until then?'

'Eat, I guess. The owners left us some ingredients – all locally sourced, I think. Some lamb shanks, potatoes, onions, garlic, veg. Kind of an emergency ration. Just as well. I'm not sure takeaways would deliver all the way down here. There's an Aga in the kitchen, so it'll probably take three hours to cook it. And a wood-burner. You and Rob will have to chop logs. Mmm. Preferably without shirts.'

Richard chuckled. 'Rustic porn, eh?' he said, getting up. 'I'll give you a hand in the kitchen.'

'Can you cook?'

'Yes. You didn't know that, did you?'

'You've never cooked for me.'

'We usually have other things on our minds, don't we?'

Lucy wanted to sigh. But she didn't.

'Yes,' she said, wondering if all this was a good idea, after all.

Perhaps she shouldn't be indulging herself in this illusion of an ordinary, loving domestic life with an unattainable man. She had to accept the relationship the way it was – sporadic, ad hoc, futureless. Hot sex for a season. To do otherwise was to doom herself to dashed hopes and heartache.

Richard stepped up to the work surface and began slicing onions in a highly competent manner while Lucy struggled to light the range. Soon enough, a glowing warmth spread through the room, and her bones too, lending a magical air to proceedings. The blatter of rain on the window added to this, much as she sympathised with poor Rob, making his haphazard way through it.

Richard didn't seem to have much to say, so she switched on Radio Four and let a drama about a 1950s public school take up the conversational slack.

'Are you nervous?' she asked, chopping the lamb while Richard sauteed onions and garlic in a frying pan.

'About what? Meeting Rob? No.'

'I am. I'm very nervous. I so want you to get on.'

He let go of the frying pan handle briefly, to put a hand on her shoulder.

'We have one very important thing in common,' he said. 'I think we'll both bear that in mind.'

'Do you cook often?' Lucy watched him put together a redcurrant sauce.

'No. Not often enough.'

She wanted to ask so many questions, but something about his manner held her back. Instead, as they ate, they talked about previous trips to Wales, their days at work, their backwoods survival skills.

This is what lovers do, thought Lucy, watching Richard intently as he shovelled lamb casserole into his mouth. The mouth that commanded her, kissed her, did unimaginably ravishing things to her . . . She so rarely saw it doing these usual things. *And then, when the meal is over . . .*

She knew that look on Richard's face.

'It seems rude,' she blurted. 'To start without him.'

'I've left some in the Aga on a low heat,' said Richard, deliberately misunderstanding.

'No, you know what I mean.'

He watched her intently for a moment then sat back.

'Fair enough,' he said. 'We'll have to leave soon anyway. Game of cards, then?'

Lucy shook her head, jittery with nerves again.

'Tell you what,' said Richard, clearing away the plates. 'You might not want to start anything without Rob, but how about you get changed? Put on a dress and nothing else.'

Lucy laughed, her eyes wide with disbelief.

'Shoes?'

'Wellington boots. And a little dress and nothing else. You have brought one?'

Lucy blushed. 'Yes, yes, I have.' It seemed shameful to be admitting that she was expecting sex this weekend - though why it should be, she couldn't quite understand.

'Go on, then.'

He finished the dishes while Lucy bolted upstairs and stripped off her jeans and top and workaday underwear.

In her suitcase she found Rob's favourite skater dress. Thank goodness all the netball and hockey kept her breasts high and perky, she thought, slipping it over her head. Of course, the minute her nipples hardened, they would telegraph her bralessness to all who cared to look, but hopefully that would be nobody but Richard and Rob. It would only take a tiny gust of wind to raise her skirt and bare all. She was definitely staying in the car. Richard could get out and help Rob with his bags when they got to the station. She would sit on the big front seat of the Range Rover, with her thighs pressed together, and wait.

Her bare feet were light and quiet on the stairs, but

Richard still anticipated her, waiting at the bottom with arms folded and an expression of quiet satisfaction.

'Just right,' he said, putting out an arm and reeling her into his chest.

Was it all right to kiss without Rob? Was that cheating?

Lucy dismissed the anxieties and let Richard's firm mouth close over hers, kissing away everything but her senses and her pleasure receptors.

'You know, Lucy,' he whispered, breaking off for a moment, his hand rubbing the small of her back rhythmically and comfortingly, 'it doesn't matter if Rob and I don't get on. It won't be your fault. We both know what we've got in you. I don't think either of us will forget that.'

'It'll be OK,' she said, for courage, the words acting as talismans.

'It'll be OK,' he repeated after her. 'Come on. Get your wellies on and get into the car.'

They ran through the rain to the Rover, belted themselves in and headed into the lane. The journey was rough but exciting; the bumpy road jolted Lucy this way and that. Richard made her sit on her bare bottom on the soft leather of the front seat, and the thrill of the journey mixed together with a potent erotic sensation so that, by the time they arrived at the station, she was sticky of thigh and her heart was bumping fast. All the way home, she would be sitting between Rob and Richard, in this tiny dress and no knickers. All the way home.

Richard pulled into the station car park and put on the handbrake.

'OK,' he said. 'Go get him.'

Lucy stared.

'Me?'

'He doesn't know me.'

'I bet he'd recognise you.'

Richard shook his head.

'He's your friend. You go and wait for him.'

'But—'

'No buts.'

Lucy huffed and sighed and spent a long time trying to make her dress longer, to no avail.

Richard eventually leant over her to open the door and she slid, very carefully and very slowly, along the seat and swung her legs to the side.

How ridiculous she would look, in her flirty little party dress and big green rubber boots. Everyone would stare. Everyone would whisper. And that was without the underwear problem.

She didn't have to go far, at least. Just a couple of yards up the pavement, under a shelter, and into the ticket office, which was, thankfully, empty. She might have been observed by a couple of taxi drivers waiting in the rank, but that was all.

It was cold on the platform and her thighs felt the worst of it. Her nipples ached and she knew they were visible through the slinky jersey material of the dress. She looked at the digital display board closest to her. Rob's train was expected in ten minutes.

She didn't dare look down the platform to see who else was waiting, for fear of catching somebody's eye. It was fairly obvious, though, that a sprawling group of young people were standing not far away from her, on their way home from a big night out at one of the town's two pubs.

She listened to their dirty jokes and friendly insults, glad that they were too preoccupied with each other to notice her.

She sank back against the wall and rested her bottom on a ledge in the brickwork, staring down at the rails.

When she looked up, there was a man on the opposite platform, watching her. She looked away immediately, but she heard his footsteps, heading for the footbridge.

She got up, intent on going back to the car until the train was actually in the station, but her way was barred by a pair of girls from the nearby group.

They looked her up and down with undisguised contempt.

'Funny way of dressing for the weather, don't you think, Bron?'

They could hardly talk, thought Lucy nervously, with their tiny miniskirts and thick white legs, cut off at the calf by fake Ugg boots.

'Must be a new thing. Farm whores. I suppose the farmers get lonely. Do you cheer them up, love?'

Some of the boys were slouching up behind them now, amused sneers splitting their spotty faces. One of them wolf-whistled.

'Leave 'er,' said another. 'You should be so lucky to have legs like that, Char.'

'Fuck off. I'm good enough for you when you want to cop a feel.'

The youngsters reverted to arguing amongst themselves. Lucy took advantage of their distraction to remove herself to the ladies' toilets – unpleasant enough, but not threatening, at least – until she heard the slow thunder of the train pulling in.

She hurried back to the platform, pleased to see that her former adversaries were safely on the train, and looked about her, seeing nobody.

Then a pair of hands covered her eyes from behind and she jumped, her wellies weighing down her legs.

'Rob!' she squealed in strangulated excitement. 'Is that you?'

'No,' he said, 'it's the Brecon Beacons Ripper. I have you at my mercy.'

She elbowed his ribs and he coughed, letting go of her. His laughing face was never more welcome.

'You made it, then?' she said dryly.

'By the skin of my teeth,' he said, picking up his bags and shaking his head. 'Fucking car. Thanks for coming to pick me up.'

On the station forecourt he looked blankly one way then the other.

'Where's your car? Nice shoes, by the way.'

'Shut up. I hope you've brought some wellies too. And if you're looking for my car, you won't find it.'

He put the bags down again and stared at her.

She nodded.

'Shit. I'm not ready for this.' He had to regain his breath for a moment or two.

He picked up the bags.

'OK,' he said. 'Lead on, MacDuff.'

Lucy stomped over to the Range Rover. Rob threw his bags in the back, then climbed up beside Lucy, who sat in the middle of the three, already belted up.

'You must be Rob,' drawled Richard, putting out a hand to shake.

'You must be Richard,' mimicked Rob, taking it.

Lucy watched the clasp bob up and down in front of her stomach, Richard's bigger hand, Rob's longer fingers, an expensive signet ring, a pair of black rubber bracelets.

'And our Lucy,' said Richard. 'A rose between two thorns.'

Her mind almost blew with the force of their two gazes. It was what she had wanted and dreaded, finally happening.

'Thanks for the lift,' said Rob, looking out at the rainy dark again. 'Filthy night for it.'

'I've seen worse,' said Richard, starting the engine.

Rob made a face at Lucy, as if to say, I knew he would be like this.

'You must be hungry,' she said. 'We've a casserole keeping warm in the oven for you. And the owner left us a couple of bottles of wine.'

'Nice one.'

They rode on in silence for a while, through the single lit street of the tiny town and out into the darkness, rainswept shapes of hills and trees their only view.

'She's not wearing knickers,' said Richard suddenly.

Lucy's heart contracted.

Rob swallowed. 'Oh?'

'I made her take them off to meet you. Seems a waste if you don't, you know . . .'

Rob looked at Lucy, who looked at Richard.

'Do you mind if we do?'

'Kiss her,' said Richard. 'Do what you want to do with her.'

Lucy turned back to Rob.

He took her by the chin. 'Did you start without me, you two?' he asked softly.

Lucy shook her head. 'We waited for you.'

He smiled, and then tilted her mouth into a long, wet kiss. His cheeks and chin were still damp from the rain, and his skin was so cold. But she felt it warm against hers, quickly, and soon all of that was forgotten, locked outside of their embrace.

His long, chilly fingers tapped a path from her knee upwards, finding the heat and shelter of her skirt, delving underneath and massaging her thigh.

Lucy hoped Richard was keeping his eye on the road, and yet she also hoped he was watching, seeing how obedient she was to his will. She had wondered, over and over, how her lovers would feel about seeing her with another man. That Richard had initiated the first opportunity was wonderful to her, a huge weight off her mind. She was grateful and she was accordingly more permissive with Rob than she might otherwise have been, letting him do anything and everything he wanted to her.

She spread her thighs wide and laid her head back, accepting the rude probing of his tongue inside her mouth. Soon enough it was mirrored by the ruder probing of his fingers. He kneaded between her pussy lips with his knuckles, grinding them in her moist slit, bumping over her swollen clitoris.

She began to make deep, throaty sounds of encouragement.

'She likes that,' said Richard. An indicator clicked. 'She likes a good fingering in the car. I should know.'

Yes, you should, thought Lucy, thinking back to that afternoon in the passenger seat of his Mercedes, her skirt rucked up and tights around her knees while he steered single-handedly, reaching over to massage her clit every time they stopped at a set of lights. They had both been strung up with erotic anticipation of her birching.

And now what were they strung up with? The possibilities seemed endless to Lucy as Rob kept his mouth firmly on hers and began to thrust slowly inside her with three juiced fingers. She let her bare bottom squirm against the leather, although it was starting to stick to it.

'How wet is she?' asked Richard, negotiating a hairpin bend.

Rob broke the kiss just enough to gasp, 'Fucking soaking,' before resuming.

Lucy jolted her pelvis forwards, moaning with satisfaction when Rob's thumb circled her clit. His hand was all over her, owning her pleasure, while Richard drove implacably onwards, a witness to her brazen lust.

The rain lashed on the windscreen and the engine purred along with her own voice.

'Make her come,' said Richard. 'Make her come all over your fingers.'

The words precipitated the flood. Lucy bucked and mewled under Rob's domineering mouth and hands, the vibrations from the engine adding to the intensity of it all.

'She loved that,' said Richard, his voice scratchy, as if caught on something sharp.

'Mm,' agreed Rob, holding Lucy close, stroking her hair. 'She always does. Don't you, kitten?'

Lucy rubbed the crown of her head into his chest, the way she had earned that nickname in the first place. She shut her eyes and let the feeling of satiety seep into her bones. The weekend had begun. And it was going to be incredible.

When a lurch and a jolt and a sudden ending of the lovely low-slung vibrations sent her into a tizz, Lucy realised that she had dozed off.

They were back at the cottage, parked in the paved yard, by the chicken coops. The rain still menaced the vehicle from all sides. Both Richard and Rob looked at her, indulgently amused.

'Better now, Snoring Beauty?' asked Richard. 'That orgasm must have taken it out of you.'

Her hairline prickled with embarrassment. She had acted shamelessly, in front of him. She snuck a sidelong glance at Rob, who had taken off his seatbelt.

'How long was I asleep?'

'Not long. Not long enough for my hard-on to go down, anyway,' said Rob.

Richard reached over and sprung the catch on her seatbelt, releasing her.

'Take off that dress,' he said. 'Then get on your knees and suck him.'

She widened her eyes at Rob, who grinned and nodded.

'Fair's fair,' he said laconically. Then he looked over at Richard and frowned a little. 'I've never done this in front of another bloke.'

'Don't be shy,' said Richard. 'I have. She can do me first, if you prefer. Whatever you're comfortable with.'

'Oh.' Rob sounded surprised and considered this for a moment. 'Right. No, it's fine. I'll go first. If that's all right with you?'

'Of course. Be my guest.'

'No, nobody's the host here and nobody's the guest,' said Rob, slightly combative.

'Sorry, you're right, just a figure of speech,' said Richard with effortless smoothness. 'We're all equal.'

'Two of you are more equal than others,' pointed out Lucy.

'True.' Rob smirked, the moment's ruffling ironed out flat by the gathering storm of his arousal. 'In which case, get on your knees and use your mouth.'

Lucy took a deep breath and pulled her dress over her head.

Richard snapped on the overhead light so that, in the streaming windscreen, she saw the reflection of her pale, naked body, her breasts high and jaunty with big, prominent nipples.

She didn't want to look at herself, so she dropped quickly

to her knees. The rubber mats on the footwell were clean and dry, at least. She pushed her breasts between Rob's blue-jeaned legs and reached up for his fly. He stroked her cheek.

'I'm hard for you,' he whispered.

Richard said nothing, but his presence was more potent than any words could have been. He was there, the watcher, judging her on her performance.

She unbuttoned the jeans then let Rob ease them over his hips to make it easier for her to lower the elasticated waistband of his boxers. Yes, he was hard for her, yes. His cock stood upright, straining for her attention, glistening at the tip.

She shuffled forwards and held on to his thighs for purchase, licking up the shaft.

Rob took her wrist and moved one of her hands to his testicles. She held them, squeezing and caressing, while she prepared her lips to stretch.

Rob had no need to be shy of showing the other man his equipment. He was a good length and thickness, possibly a little shorter than the older man, but not noticeably so. His erection pointed, straight and wide, to his navel.

Lucy positioned her mouth over the tip and began to lower herself along the shaft.

'Mmm.' She couldn't resist a little low-down moan as she felt him stretch her jaw.

Rob put one hand in her hair while the other squeezed her breasts.

'Wonderful little cocksucker,' said Richard approvingly. 'She gives it her all.'

Everything was quiet after that, save the rain and the slow sucking and licking sounds of Lucy servicing her master's cock with her mouth.

'Stop,' said Richard, after about three minutes.

Rob made an inarticulate sound of disagreement but Lucy, conditioned to obey, unsealed her lips and looked up at Richard, trying to focus her eyes.

'What the fuck?' said Rob, when he could form words.

'No, I don't mean stop entirely,' said Richard. 'It's just occurred to me that she could get on the seat between us and suck you from there. Then I could play with her.' He patted the leather space. 'Up on the seat, slut, and get back to work.'

He spoke again to Rob while Lucy arranged herself as ordered and resumed her sucking.

'I'm sorry it seems as if I'm giving all the orders. Once we're back in the house, perhaps you could take over. What do you think? Take turns? Or come up with some other way of playing this?'

'Uh – maybe discuss – over dinner,' panted Rob.

Richard chuckled. 'You're right. Now isn't the best time.'

Lucy, bent over, cramming as much of Rob's cock between her teeth as she could, flinched a little when Richard's thick fingers pulled her pussy lips wide from behind.

'This busy little pussy is going to get a lot of attention this weekend,' he said, pushing a forefinger up inside her. He moved it backwards and forwards, getting it nice and slippery, before withdrawing it and tracing it upwards, into the furrow of her bottom. He found her tight back passage and gave it a sharp, squirmy jab.

'And so is this,' he promised.

She moaned over the head of Rob's cock, and he echoed in response.

'Keep it up,' he urged. 'Suck harder.' He began to thrust into her throat, his fist tugging at her hair.

She bore down on him, feeling Richard's fingers press harder and harder on her clit, until Rob made an incoherent exclamation and flooded her throat with salty creaminess.

'She knows how to give a proper welcome,' said Richard approvingly.

He withdrew his fingers from her pussy.

Lucy knelt up, groggy and disorientated, seeing her naked body in the windscreen.

Richard placed his hands on her hips.

'I think it's my turn now,' he said.

With her position reversed, Lucy treated Richard to a slower, more stately version of fellatio while Rob flicked at her clit and speared her with his fingers.

'Open her up,' growled Richard, his fingers plucking and pinching at the back of Lucy's neck. 'Take what you want from her.'

Rob used the length of his fingers to rub and slither back and forth between Lucy's pussy lips. Nobody seemed shy any more, or awkward at the strangeness of the situation. The heat hung around them, enveloping them in a magic sex world that admitted of no other thoughts.

Lucy gorged on Richard's cock just as much as she devoured the sensation of two pairs of hands on her, grabbing her breasts, slapping her bum, filling her pussy. She wriggled back on Rob's busy fingers as she took Richard deeper and deeper down her throat, possessed by her sexuality.

When she came, Richard pulled sharply out of her mouth and let warm streams of ejaculate decorate her breasts. Some of it got on to her neck and chin.

'Leave it there,' ordered Richard.

At her rear, Rob kissed and nipped at her bum cheeks, his fingers still plunged deep.

Richard took his phone and photographed her, kneeling like that, dripping with come while Rob worked behind her.

'I want lots of pictures of this weekend,' said Richard, to Rob, who had risen from his worship of Lucy's bottom. 'One of us can take them while the other is occupied with Lucy. She's going to get more attention than she can handle, and I want it on record.'

'Sure,' said Rob. He helped Lucy back into a sitting position. 'Are you sure you're ready for this?'

Lucy shook her head.

'Not any more.'

They made her walk barefoot and naked through the mud and rain to the cottage while they hefted Rob's bags from the boot.

Flashes behind her were more likely to be from cameras than lightning.

The rain washed away the spunk, but she was caked in mud splashes up to her knees by the time she arrived on the cottage porch, shivering and soaked.

Richard wrapped her in a dog blanket and carried her into the cottage.

'Food's warming in the oven,' he called to Rob behind him. 'I'm going to get this one bathed.'

Lucy lay up to her chin in the bathwater and watched Richard, who was watching her.

'Are you scared to go back down?' she wondered aloud.

'Scared?' Richard curled his lip.

'Yeah. How do you make small talk with the man who doms your submissive? It's not exactly the kind of thing the advice manuals cover.'

'Well, you might be right,' admitted Richard. 'I'd rather we were all together as much as possible. You provide a focus.

We both like being cruel to you. Apart from that, what do we have to discuss?'

'Do you know many other doms?' Lucy reached out for a towel, which Richard passed to her.

'No,' he said after a pause. 'I don't.'

'You could talk about that. Wouldn't it be a relief? I'd love to meet another submissive and talk about it without feeling like a freakshow. I mean, I know lots online, but to have an actual conversation, over a couple of drinks? I think it'd be special.'

'Women are more interested in that kind of thing,' said Richard dismissively. 'I don't need a social aspect to my kink.'

'You're the strong, silent type,' said Lucy, leaning back against Richard as he rubbed her dry. 'It's a pity, in a way. I think Rob would like to talk about it. I think that would mean a lot to him, actually.'

'Do you?'

Richard pulled the towel off her and began to apply body lotion, generously, and with particular attention to her breasts and bottom.

'Yes, because I think he has some funny ideas about what you have to be like to be a dom. And you are it. You are the man who defines dom-ness, in his imagination. Powerful, older, rich, good suits, all that. I think he's worried he doesn't measure up. But, you know, he does. I try to tell him that a good dom can look like anyone, come from anywhere, have any job. But he finds it hard.'

Lucy sighed.

'You think he feels threatened by me?' Richard paused with a handful of lotion, arching an eyebrow.

'Of course he does.'

'OK.' Richard rubbed the last of the moisturiser over

the twin curves of Lucy's rear, then he smacked it, hard and resoundingly. 'Did you bring us here so you could choose between us?'

Lucy stared.

'Of course not. Why would I do that?'

'Well, I did wonder. It's natural, I think.'

'Richard, I've got two fantastic lovers. Why would I want to change that? I want to keep you both. I just think it'll be easier if you know each other and if we can perhaps do the odd thing together now and again. That's all. Don't ever think I want to lose you. Don't ever.'

Half-laughing, half-crying, she pressed herself into Richard's embrace.

Richard said nothing until he drew apart from her and asked, 'Are you cold?'

Lucy looked down at her nipples for the answer. They were erect.

'Um, a bit,' she said. 'Why?'

'I'm not sure you deserve to get dressed yet, but if you're very cold . . . But the fire is lit downstairs, I think. I heard Rob muttering under his breath and striking matches. Perhaps you'll be warm enough.'

'I'll freeze!' Lucy hugged herself and made a beseeching face.

That seemed to make up Richard's mind.

'Of course you won't,' he said briskly. 'Get downstairs. Why on earth would you need clothes anyway?'

'Am I in trouble?' she asked, turning to face him at the bathroom door. 'For this?' She waved a hand, indicating the whole cottage and the scenario itself.

'You're always in trouble, Lucy,' he said. 'You embody it. Downstairs with you, now.'

Knowing Richard's 'no more answering back' voice well, Lucy flitted down the staircase to find Rob sitting in the best armchair by the crackling fire, an open bottle of wine and three glasses on the coffee table.

'You finished your dinner?' she said, plonking her bare bottom on a low leather-patched stool by Rob's feet.

'Yes,' he said, smiling. 'Is this your after-dinner outfit? I like it.'

'Oh, it's just an old thing I threw on,' said Lucy, smiling back. 'You seem very relaxed. I'm so glad.'

'This place has that effect,' he said. 'Or it could be the food and wine. Though I haven't had any wine yet. Do you want some?'

'I'll pour.'

She stood and bent over the table, making sure her profile was displayed to Rob at its best advantage.

'Isn't Richard coming down?'

'I expect so. He might be getting changed, or unpacking a few things. Are you OK? Comfortable? Didn't get too wet?'

'I'm fine,' said Rob.

He was wearing boots, rather tight jeans and a dark long-sleeved T-shirt; he looked casually mouthwatering. There were still traces of his cold, rainy journey in the high colour of his cheeks and the slickness of his off-blond hair, now a shade darker from damp.

Lucy handed him a glass of wine, and poured one for herself.

'Cheers,' she said, raising it, sitting as close to the fire as she dared without roasting one side of her body.

It was odd, how quickly she adjusted to her nudity. The self-consciousness she had expected to feel was a long way back in her mind – which was a little disappointing because, if she was honest, she had hoped for a stronger sense of shame. Instead she felt calm, warm and like an artist's model, taking everything in her professional stride.

Something would have to be done about that, she thought.

'Are you nervous?' she asked.

'Who, me? God, no, too busy enjoying not still being on that endless journey,' he said. 'And you make a nice visual accompaniment to the wine.'

His eyes were ravenously bright, observing her over the curved rim of the glass.

Lucy felt an additional warmth, above the fire. She thought of how Rob had seen her earlier, in the car, her bottom in his face while she sucked Richard's cock. He had seen her at her sluttiest. He was still here, apparently unfazed.

'The journey wasn't all bad, I hope,' she said with a smirk.

He returned it, swallowing his wine slowly and with relish.

'No, not all,' he agreed. 'The last bit was good.'

'Did you mind,' she said, dropping her voice to a whisper, 'Richard being so bossy? He didn't mean to put you out.'

'He didn't. Honestly. It's fine.'

A creak from the stairs broke their brief communion.

'Richard,' piped Lucy, returning to the bottle. 'Will you have some wine?'

'Mm, don't mind if I do.'

As he reached the foot of the stairs, Lucy saw that he had not been getting changed. He had, however, been unpacking some items from his bags.

These items were placed on the rug beside Lucy's footstool.

'Oh,' she said, her voice faltering as she handed the wine to her master. 'I really am in trouble, then?'

She retreated back to the footstool and cast her eye over

the rug with heavily pantomimed dismay. A broad-backed hairbrush, a two-tailed strap, a riding whip.

Richard took his seat in the other armchair and sipped at his wine.

'So, Rob,' he said. 'Do you mind if I call you Rob, by the way? It's how Lucy always refers to you, but if you prefer—'

'No, Rob's fine. I sometimes have Lucy call me 'Dr Sherburn' but I'll let you off.'

'Doctor?'

'Rob has a PhD,' said Lucy eagerly, but Richard nudged his leather-shod toe between her bottom cheeks and shushed her.

'We'll hear from you, young lady, when you're spoken to,' he said.

Rob smiled tightly into the fire before looking back at Richard.

'What she said. No medical training. Just an abnormally huge and useless knowledge of post-war social policy.'

'Yes, she said you were an academic. At the LSE, was it?'

Rob nodded.

'I'm a lowly post-doc with a couple of seminar groups at the moment, but I'm having something published later this year and hoping it'll whisk me into the starry heights of, I dunno, a lectureship.'

'That's where you see your future?'

'I'll be honest, Richard, I don't see my future at all. I don't have a plan. I never have. Bloody hell.' He shook his head, vigorously, and took another slug of wine. 'I'm sure you don't want to hear my life story. Or my loaf story, as I should perhaps call it.'

Richard smiled. 'On the contrary,' he said politely, but Lucy didn't think his heart was in it. Why would it be?

Richard was a go-getting corporate bastard who had never tolerated a rival in his life. Why would he start now? Her nerves flared up again, tormenting butterflies with sharp antennae.

'We're not here to bore Lucy with this kind of thing,' Rob proclaimed. 'And I think you must agree with me, Richard, given what you've brought down with you. I'm guessing a quiet post-prandial game of Scrabble isn't on the agenda.'

'You're not wrong. Or, well, I don't think you are. If you'd prefer to play Scrabble, of course, that's an option.'

'Oh. No, it's fine.'

'What I mean to say, and I'm coming across clumsily, for which I apologise, is that I don't have an agenda. I just have some preferences. If they aren't yours, then we can rethink the plan. In short . . .'

'You're both in charge,' translated Lucy. 'You both get to tell me what to do, but you don't get to tell each other what to do. The scene has to be negotiated between you.'

Both Richard and Rob stared at Lucy.

'Didn't I say something about speaking when spoken to?' said Richard.

Lucy gripped the sides of her footstool and hung her head.

'Sorry, sir,' she whispered.

Richard turned back to Rob.

'She spoke out of turn, but her words are no less valid. That's exactly what I was trying to say.'

'I never thought of you as in charge to begin with,' said Rob, a tad belligerently. 'I don't play second fiddle to anyone.'

'And neither do I. So this isn't going to be easy. If Lucy isn't going to get torn apart in a battle of dom wills, we have to play this very carefully.'

'OK. I see what you mean. It's fair enough. So, what do we do? Take turns?'

'I think, as an opening position, that makes the most sense. Perhaps when we know each other better we can play as a threesome, but for now, well, do you want first dibs?'

Rob laughed.

'Are we back in the playground? We'll be playing cops and robbers next, handcuffing each other to the climbing frame.'

Lucy thought that sounded pretty good, but she kept her own counsel, knowing that she had already chalked up a punishment from Richard.

'I'll go first if you prefer,' said Richard, shrugging and sipping at his wine.

'No, you're fine. We need to get the measure of each other, don't we? You watch how I am with Lucy and then I'll watch you.'

Richard nodded. 'Maybe I'll pick up a few tips.'

Rob put down his glass and stood up.

'Right,' he said. 'That's put me on the spot. What's it going to be?'

Lucy could see that Rob was a little bit flustered, now that he was called upon to perform. He would want to impress Richard and that would put him off his stride.

She wriggled suggestively on her stool, hoping he would understand that she wanted some attention to her pussy.

The little shimmy seemed to inspire him, and he crouched in front of her, his mesmeric blue-green eyes fixed upon hers.

'Spread your legs,' he said. 'Show us the goods.'

Lucy obeyed, parting her thighs wide until she was split as far as she could be.

'See that?' said Rob to Richard.

Richard's reply was the flash of his camera app.

'Have you ever,' Rob asked pleasantly, 'had a girl with such a fat, juicy clit?'

'Now you come to mention it, I don't think I have.'

'I think it's the fattest, juiciest clit in the world. It's always so swollen and needy. It's like it needs to be frigged non-stop. Sometimes I forbid Lucy to touch it for a few days in a row. That's one of my worst punishments. She told me once that when she isn't meeting up with one of us she likes to masturbate at least three times a day. Don't you think that's shameful, Richard?'

'She's a little tramp.'

'One of the things I like to do is to get her to come in public, just by rubbing herself against a seat. She can do that, you know. Did you know that?'

'I must confess, I didn't.'

'You should try it. Next time you're out together. I made her do it on a train once. The carriage was almost empty, but there were a couple of guys further down the aisle. She humped that seat until she couldn't hold back. God, it turned me on. Had to have her at the back of the station car park as soon as we got off. Do you remember that day, Lucy?'

'Yes, sir.'

'That train seat was a bit like this stool – that velvety material. Or you can have her stuff something in her knickers so she's got that clitoral friction whenever she moves. She never lasts long. Anyway, we'll come back to Lucy and her easy orgasms. Hold your tits up high for us, Luce. Yeah. Squeeze them. Nice and tight. Stroke the nipples. Did you bring any nipple clamps, Richard?'

'No.'

'I did. I'm saving them for later though. What I like is when Lucy humps a chair and strokes her nipples at the same time. I love that. I make her look me in the eye the whole time. It's especially enjoyable in a public place, and I guess your presence takes us halfway there. Lean forward, Lucy, and ride that stool.'

Lucy shut her eyes for a moment. Rob knew that this was one of the commands she found hardest to obey. Because he knew it, it was one of the kinks he explored with her most often. He loved her discomfiture and her embarrassment, which seemed to get worse every time instead of better.

She proved herself his willing slut time after time, but his appetite for this kind of display had only grown. One day, she thought, he was going to get her arrested.

But not today, because only Richard's eyes rested on them, and they were burning with curious lust.

Rob was right about the upholstery of the stool. It was very reminiscent of the stiff fuzz in that railway carriage. It prickled against her bare thighs and now she did not even have the protection of knickers. When she leant forward, the pile felt thick and dry against her clit.

She was so wet, though, that it scarcely mattered. She pushed out her bottom, bent low and cupped her breasts in the way Rob always liked.

It was excruciating to know that Richard was watching her from the side of the room. This was an aspect of her sexuality he knew nothing about: her love of being humiliated in semi-public settings. She felt guilty, as if she had been concealing an important truth from him, and now it was all coming out.

But perhaps he wasn't into this kind of thing, anyway. After all, there were things she did with Richard that Rob never suggested. Richard was much more into tying her up and using sex toys than Rob was, for example.

Rob was all about mind control and unbroken eye contact.

And this was what he was doing now. He pierced her skin with his penetrating gaze, making her hold it as she began to shift about on the stool.

'Nice and slow to start,' he said approvingly. 'That's it. Stretch those thigh and arse muscles. Move those hips. Ride that pony, Lucy, ride it. Don't stop. How does it feel on your clit?'

'Rough.'

'Bad?'

'No. Not bad.'

She began to jerk, squeezing her gluteal muscles, working hard to get the level of friction she needed. She wanted to get this over with as quickly as possible. But now that little itch had taken fire at the core of her, and was starting its inexorable spread outwards. She would need to buck vigorously over the stool cushion to get where she wanted to be, but that was too much. Too slutty, too embarrassing, too blatant. If it was possible to preserve any vestiges of decorum whilst shagging a footstool in front of two men, she would try to do it.

'She's getting there,' said Rob. 'See her, hard at it. Work it, girl. Ride.'

'Perhaps she needs the whip,' suggested Richard. 'Do you think she's making enough effort?'

Damn, it sounded as if Richard was really enjoying the spectacle. And his suggestions were not welcome.

'That's a great idea,' said Rob, 'and I would. But I like to hold her eye contact. She hates it, you see. She hates to know that she can't hide from me. It makes it so much more satisfying.'

'Good point. But for the future, since there are two of us—'

'Yes, for the future. Ride it, Lucy. Get that bum out, get down low.'

The stool was beginning to jolt around on its legs. Vaguely, Lucy hoped she wasn't going to break it.

The pressure was building and it told in her expression: she knew because Rob's smile was getting broader and wickeder by the second, his eyes shining bright.

She had to let go of her breasts and grip the front of the stool so as not to tip over.

'Sorry, sir,' she grunted as they began to swing in rhythm with her lunges. Her clit, fat and juicy as Rob had said it was, mashed into the velvet, the sensation of it getting stronger and stronger until she felt it taking over the whole of her lower body.

She bumped up and down, wailing out her orgasm. Rob's hand shot out and held her by the chin, stopping her from withdrawing eye contact at the crucial moment. She always tried, always failed. She had to come with his keen eye upon her, his crooked smile of triumph twisted across his face.

It always made her want to cry, once the shudders of pleasure had died away.

Rob knew this, and he always knelt down and kissed her, wrapped his arms around her, reassuring her that he didn't think she was a freak, or if he did, she was no more so than he was. His eyes upon her gave her the strongest sense of being owned that she ever felt – much more than a whipping or a fucking in bondage or anything. That sense of utter emotional nakedness was what being owned was, to Lucy.

'OK,' he said softly, pulling her up from the stool. 'I think I want one of those.'

He unbuckled his belt and dropped his jeans and pants to his knees, looking rigidly away from Richard, then he sat down on the stool, his erection pointing up at Lucy in accusation. *You did this.*

'Climb on board,' he said, pulling her on to his lap.

She straddled his thighs and lowered herself down, holding his shoulders for steadiness. She lined her pussy up with the rounded head of his cock.

She thought of Richard, standing behind her with his camera. He would be able to see Rob's cock disappear all the way inside her with its almost insulting ease.

'Mmm, take it in,' murmured Rob. 'Spread your legs good and wide so Richard can see.'

Flash, flash.

Lucy pictured it; her pale bum bent towards the lens, thighs parted, thick stalk planted halfway up her.

'She's tight, isn't she?' said Richard.

'Mm, always so fucking tight,' agreed Rob. 'That's it. Suck me in. You want all of this, don't you? You love a big, thick cock stretching you.'

'Filthy,' breathed Richard, snapping away again.

Rob's hands grabbed Lucy's bum cheeks and spread them apart. This made his cock glide in even more easily, and caused her little pucker to twitch.

'Show the man your arsehole, Lucy. We've all seen it. We've all fucked it. Haven't we?'

'Yes, sir.'

'I've heard how much Richard likes to use it. Well, I bet he'll get his go soon. Don't you?'

'Yes,' wailed Lucy, finding the widespread condition of her arse wildly arousing. Now she was dirty, and shameful, and utterly submissive. She had no purpose in life other than to be used and owned by these men. She was the dirt beneath their boots. Whatever they demanded of her, she must obey.

'I can't wait,' said Richard dryly.

Flash, flash.

'In the meantime . . .' said Rob. He dipped a finger in Lucy's juices, rubbing her clit for a cruelly brief moment, then he returned it behind her, into the furrow still exposed by one hand on her left bottom cheek, and pushed against the hole.

She made a tiny, barely there squeak of protest.

'What? Not in front of Richard? Don't you want him to see how much you like having your arse fingered while I'm fucking your pussy? I'm sure he knows already.'

'I do,' said Richard, helpfully.

Flash, flash as the finger slid in and the bouncing increased in vigour.

'You like it with a butt plug in, don't you, Luce?'

'Yes, sir.'

'You like to have both holes filled, don't you?'

'Mmm.'

'What if you could have a different cock in each?'

That last question was from Richard.

'Oh God,' was Lucy's fervent reply.

As she worked Rob's thick tool inside her, she imagined, for the hundredth time, the scene Richard had suggested. It had been on her mind ever since she met them – servicing them both, a good little whore with two masters.

She ground down, pushing her bum right out, wanting it in Richard's face, or rubbing the lens of his camera. Rob's finger felt much bigger than it really was in her tight back passage. He jabbed it back and forth in rhythm with his cock.

'How does she look?' asked Rob, panting heavily now.

'Like a dirty slut,' said Richard. 'Loving it.'

She had succeeded in getting the position she needed to bring on that first sweet tickle on the path to orgasm. She recognised it so well now, and she had the timing of it down to a fine art. She would need to ask permission in five . . . four . . . oh, it felt good . . .

'Please, sir, may I come?'

Rob rammed his finger hard up her arse.

'What do you think, Richard?'

Oh, please don't delay permission! Please!

'Does she deserve it?' pondered Richard.

Yes, I bloody do!

She held herself still, unbearably poised on that fatal brink.

'She's worked hard,' Rob admitted. 'Her pussy'll be sore if she works much harder. And we don't want that, do we? We've got lots and lots more plans for her pussy.'

'That's true,' said Richard. 'We don't want to wear it out too soon.'

Through the red cloud of sexual frustration warping all her thoughts, it occurred to Lucy that Rob and Richard worked well together. They seemed to pick up on each other's cues without effort, harmonising their domination of her. Was this a good thing or did it bode very ill indeed for her? She couldn't quite decide.

'All right, toots,' said Rob at last. 'You can come.'

No sooner did he speak the words than the first flood overwhelmed her, falling away in spasmodic echoes until her climax had been fully wrung out of her.

Looking at Richard's photographs afterwards was an interesting experience. She hadn't realised how she writhed, her back twisting like a snake at the moment of orgasm. She looked as if she might wrench her spine.

But for now, object achieved, she had to oblige Rob. He didn't need much work, his pelvis jerking upwards, slamming into her until she felt she might break.

He went at it a little too hard and the stool tilted backwards.

Lucy, with Rob attached, fell back into Richard's waiting arms.

Rob came in a mess of limbs and confusion on the hearthrug, on top of Lucy.

'Are you OK?' asked Richard, half-laughing, as they tried to disengage.

'We'll live,' gasped Rob, pulling out and reaching for the tissues.

Lucy lay in heavy-lidded languor in Richard's lap, letting Rob dab at the mess he had made of her.

'Pour us some more wine, Lucy. We all need a little break before Rob hands you over.'

The perfect decadence of sipping at spicy red wine, splendidly naked, between her two lovers, pleased Lucy. She yawned and leant against Rob while he discussed the economic recovery with Richard. Sometimes she summoned her escaping wits to make a contributory point but, more often, it was nicer to half-drowse in the shelter of Rob's arms.

'Anyway,' said Richard, stretching his arm over to the table to put down his glass, in a manner that struck Lucy as a statement of intent. 'We've banished the national debt and made our five-year forecasts. Now I think there's the matter of an outstanding punishment.'

Lucy groaned and tried to burrow into Rob, but he withdrew his arm and moved away from her down the sofa, shooting her a look of stern disapproval.

The formal handover was in progress.

'Stand up, Lucy.'

Richard had straightened his back and clasped his hands in his lap. He was the epitome of businesslike. Lucy knew there was no use appealing to Rob and it would be unfair to try him anyway. She wasn't here to play the two off against each other. She was here to try and create a third way.

She got to her feet and stood in front of Richard, her eyes downcast, head hanging a little.

'Remind me of the little problem we need to address, Lucy.'

'I spoke without being asked, sir.'

'That's right, you did. More than once. I wonder how I can drive this lesson home. What do you think, Lucy?'

'Me, sir?'

'Yes, you. What sort of punishment works for you?'

She hung her head still lower. She hated when he made her admit this.

'Lucy,' he prompted gently. 'You know what helps you with your behaviour, don't you? What's most effective?'

'Spanking, sir,' she whispered.

'Speak up. I don't think our friend caught that.'

'A spanking, sir,' she said, fighting to keep rebellion from her tone.

'Yes. We've found, haven't we, through a hard process of trial and error, that the one thing guaranteed to improve your behaviour is a sound spanking. Lessons don't seem to go in through your ears, so we've resorted to delivering them through your bottom. That's the kind of girl you are, isn't it?'

'Yes, sir.'

'A sore bottom works wonders, doesn't it?'

She gritted her teeth. He loved to prolong the embarrassment. He could keep this up all night if he really wanted to.

She had to maintain her meek tone, but it wasn't easy, especially with Rob, lounging on the corner of the sofa, grinning from ear to ear.

'Yes, sir.'

'Have you noticed that, Rob?' asked Richard politely.

'Yes, I have. She needs plenty of them, too.'

'Quite right. The more spankings she gets, the better she behaves.'

He waved a hand at the implements, which had been awaiting their moment with such patience.

'How shall we choose, Lucy?'

'I don't know, sir.'

'Which of those is the worst?'

'It depends. Depends on how hard they are used, how many strokes. Lots of things.'

'Well, now, it's Friday night. We're here until Sunday evening. Perhaps we shouldn't go in too hard too soon. What do you think, Rob?'

He inclined his head. 'Don't want her stretchered off the pitch before full-time,' he said, which made Lucy laugh a lot because Rob hated football, so it was the most unexpected metaphor for him to use.

'Something's amusing you?' said Richard severely. 'Or is it relief that you aren't going to get your full just desserts quite yet?'

'No, sir, nothing, sir.'

'Really? Because I'd be very relieved if I were you. I'd be thanking my lucky stars, and my lucky masters.'

'Thank you, sir. And sir.'

'I think, in that case, I'm going to use the belt this time. Fetch.'

He snapped his fingers.

Lucy knew this was the signal for her to drop to her knees and crawl. She made her way over to where the strap lay and spent some fruitless moments trying to get it between her teeth without using her fingers.

'No hands,' reminded Richard when she was tempted to just nudge the thing into an easier position.

She huffed and tried again, succeeding at last in getting the thick leather between her teeth, biting down on the shine. God, it smelled good.

She scurried back to Richard, sat back on her heels and offered her gift to him. He took it from her mouth and thanked her.

'Now, you need to pick that stool back up and bend over it, with your palms flat on the seat.'

The stool was having a rough evening, it seemed. First masturbated over, then shagged on, and now it would be the venue of an incident of corporal punishment. Lucy wondered if it had often been so ill-used.

She put her hands down on the threadbare fabric. Luckily it didn't seem to have any traces of its earlier employment on it but, when she bent lower, she could smell sex, a potent mix of her and Rob. Well, perhaps that would help her through the ordeal to come: a little reminder of pleasures past and, hopefully, future.

'Legs absolutely straight, slightly apart. I shouldn't have to tell you this.'

She arranged herself into Richard's preferred posture, wanting to snap back that she couldn't be expected to remember every detail of both her lovers' tastes. Rob nearly always had her over his knee; it was Richard who liked the more formal presentations.

She heard the sofa creak and watched him get out of it

through upside-down eyes. She could only see his legs now, pacing behind her, and the long dangle of the strap from his hand. He'd need to put some distance between them to get a decent swing. She shuddered, her thighs suddenly trembly.

From the corner of her eye she saw Rob sit forward, perching on the edge of the sofa.

'How many strokes?' asked Richard.

Was he asking her?

No, it transpired he had addressed the question to Rob.

'How many would I give? Well, that would depend on a lot of things. I think you're the best judge, to be honest. I sometimes use my belt on her, but it's hard and fast when I do and I don't count. I just stop when I think she's had enough.'

'I see. Has she ever safeworded with you?'

'No. With you?'

'Yes, a couple of times.'

'You've taken her a bit further than me, then. You'll know her limits.'

Richard seemed gratified by this, as if it made him the senior dom. He who spanked hardest won at life, apparently. Lucy wasn't sure she agreed with this philosophy, but it had its merits.

She pushed her bottom out, the way he always insisted she did and waited, eyes shut, lungs prepared for some serious breath control.

'Don't you do a warm up first?' asked Rob.

Lucy exhaled heavily. If they were going to chat about it all night, they could at least let her out of this demanding position. Her muscles were tense and beginning to wobble already.

'Sometimes,' said Richard. 'With a heavier implement I usually would. The cane? Maybe, maybe not. Sometimes you want her to feel the full impact, no holds barred. Sometimes you just want a bit of sensation play. But this strap is probably OK to use without one. It's not the worst weapon in the armoury by a long chalk.'

God, what a pair of geeks, Lucy thought, exasperated now. Spanking geeks. The worst kind.

'It's more a tawse than a strap, though, isn't it? With the split tail. I thought they were pretty fierce. Never used one myself,' Rob disclaimed.

'It's not the same thickness as a classic tawse, and it's more supple. It'll sting rather than pack a real punch. You'll see her bum turn slowly red, but there won't be bruising or welts.'

'Nothing better than watching a bum turn slowly red,' said Rob appreciatively.

Lucy begged to differ. Well, she didn't beg out loud, because she knew exactly where that would get her, but she thought about it.

'Perhaps you'd do the honours with the camera,' suggested Richard.

'Glad to. Totally.'

Rob came to stand on the other side of her.

'Do you mind?' he said.

'Go ahead.'

She felt Rob's hand on her bottom, stroking it gently, over the curve and downwards, his fingers dancing delicately on her inner thigh.

'What's good about this,' said Richard, 'is that she's already come twice. I think it hurts more when she isn't very aroused to begin with. I sometimes make her come before I punish her for that very reason.'

'That's a very good point,' said Rob. 'I hadn't thought of that.'

'I think this weekend is going to be very productive. We're learning a lot from each other already.'

Lucy grimaced. This was the kind of information she felt didn't really need sharing.

'OK,' said Rob, stepping back. 'I've got the camera set up. I think we're ready to go.'

'Lucy,' said Richard. 'I'm going to ask you to count in the usual way. Is that clear?'

'Yes, sir.'

At last it was going to start. The sooner it started the sooner it would be over with.

The first stroke lashed down, catching her under the curve of her bottom, snapping sparks from her skin. It stung, but it was a pain she always relished, a kind of sharp, exquisite tang. It was there and gone in a second and it took its time to build up into a sustained burn.

'One, sir, thank you, sir.'

'We didn't decide how many, did we?' said Richard, laying on the second.

'Two, sir, thank you, sir. No, sir.'

He laid two more very quickly, so that she had to count them together.

'How many do you think, Lucy?'

There was a form answer to this question.

'As many as you think necessary, sir. Ow! Five sir, thank you, sir.'

'That's right. So I'm considering this now.'

The sixth stroke was very hard, right across the centre of her bottom. She rocked a little and curled her toes, but breathed through it.

'Given that the situation is novel,' he said, after she had counted, 'I'm inclined towards leniency. However, you transgressed not once, but twice, so I think I should take that into account, too.'

The seventh stroke sizzled, heating up the tender skin at the tops of her thighs. She made a curious cross between a yowl and a whimper.

'Seven, sir, thank you, sir.'

'I'm going to stop at twenty,' he said. 'Although I know you can take a lot more. But we have the whole weekend ahead of us and, for that reason, I don't want to peak too soon. Two whole days with your bottom at our disposal. I don't think we'll be able to resist making the most of it, do you, Rob?'

'I'm pretty sure we won't.'

Lucy pushed her bum out. Twenty was nothing, with that relatively lightweight strap. Not that it didn't burn and sting like buggery – every stroke felt like one more than she could take. But she knew how far she could go and it was substantially beyond twenty with the strap. That would barely get her into subspace. In a way, this was crueller than a thorough thrashing. But, of course, there would be more to come . . .

Strokes eight, nine and ten were teasing flicks on and between her thighs. She hated it when he did that, but his aim was uncannily accurate, and he was always able to create the maximum discomfort with the minimum effort.

Halfway through now, with the camera flashing away like a strobe light.

'Have you ever whipped her pussy?' Richard asked, taking a half-time break of half a minute or so, rubbing her bottom to keep it properly sensitised. He didn't want to numb her. He made sure she felt every nuance of that punishing leather.

'Yeah, well, not whipped so much. I've spanked it with my hand.'

'She absolutely hates it,' Richard confided. 'I've a small, very thin strap that I use. It never fails to make her sob.'

'Really? I've only done it to warm her up a bit. Maybe you'll have to show me how you do it later on.'

Please don't. But the thought turned Lucy on and she hoped she'd find herself, in due course, lying with her legs wide open while Richard reddened her poor spread lips, making her gasp every time a stroke caught the tip of her clit. It was horribly painful, but the heightened arousal afterwards was out of this world.

But for now, her bottom was in the line of fire, and the second half of her punishment was laid on with steady, sustained force. It could only have lasted a minute, if that, but to Lucy it seemed to take forever. The room rang with the crack of the strap and her answering grunt, then her increasingly feeble-voiced count.

Her legs began to tremble, perhaps because she knew the end was near and she had given herself tacit permission to lose control. Having slipped her grip on herself, she began to wail after the next five strokes, and twist her hips.

'Stay still,' Richard warned her. 'You don't want this wrapping around.'

No, she didn't. She'd learned that lesson the hard way. Too much dancing around and trying to get out of the way of the strap resulted in its landing in an even more painful spot than her bottom. Back in her early days, she'd sometimes tried to shield herself with her hands, but a few smart strokes to her errant palms had cured her of that impulse.

Now she knew that her best way of making it through a punishment was to do as she was told and maintain her position. Bottoms were sensitive, but far less so than other body parts. In this, as in every maddening thing, her doms knew best.

The last three strokes nearly broke her, placed one on top of the other so that she cried out for mercy on the final fall of the strap.

A pointless time to beg for it, she reflected, but she couldn't help herself.

Both Richard and Rob found the irony amusing, Rob cooing with fake sympathy.

'Poor Lucy,' he said. The camera clicked. 'God, her arse looks fantastic. You haven't missed a spot.'

'Thanks. I can be a bit anal about it, actually. I have to have the perfect shade and the perfect coverage and so on. I'm even worse with the cane. If one stroke goes awry, it puts me out and I have to try again once the marks have faded.'

'I think doms are allowed to be anal,' said Rob.

'Boom boom,' said Richard.

Lucy grinned, despite the sweat on her face and the still-throbbing state of her backside. It was over and she had survived.

She awaited permission to break her position, but it didn't come.

'Actually,' said Richard, 'speaking of anal . . .'

She clenched.

Did Richard mean to take her arse in front of Rob? How utterly humiliating, rude and debasing. In other words, what a turn-on.

She made a little sigh of trepidation.

'What's that, slut?' said Richard, giving her sore bottom an extra smack. 'Don't you think I have the right to use you as I see fit?'

His low voice, always slightly menacing, even in jest, made her shiver.

'Of course you do, sir,' she whispered. 'It's just that—'

'Go on?'

'I'm embarrassed, sir.'

He laughed. 'So you should be. You're about to show your other master just what a shameless little bum-slut you are. Though I'm sure he knows it.'

'Oh yes,' confirmed Rob. 'She loves it, no doubt about it.'

'And I think I've earned it,' said Richard. 'Rob, there's a tube of lubricant in my inside jacket pocket. Could you fish it out for us?'

Lucy had to resign herself. There was no way she was getting out of this without safewording. And besides, her tired clit was swelling back into vibrant life at the thought; her spanked thighs were steamy with heat.

There was nowhere to hide. Both these men knew her well. Every dirty secret she had was in their possession. There was no chance of pretending to be a coy flower now. The difficulty for her was that one knew things that the other didn't, and now everything was going to be laid completely bare. She would never be allowed to forget it.

'Keep that position,' instructed Richard, coming closer.

She wanted to stand, to stretch her spine and still the trembling of her knees, but that was going to have to wait. Richard's hand, with lubricated fingers, slipped between the scorched cheeks into the hot furrow.

'You've already had Rob's fingers up here tonight,' he said softly, circling and probing. 'He knows you love to be filled.' One slippery finger slipped in, followed by another, stretching her.

She concentrated hard on not clenching, breathing,

keeping open and relaxed. Her pussy itched now, longing for some attention on its own account.

'Especially after a strapping,' said Richard. 'You spread your cheeks without thinking twice when they're good and hot, don't you?'

'Yes, sir.' An agonised gasp.

The fingers speared and scissored, preparing their territory.

'I think what would make this special,' said Richard, 'what would make this different, would be for Rob to sit in front of you and watch your face while I'm having your arse.'

'Ooh, no,' wailed Lucy. 'Please.'

But Rob was there, kneeling down in front of the stool, and his smile was more encouraging than cruel. He put his hands on top of hers, holding her there.

'You can do this,' he said. 'Do it for me. And Richard,' he added swiftly. Lucy had to assume that Richard had just given him A Look.

'Sometimes I don't let her come after a punishment,' said Richard. 'For the rest of the day. She hates that. Don't you, Lucy?'

'Yes, sir.'

'Anal sex is best for that, I find. OK.'

He removed his fingers and she heard him getting rid of the lower portion of his clothing.

Rob, his eyes furtive, gave her a swift kiss on the lips.

'Good girl,' he whispered.

For some reason, this made her feel even more exposed and small. Rob approved of her having anal sex with another man in front of him. She really was in a foreign place, away from all the cosy concepts of love and romance she'd grown up with.

Sometimes it scared her.

Richard penetrated her with his usual slow consideration, but she wished he'd just shove it in and take it fast. Every moment with Rob's eyes upon her, watching her take a cock inside her tight, sore bum was excruciating. Not physically: she was used to the discomfort, the sharp moment of pain and then the strange fullness. But she couldn't meet his eye and tried to blank him out of her consciousness, shutting her eyes to him.

As if Richard could see this, he said, 'Look at Rob. Look at your master. Let him see you getting fucked.'

'I can't,' she gasped, and Richard stopped after one hard thrust and held himself inside her to the hilt.

'I beg your pardon?' he said, taking hold of her hair, pulling her head up.

'You can,' said Rob. 'Look at me, Lucy. I'm ordering you to.'

The relief of having no choice flooded through her, raising her eyelids swiftly.

It had to be done. She would do it.

'Is she looking?' asked Richard.

'Yes.'

'Right. Now, let me fuck this tight little arse.'

This he proceeded to do, in big, salutory thrusts, making it clear to her that he owned the narrow space he occupied and would do what he wanted in it.

She looked at Rob, who maintained an almost unblinking stare throughout, her vision blurring as the thrusts became ever stronger, an extra punishment, adding to and augmenting the existing pain in her bottom.

She wanted him to touch her clit, or to be allowed to touch it herself, but she didn't think Richard had that in mind for her tonight. He was putting on a show of dominance, and she suspected it was more for Rob's benefit than hers.

If Rob objected, he didn't seem about to say so.

He looked so grave and stern. When he smiled, you couldn't possibly imagine that he had this expression in him and yet here it was, keeping her in her place better than a hundred shackles and straps.

She took the pain for love, took the humiliation for love, took everything either of these men had to give her for love, love, love.

Richard grabbed her hair and pulled hard, then he came, hot and steamy inside her, filling her.

Rob crouched closer, stroked her damp cheek, whispered, 'Good girl.'

Her wobbling arms collapsed beneath her and she accepted Richard's full weight on her back as she folded her body over the stool seat.

'Well,' said Rob, after a mingling of grunts and pants that drowned out the hammering rain on the window panes. 'Shall I open another bottle?'

The three of them nestled on the sofa, in various states of undress, covered in blankets, sipping at their wine.

In the middle, Lucy was cradled by two arms, her head on Rob's shoulder, while Richard stroked her feet.

'Am I crazy,' she said, yawning, 'or is this a really promising start to the weekend?'

'Both,' said Rob at once, and she flicked at his chest.

Richard's laugh was redolent of red wine and relaxation.

'I'm having all kinds of ideas,' he said. 'How about you, Rob?'

'Oh yes, I'm full of sadistic creativity tonight. For instance, I'm thinking we ought to send Lucy outside naked in the rain to collect the eggs from the henhouse tomorrow morning.'

Richard took up the theme. 'Yeah, but she can wear her wellies. Nothing else. You like rubber, don't you, Lucy?'

'Not that kind,' she said, stretching out between her two bookend lovers. 'I did bring my latex spanking skirt though.'

'Oh, God, I love that thing,' enthused Rob. 'Have you seen it, Richard?'

'More than once. She was with me when she bought it, actually. I remember her modelling it in the changing room of the shop. I had to test drive it, you see. Make sure it worked.'

'You spanked her in the changing room?' Rob sounded impressed.

'Yep. Remember that, Lucy?'

She cringed a little at the recollection.

'Everybody heard,' she said.

'Mmm,' said Richard, apparently reliving the scene. 'You can wear that tomorrow.'

'I'm in for a busy day then,' she said happily, snuggling.

'What do you think about tomorrow, Richard?' asked Rob. 'Are we on the same page enough to play a double-hander, do you think?'

'What, top her together, instead of in turn?'

'Yeah. I think we can read each other pretty well. Should we give it a go?'

'I don't see why not. What do you think, Lucy?'

Lucy bit her lip. 'I think that's the scariest thing I've ever heard. And also the hottest.'

'That's settled then. So, if we're going to be up to fun and games tomorrow, we ought to think about getting some sleep.'

Rob removed his arm from Lucy's shoulder, looking over at the staircase.

'Oh! Sleeping arrangements!' Lucy remembered that

there was one double room and one single. 'Who's going to take the back bedroom?'

Rob and Richard looked at each other. Nobody volunteered. Nobody spoke. Nobody blinked.

Lucy woke up the next morning dimly conscious of the rain still falling, as it had done in her dream. Her limbs were pleasantly sore from last night's exertions, but not so much as to put her off getting up to more mischief today. Her back passage was still a little stingy from Richard's vigorous use of it, but the effects of the strapping were long gone, her bottom cheeks back to pristine condition. Her pussy, she realised straight away, was wet and felt empty, needful of attention.

Who would be able to help her out with that?

On her right side, Richard lay, sprawled on his back with his limbs all akimbo, exhaling little half-snores at the ceiling. His eyelashes were long and sooty-black on his cheek and his morning shadow darkened his chin like a drawn-on beard. He looked so boyish in sleep, so unlike the elegant, rather autocratic man she knew by day.

On her left, Rob was curled up in a foetal ball on his side, and his more youthful face was noble, like a marble knight on a cathedral tomb, straight-nosed and full-lipped.

She kissed first Rob and then Richard. Rob woke immediately, his eyes shining into life, while Richard muttered and twitched and turned over.

'I'm not having that,' said Lucy, wriggling into a spoons embrace with Rob, letting his hand wander down her hip and between her thighs while the other cupped her breasts.

She began to massage Richard's shoulders, bending forward to breathe hot kissing breath on the back of his neck.

He sighed and shifted, then twisted his neck to face Lucy, his eyes momentarily confused.

'Oh, we're here,' he said. 'That's right. Morning, Robert.'

'Morning,' said Rob, laconic as he pushed his fingers between Lucy's pussy lips and rubbed her clit.

'Is this a private party or can anyone join in?'

Lucy moaned and rubbed her head back against Rob's chest.

'Nothing's private when you sleep three in a bed,' said Rob. 'Get stuck in.'

Richard's fingers joined Rob's, another hand at her breasts. She reached forwards and wrapped Richard's morning glory in a curling embrace, squeezing and pumping the shaft. In the meantime, Rob's cock insinuated itself between her bottom cheeks and eased up and down in the crack.

Lucy came first, her tongue tied up by Richard's, her genitals thoroughly invaded by two sets of fingers, then Richard; then Rob finished himself off inside Lucy's pussy from behind, while Richard stroked her breasts and sucked her nipples.

'Happy new world,' yawned Lucy, and it certainly seemed like it.

Prisoner 39

Mile after mile after mile of green, dotted with white puffs. That would be the sheep.

Emma looked away from the train window, needing to find something less monotonous to fix her attention on. It didn't matter what, as long as it calmed the nerves raging in her stomach.

She couldn't concentrate on her book, though, hearing a different voice in her head, locking the poor author out.

It'll be fine, it's an experience anyway, even if you don't enjoy it after all. Allyson will be there. She can read you: she'll know if things are going too far.

She shut her book, and looked back out at the suffocating green.

Who would the other people be? Both men, she knew that. But would they be men she had played with before, or total strangers?

She rewound the conversation she had had with Allyson, the pair of them sleepy after post-spanking sex, about her fantasy. She could have left it at that – a kinky dream. But she should have known that Allyson was all about fulfilling such dreams, and it was well within her power. She knew everyone, and guarded a slew of secrets of the Rich and Famous. She only had to snap her fingers and whatever she asked was done.

It's ridiculous to be nervous. You're an old hand at these kinds of games.

But then, the nervousness was part of the fun.

The train began to slow and Emma thought she might be sick.

She took her overnight bag down from the rack and slipped quietly into the toilet cubicle. When she came out, there was one little addition to her outfit – an ID pass clipped to her coat lapel.

And thus Emma Frayne, resting actor and sometime sex worker, became prisoner thirty nine.

She looked out for Allyson on the platform, but there was no sign of her. She must have sent one of the others. As her fellow passengers slowly filtered through the station exit, she scanned the place for likely characters.

It was him. It had to be the man in the blue serge uniform.

She stood with her back to the wall, trying to be unobtrusive, wondering why he didn't come over straight away. Perhaps it wasn't him then, which would be strangely disappointing. He was rather attractive, in a burly, whiskerish kind of way.

The mystery was solved when another man came out of the gents' toilets and spoke to Blue Serge. This new man was somebody she recognised: she and Allyson had played with him before. Not at the club either; they had gone to his home, which was a prime piece of property porn. He was that banker. Richard, was it?

This was more than satisfactory. She'd fantasised about

him more than once since that intense and pleasurable week-end, and had vaguely hoped they might meet again.

With the platform now empty, it was safe for the pair to approach her.

'Prisoner thirty nine?' asked Blue Serge, giving her a blatantly lecherous once-over.

'That's right,' she said, trying to sound brave. It was remarkable how quickly she could fall into this meek, craven mindset.

'You'd better come with us.'

Blue Serge put his hand around her upper arm and led her out behind Richard, who had neither spoken nor looked at her.

Unexpectedly, the car wasn't in the station car park. Instead they walked on, down a long single-track road that led away from the town to some woodland. It was perfectly dark and deserted and quite silent, except when another train flashed by, all warm light and distant people: people going to safe places; people she should perhaps envy.

Richard stopped abruptly. It took Emma a moment or two to realise that a car was parked under a nearby tree. She didn't know much about cars but this one looked expensive.

She was still eyeing its silver sheen when Richard turned and began addressing her.

'Prisoner thirty nine, you have accepted a place on the government's new Short, Sharp Shock disciplinary programme in preference to a longer custodial sentence in an ordinary prison. Could you please confirm for me that this is the case?'

'Er, yes, it is,' she mumbled, startled by how convincingly Richard adopted this pitiless, judicial tone.

'Good. You will be with us for a weekend, and I think you must realise that it isn't going to be a luxury mini-break. Hmm?' He raised an eyebrow.

'Yes, yes, I realise that,' said Emma.

'When you speak to me, or any other member of staff, you will be respectful and call us 'sir' or 'ma'am' at all times. If you forget, you'll incur punishment, is that clear?'

'Yes, sir.'

'Now then, first things first. Blake, get the uniform out of the boot. Prisoner, remove your clothes.'

'What? Here?' She looked around wildly. Nobody was around, or likely to be, it was true, but – 'What if a train comes past?'

'What if it does?' said Richard laconically, while Blake snorted over by the car. 'You've broken two rules already, my girl. Failure to use the correct honorific, and failing to obey a direct order in a timely fashion. If I were you, I'd start making up for that right now.'

I can say 'Colditz' and all this will be over. I can go back to the station and . . . No.

Emma looked up at the night sky, clouded and vast. A dream was coming true. She bit back a smile and took off her jacket.

She bent her head, avoiding the eyes of Richard and Blake, who watched her every move with grim satisfaction.

Off came the jumper, off came the jeans, the denim rucking around her pale legs. She looked back at the railway line as she stepped out of them.

Nobody was there.

The night air played, lewd and cold, about her bare skin and she shivered and hugged herself.

'Underwear too,' clarified Richard.

She gasped and gave him a quick pleading glance, which he rebuffed, folding his arms.

She unhooked her bra and put it on the ground with the rest of her clothes. The cold made her nipples stiffen with a pang until they felt unbearably tight.

'Underwear is a privilege,' said Richard as she peeled down her knickers. 'You haven't earned it.'

Now that she was fully naked, Blake stepped forward with some white material over his arm.

'You'd better put it on her,' advised Richard.

The low rumble of an approaching train made Emma jump in alarm and hold out her arms to Blake.

He put the thing on her. It was a kind of shift made of a heavy canvas-like material that felt coarse and aggravated her nipples. It fastened all the way down the back with large hooks and eyes, leaving a long split of bare flesh in the middle where the metal clasps met. The area around her bottom was cut away, rendering it permanently bare.

Blake was clipping the hooks and eyes together when the train thundered past. The way they were standing meant that nobody could have seen anything but a woman in an odd white dress, but Emma still wailed and tried to cover her bottom with her hands.

Blake pushed them roughly away and slapped her bottom hard.

'No,' he said. 'It's forbidden for you to cover it.'

'That's right,' said Richard. 'While you're with us, your bottom will be bare at all times. In fact, it'll be a number of other things too, including red and sore, but bare in the basic necessity. Now, we have those two rule breaches to deal with. Bend over the bonnet of the car, please.'

The temptation to plead was almost overwhelming, but Emma knew that it would only end up the worse for her, so she trotted obediently to the vehicle and bent, palms down, over the sleek, silvery surface.

'Two lessons,' said Richard, stepping up behind her. 'Respect and unquestioning obedience. Learn them well.'

He commenced dealing a hard and fast spanking, peppering both cheeks with painful rapidity. Emma, although no novice, found his devastating technique became difficult to bear very quickly. She was able to swallow her squeals, but the squirms were unstoppable, shameful for a woman who prided herself on being able to take very long, very severe punishments.

She didn't want to beg, but really, if he didn't slow down soon . . .

Luckily, he seemed to tire of his high-octane performance after a minute or so. He ordered her to her feet, frowning at the palm of his hand.

'See what she's done to me, Blake,' he said.

Blake sucked in a breath. 'You'll need to be bringing out the heavy stuff,' he said, shaking his head.

'Well, we have plenty of implements,' said Richard. 'Every single one of which is going to make its acquaintance with that bottom. Now, into the car with you. Blake? Sort it out, please.'

Emma felt Blake's hand on her warm bottom, pushing her towards the back seat of the car. Once she was inside, feeling the leather upholstery cool and smooth on her chastised skin, Blake produced a pair of handcuffs and locked her wrists together.

The journey was passed in silence. It seemed even Richard, for all his vast wealth and contacts, hadn't been able to get hold of a real prison wagon. This luxury car didn't quite project the right mood, so stern and concentrated reflection was required, to keep the mindset in place.

Emma was dying to ask Richard about his new girlfriend. Allyson had said they were getting quite close. She'd also said that he shared her with another dom. What would it be like,

Emma wondered, to be in that kind of relationship, with two lovers who cared for you? She felt a twinge of something.

Stick to the motto, Em. 'You can tie me up but you can never tie me down'.

The cottage was much more rustic and charming than she'd imagined. She'd thought of a blank-fronted, grey stone chiller of a place, high on a slate cliff. This was a pretty haven nestling in some foothills. Still, it was hard to find exactly what you wanted, she supposed, and none of them were professional location scouts. Like the car, the cottage would have to be reframed by her imagination.

'Let's have you,' said Blake, gruffly, pulling her out of the back seat and marching her towards the front door, Richard leading them once more.

They had to duck under the lintel. There, at a desk in the living room, sat Allyson, in a perfectly tailored dark skirt suit, looking over some papers.

'Ah,' she said, looking up, 'new arrival. Thirty nine, is it?'

It was unsettling, Emma thought, how Allyson could fake complete unrecognition. Even she found it difficult, and she'd been to RADA.

'Yes, ma'am,' she whispered.

Richard and Blake lurked over her shoulders, casting a shadow of forceful authority.

'I've been looking over your records, thirty nine. They make very disturbing reading.' Her stare hardened, and the mouth Emma had kissed so many times was set in a straight, cruel line. 'The same words keep coming up over and over again – spoilt, selfish, wilful, insubordinate. You're from a good home, but you've brought disgrace on your family, who spent thousands on your education only to have you throw it back in their face. You're here because you were caught on CCTV performing a lewd act on some random stranger in a public place. You had to plead guilty, in the face of overwhelming evidence, but you still tried to worm your way out of it by offering sex to pretty much everyone involved in the case, from the arresting officer to the judge. Aren't you ashamed of yourself?'

'Yes, ma'am.' Emma's cheeks were flaming hot. Allyson played her part so perfectly that she almost believed the accusations being made against her.

'I'm not convinced. You're here to have your ways changed, young lady. By the time you leave this place, you will be very sore and very sorry, but ready to embark on a new stage in your life. A stage you will never have to feel ashamed of.'

Emma nodded.

'Is that all you have to say? A word of gratitude would be nice, or some acknowledgement of the hard work we're going to do for your benefit.'

Emma nodded again. Her throat was dry, but she managed to force out the words, 'Sorry, ma'am, thank you, ma'am.'

'Well.' Allyson rose to her feet. 'Now the pep talk's out of the way, I think we should move on with the orientation.'

Orientation? What was that supposed to mean?

She soon found out.

'Blake, could you fetch the spanking bench from the outhouse, please? And Richard, we'll need a strap, a paddle and a cane.'

Emma gasped, not that she was surprised. Allyson and Richard both knew she could take a tough thrashing. But could prisoner thirty nine? This was the question.

'What's the matter, thirty nine? Never been spanked before?'

'N-no, ma'am.'

'But you knew you had this coming?'

'I wasn't sure what the judge meant by corporal punishment.'

'Ah.' Allyson exchanged a significant look with Richard. 'This is what comes of banning the cane in schools. None of them know the right terms any more.'

Richard shook his head, reaching inside a cupboard in the Welsh dresser to remove the implements Allyson had called for.

'You will be answerable to all three of us, thirty nine, and so each of us is going to give you an introductory punishment, just to give you a taste of what you have to come. Unless, of course, you behave absolutely impeccably. But nobody ever does, alas.'

Allyson almost winked and Emma found herself slipping out of role, her lips twitching upwards. The sight of Richard with the strap, paddle and cane was mouthwatering. She thought of his strong, suited arm, reaching back, stopping for a quivering moment then speeding down with its special delivery.

Deliver me to evil.

She smiled in earnest at the stray thought, eliciting an immediate frown from Allyson.

'Something amuses you? See if you find *this* funny.' She took the wooden paddle from Richard and slammed it down on the desk so Emma jumped high in the air and clamped a hand to her mouth, suppressing a shriek.

Blake re-entered the room, carrying a kind of padded step-ladder affair with leather cuffs attached at strategic points.

All attention was turned to him as he set it down in the middle of the room and beckoned Emma towards him.

'You're really going to?' said Emma haltingly.

Blake laughed. 'Didn't you know?'

'Apparently she thought "corporal punishment" was something to do with the army,' drawled Allyson. 'But realisation is dawning, isn't it, thirty nine?'

'Yes, ma'am, but—' She turned tragic eyes to her lover, but received only a pitiless stare in return.

'If you can't do the time, don't do the crime,' said Allyson softly.

'Maybe prison after all?'

'Uh-uh. Too late for that. You've signed the consent form.'

'But I didn't know!'

'Oh, come on,' said Richard. 'You would have had all of this explained by your lawyer. Trying to wriggle out of it now because you've changed your mind won't wash. I know a spanking compared to a prison sentence seems like a good deal at the time, but when you're faced with the reality of it, you lose your nerve. It happens to everyone, thirty nine. But they have to be dealt with. It's summary justice. And it's for your own good.'

He said the last sentence with a smile that chilled Emma's heart.

She really ought to stop stalling. She could barely wait to feel his familiar strength and firmness as he laid the strokes on her.

They all liked to pretend otherwise, though, so she shot one last desperate glance at the door, as if expecting a dramatic, last-minute reprieve, then stepped forward with a heavy heave of her chest.

Blake ordered her to kneel on the lower step and bend with her stomach on the upper. The padded leather was at least comfortable, though the straps buckled around her knees weren't so much.

'By the time you leave, you might be able to take punishment without being strapped down,' said Blake, pulling tight. 'But we don't take chances with the new girls.' He looked over at Allyson. 'Do you think she's a screamer? Should I gag her?'

Allyson took Richard into a corner and conferred with him in a low voice.

Emma couldn't hear everything they were saying, but she gathered they were discussing the safety or otherwise of a gag. Allyson thought that she knew Emma's limits so well that she could stop before she got close to safewording. But Richard pointed out that the situation and role was unfamiliar and might affect her tolerances. Allyson conceded this.

'No,' she said to Blake. 'Let's sound her out first. If she's a screamer, we can gag next time. Besides, I don't mind a few howls of pain, do you?'

'Not at all,' said Blake.

'And I love to hear all the desperate apologising, and begging, and promising to be good,' added Richard. 'Don't you?'

'Oh, yes.'

'Music to my ears,' said Allyson. 'OK, then, let's start with Blake and the strap. Give her thirty, hard.'

Emma liked the strap, but she didn't know Blake and was a little anxious that he might not be as expert as his co-conspirators.

The first stroke was a relief, falling in the right area, a good sizzling lick that set her up for more. She had had tops who hit too high, or let the belt curl around her hip, and that wasn't fun.

Blake was able to handle his leather, and Emma relaxed into the strapping, enjoying the growing heat, identifying his rhythm and adjusting her breathing accordingly. The leather had to be very thick to really hurt her, and this was a lovely supple length, stingy but not thuddy, almost a luxurious sensation.

But, of course, thirty nine wouldn't see it that way.

Emma was ten strokes in before she remembered that thirty nine would be flapping and squealing. Unless she was the silent, defiant, stoic type. Yes, that's what thirty nine would be. Full of stubbornness, determined not to show weakness.

If they wanted to break her, they'd have to work at it.

So she let out no more than angry panting, letting her fingers curl, white-knuckled, around the metal bar of the spanking bench.

'You've got a fighter here,' commented Allyson as the strap fell, over and over, getting hotter now, getting sore.

'We've had plenty of fighters,' said Richard. 'None of them have beaten us. In the end, you'll be just as sorry as the others.'

Emma gritted her teeth and shut her eyes through the last ten strokes. Blake could have been harder on her. He could have hit the same spot over and over. He could have concentrated on her tender thighs. He could have swung wider, put more force into it. But this was an introduction. Of course, there was plenty of time for that.

'A good thirty,' said Allyson. 'Thanks, Blake. Now she knows what it's like to have a bright red, spanked bottom. How does it feel, thirty nine?'

'Fine, ma'am,' said Emma through still-gritted teeth.

'Fine, eh? Well, it looks lovely. Let's just give you a minute or two to get used to it before I take my paddle to you. You won't be feeling fine after that, I promise.'

The three of them sat around Allyson's desk and chatted

about the journey and the weather for what seemed to Emma an intolerably long time. They knew she'd just want them to get it over with, but they weren't going to give her anything she wanted.

Blake, she learned, was a paramedic and he had a long conversation with Richard about this. It seemed he and Richard were meeting for the first time this weekend, although both of them knew Allyson.

It was boring and annoying to be bent over a stepstool, bare, stinging bottom on display, while people behind you droned on about their work as if you didn't exist. She kicked in her bonds, frustrated, and heard Allyson laugh.

'Somebody wants more attention,' said Blake. 'She hasn't had enough, has she?'

'If attention's what she wants, attention she shall have,' vowed Allyson. 'I've got a nice wooden paddle here, thirty nine. You'll see that it feels nothing like the strap. I wonder if you'll find it better or worse?'

'A lot of our inmates hate the paddle most of all,' said Richard. 'Though the majority fear the cane more.'

'You'll be able to do a full comparative study very soon,' promised Allyson. 'Now. Stick that bottom out nice and high. You're going to get twenty.'

The first stroke landed with indecent loudness, fat and full on the centre of her backside. Emma couldn't help a whimper. She really wasn't a fan of the paddle.

'This'll get the message across,' said Allyson, in a low, fierce whisper. 'You can't ignore it. I'm going to have you begging for mercy.'

Emma had learned how to cope with the paddle, but it had been a long, hard road. Thirty nine was at the very beginning of that road and, for Emma, it was rather liberating to be able to give voice to hearty yells of protest each time the wooden oval seared into her skin. Only a few strokes in, it really was like being paddled for the first time. The panic of feeling that she couldn't take it flooded into Emma in a rush – a response she had thought to have overcome and controlled long ago.

'Oh, no,' she whimpered at about stroke six. 'Please, no.'

'What's that?' asked Allyson, dealing stroke seven with relish. 'Not so easy to take, eh?'

'Ow, no, I can't!' She tried to move her bottom away from the inevitable descent, but the knee straps held her in place.

'We'll remember this,' said Allyson. 'Any bratty behaviour from you, and the paddle comes straight out. Wherever you are, whatever you're doing, you'll be touching your toes for twenty hard strokes. Better get used to it.'

Eight, nine, ten. Nothing of Emma existed except her bottom, a constant flare of pain consuming all her energies.

'Ow, it's horrible! I'm sorry! I'll be good!'

Five more in such rapid succession that she howled.

'That's better,' said Allyson. 'You'll certainly be getting more of this.'

'Nooooo!'

Emma twisted her neck around. Allyson had stopped. Surely there were five more to go.

Allyson looked weird, almost worried.

'Five more,' prompted Richard.

'Yes, yes, I know,' said Allyson hurriedly. 'Just . . . No, it doesn't matter. Five more.'

The last five were the hardest yet and Emma knew that just one more would have broken her and brought the tears out. As it was, she lay there, grateful for avoiding that particular embarrassment, letting the alarming throb slowly recede, leaving tight skin and residual sting behind.

Allyson bent down to her ear.

'You sure you're all right with this?'

Emma nodded.

'Any time you want to stop . . .'

'I'm OK. Thank you. Love you.'

'Love you, too.'

She straightened up and slapped the paddle into her palm. 'Take note, gentlemen,' she said. 'This is what she needs.'

'Better take another break before the cane,' said Richard.

'Good idea,' said Blake. 'No point caning a numb bum.'

They all agreed with that, laughing. Richard went to make them a cup of tea.

Allyson took a number of photographs of Emma's bottom, promising to put them online on the government's 'Crime and Punishment' gallery.

'Won't that be a service to the community,' she gloated, holding Emma's chin in her hand and forcing her to look up at her. 'You'll be a living deterrent. You never know, you might put someone off a life of crime. "Don't want an arse like hers, ouch, no thanks," they'll say. We'll have a little picture of your face next to it too, and your name and all the details of what you did. It'll be out there for all to see, forever. I'll get some snaps of you after you've been caned, too. I always love a caning photo.'

Emma saw Richard go into the kitchen and return with a bottle of sherry and some glasses.

'I don't believe in caning drunk,' he said, 'but just a quick snifter shouldn't hurt.'

The cork popped, the liquid glugged, the glasses tinkled.

Emma's mouth was dry. Nobody was offering her a drink.

'When are the others getting here?' Blake's voice.

The others?

'They shouldn't be too long now,' said Richard. 'Unless Lucy's managed to leave the motorway at the wrong exit. She does have a bit of form for that.'

Emma knew better than to speak, but she made a tiny strangulated noise in her throat. Wasn't Lucy Richard's new girlfriend? Surely she was too inexperienced for a scene like this. And besides, Emma didn't want the group focus diverted to any other bottom but hers. Part of the attraction of this whole scene had been the undivided attention of three hardcore tops.

Allyson cleared her throat and spoke a bit louder, obviously picking up on Emma's unease.

'Young Lucy has been sent here as a warning, a kind of caution. She is to watch what happens to girls who don't mend their ways before it's too late. Her guardian and escort, Dr Sherburn, is accompanying her to pick up a few disciplinary tips of his own. I hope prisoner thirty nine's fate will serve to convince her to improve her behaviour.'

Oh, OK. They aren't joining in. Just watching.

'How's that whole three-way thing going?' Allyson's voice was lower now, the question directed at Richard.

'What, with Lucy and Rob? Well. Very well. Much better than I expected, if I'm honest.'

'No jealousy or competition?'

'Nothing like that. Well, perhaps a little. Especially the competition. But it keeps me on my toes, which isn't all bad.'

'I couldn't share a sub,' said Blake.

'Well, perhaps you'll never have to,' remarked Allyson. 'But you haven't found one yet, have you?'

'Not permanently,' said Blake, with a trace of a sigh. 'I'm still looking.'

'In the meantime,' said Richard, and glasses clinked again, 'here's to play parties.'

'Abso-bloody-lutely,' said Blake, and they all laughed.

'Well, then,' said Richard, after a pause. 'I can see a bottom not too far away whose impressive colour is beginning to fade. Better do something about that.'

'Can't wait to see what she makes of the cane,' said Blake with bloodthirsty enthusiasm.

Emma clenched her buttocks, then relaxed them, remembering that clenching was not allowed. But surely prisoner thirty nine would clench as a matter of course?

The gluteal muscles came back into play.

She heard Richard's footsteps across the wooden floorboards, then the deathly swish of the cane, making her twitch and squeal. But it didn't land on her. He had done it merely for effect.

'This is the most feared of our implements, thirty nine,' said Richard softly.

Emma saw the slender rattan glide in front of her face, then it was held there, vibrating slightly, it seemed. Or perhaps Richard's hand was shaking.

'Take a good look,' he said. 'Does it look cruel?'

'Yes, sir.'

'That's because it is. It will be like nothing you have ever felt before, and its effects will linger. It's a most effective reminder. How many strokes, Governor?'

Allyson laughed.

'We usually start with six,' she said. 'But I'm going to make it ten for this one. She's a tough nut to crack.'

'Ten it is.'

Emma groaned and tried to prepare her body for the coming onslaught.

She knew she could take ten strokes – she'd taken many more in the past – but her role was beginning to invade her headspace, tricking her into thinking she couldn't possibly cope.

Richard tapped the cane lightly across her bottom then rested it there for a moment, sizing up his stroke.

She shivered.

He pulled it away and let it whoosh back down, a perfect line, bearable at first then flowering into intense, white heat that made her hiss and catch her breath.

'What do you think, thirty nine?' asked Allyson from the back of the room. 'Will ten be enough?'

'Please, ma'am,' she gasped. 'Please don't!'

'Regrets, she's got a few,' said her unsympathetic lover.

The men laughed.

'You deserve it, thirty nine,' continued Allyson. 'Every stroke and more. And you needn't think you won't be getting caned again this weekend. You're going to learn some respect. I'm going to personally make sure of it.'

Richard was one of Emma's favourite caners and he didn't let her down, scoring a work of welted art across her poor buttocks. But prisoner thirty nine was not so appreciative of his skills, yelling until she was hoarse, putting her hands over her bottom so that Blake had to come and hold on to them, writhing like fury in her bonds.

Emma swam and floated in the sharp, sizzling sting while thirty nine begged for mercy and choked on her tears. Had she split into two? It was almost as if she had. The cane had sliced her apart, giving half of her to pleasure and the other to pain.

Dimly, somewhere around the eighth stroke, her thirty nine self realised that the ordeal was almost over and clung to that knowledge like a life raft.

But the Governor had said there would be more to come.

Fresh tears joined those already blurring her eyes. She was so rarely able to cry during scenes that this seemed like a victory. Yes, role-play was the way to do it. It allowed her to release her emotions in a way that cool, controlled Emma somehow couldn't. This had been a brilliant idea. She had known it would work and she was right.

The last two strokes were like marks of honour, the crowning achievement of an endurance test. Emma gave herself up to her sobs, amazed by them, wanting to see where they might lead her.

'That's good, thirty nine, that's very good,' said Richard, softly, crouching in front of her, cane still in hand. 'You're feeling sorry, I can see. You're ready to change. Aren't you?'

She nodded, and let out some more strange noises.

'Help her up,' said Allyson.

Come over to me. Come to me. Take me in your arms and tell me everything's all right and I'm forgiven.

But Allyson stayed where she was.

It was Richard and Blake who unbuckled the straps, then took one each of her upper arms and lifted her gently to her feet.

'Put her in the corner,' said Allyson. 'I'm going to sort out some food.'

She disappeared into the kitchen without even catching Emma's eye.

Emma's legs trembled so much that she could hardly stand in place. She leant her forehead against the wall and let it support her. Richard placed her arms behind her back, folded above her bottom, which was to remain on view.

It was probably against regulations but he didn't seem

able to resist brushing his fingertips over the ridges he had placed on her skin. His voice was low, and a little thick, when he said, 'Stay there until you're ordered otherwise.'

She stood still, listening to the sounds coming from the kitchen. Blake went in to help and the buzz of their conversation was, tantalisingly, too quiet to decipher.

Richard sat quietly, his presence only occasionally given away by little jingles from his iPad every now and again. She knew he was looking at her striped bottom. She wished she could see it herself.

She had stopped sobbing now, but couldn't seem to help sniffing rather a lot. Surely he could offer her a tissue? A runny nose seemed a humiliation too far, after everything else.

Sometime after she had gone to the corner – it could have been ten minutes or half an hour – she heard the sound of a car engine outside.

The armchair creaked. Richard must have stood up.

'Al, they're here,' he called, then a burst of colder air came in, soothing Emma's bottom just a little.

She heard other voices, greetings, kisses.

The front door shut and Richard said, 'Right, all normal service is suspended – as from now you are visiting Facility Fifty One. Don't look so spooked, Lucy. You've seen a caned bottom before.'

'Yeah, just. Ouch.'

The men laughed, but they soon remembered what they were here for.

'Miss Ward, this is prisoner thirty nine. Dr Sherburn has brought you here in the hope that she will be an example to you. Is that right, Doctor?'

'Quite right,' said Rob, with whom Emma was not familiar.

'You see her now recovering from her introductory punishment. It's the first of many – an acclimatisation. By the time she leaves this place, she will be extremely penitent and vowing never to return.'

'I'm sure,' said Lucy.

'Ah, great timing.' Allyson was back in the room, and Emma could smell what she was bringing with her. Spaghetti bolognese, she thought. Her stomach rumbled. God, she was hungry.

'Richard, could you get that spanking bench out of the way, we're going to need to extend the table.'

Richard obeyed Allyson's command quickly. Emma heard the straps jingle and the stepstool contraption creaking back into its smallest configuration.

Plates, cups, knives, forks, serving bowls being laid down on placemats.

She wanted to ask permission to come to the table, but nobody mentioned her or spoke to her. Was she supposed to stay here while they ate? Could they really be that cruel?

'Good, take a seat, everyone,' said Allyson. 'How was your journey?'

Emma felt a sickening wave of dismay wash over her, as knives and forks were taken up, and Rob and Lucy talked boringly about traffic and the weather.

She really was excluded from the meal. But they couldn't let her starve, surely?

'What do you think of the view in here?' asked Allyson, slyly, after Lucy had raved about the mountains, and valleys, and winding roads.

'Very pleasing,' said Rob. 'Great work with the cane. I bet that was Richard's hand.' Lucy just coughed and giggled.

'Got it in one,' said Blake. 'I'm going to ask him to give me lessons.'

'Perhaps you could practise on our Lucy,' said Richard.

'Perhaps not!' This, of course, from Lucy.

'Don't forget what you're here for,' Rob warned her. 'Lessons for you, too. If you can't behave, you might find yourself side by side with the prisoner.'

'Doesn't she get food?' asked Lucy.

Emma could have kissed her. Here was the question she wanted answered.

'Of course,' said Allyson. 'But eating good food at the table is a privilege she has lost for the time being. When we've finished, she'll get a bowl of porridge to eat kneeling on the floor. I doubt she'd want to sit down, anyway.'

'I suppose not.'

Porridge! Emma tried to block out the vision she had of a plate piled high with spaghetti and sauce, topped with Parmesan, surrounded with salad, a plate of garlic bread at the side. Not tonight.

'What did she do?' asked Lucy.

'Disgraceful behaviour,' said Richard with relish. 'Public lewdness with a group of strangers. Both men and women.'

'Oh, I say.' Lucy sounded shocked.

'Don't pretend you're any better than her,' Rob rebuked her. 'You know I have to keep your whorish ways in check. That's why we're here.'

'When she was caught and arrested,' said Allyson, stridently, 'she had one man's cock in her pussy, another up her arse and she was licking a woman's clit. She was in the cloakroom of a public nightclub and customers were coming and going the whole time. Though, of course, a lot of them stopped to watch. Most of them had already felt her up on the dancefloor. That was prisoner thirty nine's idea of a good night out. Every week.'

Emma swallowed hard. Allyson was teasing her, turning her on.

She had been warned before the weekend began: 'You'll get no orgasms, my girl.'

Please don't turn me on. I'm wet enough already with the throb of the cane and the sensitivity of my hot, stretched skin. I can't take much more.

Now she was glad of the hunger, concentrating on it instead of listening to Allyson's inflammatory words, which she tuned out as best she could, catching snatches here and there.

'. . . wide open . . . sucking her nipples . . . she came three times in a row . . .'

The words became blank, empty of meaning, while she thought about food, every kind of food she had ever eaten.

Finally, they finished their meal and Allyson went into the kitchen for the ceremonial bowl of porridge.

She was made to kneel and eat it from the floor, spooning it into her mouth in great, greedy gulps. It was cold, but she didn't care. She didn't care that everyone watched her, laughing or tutting over her table manners. She didn't care about anything now, except being prisoner thirty nine and getting Allyson alone.

'It's time you were in bed, thirty nine,' said Allyson, taking the empty bowl from under her nose. 'Early nights for you. I'll take her up. Rich, is there another bottle in the fridge?'

Emma's upper arm was braceleted with Allyson's fingers, hauling her to her feet and nudging her to the stairs.

'Go and brush your teeth,' ordered Allyson. 'Then you can get your nightshirt on.'

The nightshirt didn't cover her bottom. It was made of some rough kind of grey flannel that rubbed her nipples. Allyson commented on how hard they were, watching her change.

She laughed, a little callously, then her voice altered.

'This is good for you, yeah, babe?'

Emma nodded, but she could feel her emotions welling at the abrupt kindness in her lover's tone.

'But, just a hug would be nice.'

'Aww, come here, darling.'

The women embraced, long and deep, Emma shedding a few tears on Allyson's smart, silk shirtsleeve.

'So proud of you, babe, so proud,' whispered Allyson. 'You're special, you know that?'

'I love you,' said Emma. 'Oh God, look at your shirt.'

Allyson tutted and pretended to frown.

'Naughty girl,' she said, patting the wet patch. 'I won't spank you for it, though. Not right now.'

'You can if you like.'

Allyson kissed her, cupping her wet cheek in one hand.

'You'd better get some sleep,' she said. 'You're going to need it. Tomorrow you're back to being thirty nine.'

'How do you know those other guys?'

'Blake? He's my cousin.'

'He's a paramedic?'

Allyson laughed. 'Yep. But don't worry. I'm not planning on having to use his professional services this weekend. I'll take care of you, babe.'

'What about Rob?'

'Him I don't know. But I intend to find out more. I'll let you know. Sweet dreams, my darling little slut. Wait till this is all over and I'll give you the seeing-to of your life.'

Emma, now face down on the bed, moaned with happy anticipation. The blankets were scratchy and the mattress thin, but she could have slept in a skip. A good whipping always did that for her.

'Don't make me think about sex,' she begged, with a yawn.

'No, best not,' Allyson agreed. 'Don't you dare touch yourself either.'

She bent and kissed the top of Emma's head.

'Night night, sleep tight, make sure the bugs don't bite. Tomorrow's going to be a long day.'

Perversion Therapy

'I haven't seen you around. On the scene, so to speak.'

Allyson offered the wine bottle to Rob, who took it and poured himself another glass.

He then settled his arm around Lucy, re-establishing the link that led from him to her to Richard, on the sofa, and smiled at his interlocutor.

'No,' he said. 'I've never been a scene kind of person.'

'How do you know if you haven't tried it?' Allyson's challenge was friendly enough but her eyes were hard. Rob had been told she could be difficult if you rubbed her up the wrong way. 'You should come to the club. Meet some of the girls.'

'Well, I'm trying it now, I guess,' he said. 'And I'm liking it so far. I wish I hadn't missed the show.'

'Perhaps we could do a repeat performance with Lucy?' suggested Allyson, slyly.

This prompted a squeak of alarm from the submissive in the room, who clung to Richard and curled into a defensive ball.

'I'm not sure she's ready for that,' said Richard.

'Ah, proper knight in shining armour, you are, Rich.

The gentleman sadist. Always liked that about you. Anyway, shouldn't bad girls be in bed? If we're doing this by the book.'

'That's a good point,' said Rob. 'Lucy's here to learn. I suggest you go up before we're tempted to take Allyson up on her idea. Oh, but which room?'

'I've put you three in the big bed upstairs,' said Allyson. 'I'll take the sofa bed down here. Blake's on the air mattress over by the fire. You'd better not snore, Blake.'

'I'd better not drink much more then,' said Blake, putting down his glass.

'Run along then, madam,' said Richard, helping Lucy up and on her way with a smart smack to her bottom.

'Ow,' she protested, but she didn't try to argue, knowing better than that by now.

She climbed the stairs, looking down at them reproachfully before disappearing from view.

'So, then, Rob,' said Allyson, returning to her interrogation. 'If you aren't on the scene, how did you get into this? Have you been doing it long?'

'Oh, you want my story?' said Rob.

'Please.'

'Well, all right then. It all started in my PhD year when I was sharing a house with some other students . . .'

Everybody asked him how he'd done it. How he'd managed to get himself lodged in a house with three female flatmates.

The guys at the pub toasted him, lost in admiration, but they didn't know how difficult it was for him. OK, not difficult so much as awkward.

Their boyfriends – for they all had one, gallingly enough – regarded him with suspicion. All the women he came into contact with assumed he was either seeing one or other of his flatmates, or that he was gay. It was shagging suicide. He didn't get laid for six months, even though he was good-looking, and personable, and popular.

Then came the day that he returned home from the library to find Ruth, his favourite flatmate, sobbing as she peeled vegetables over the kitchen sink.

'What's up?' he asked, though as a rule he tried to avoid this kind of thing, heading to his room if there was a whiff of it in the air. But today he happened to be hungry and he knew that there was cold pizza in the fridge, so the peril must be faced.

'Do you think I'm a lazy slob?' she asked, sniffing madly.

'Do I? No. God, no.'

Actually, she was, a bit. Nothing terrible, though. Frankly, she was about as untidy as he was, in terms of leaving mugs under the bed for weeks on end and empty DVD cases all over the floor. But it wasn't that bad, was it? It wasn't up to *How Clean Is Your House* levels. Yet.

And she'd never peeled a vegetable before. This was new. She had PickupaPizza on speed dial, just as he did.

But he worked harder than she did. Ruth rarely got out of bed before two in the afternoon, and was constantly making horrified remarks about how behind she was with her PhD studies. She spent half the week at her boyfriend's place, and the other half mooching around the house watching *Cash In The Attic*. Rob privately thought she should get a job if she wasn't interested in the academic side of things, but of course if he said that it would be furiously debated and held against him for all time. He wasn't her supervisor. It wasn't his problem.

She wasn't his vision of a slob, though – she had nice nails and she dressed well, if a little outrageously sometimes – so he wasn't being entirely untruthful when he repudiated the suggestion. And she was sweet. And a bit sexy. Who in their right mind would call a sweet, sexy girl a slob?

'Did someone say you were?'

He took the cold pizza from the fridge and munched on it, enjoying its chewy, stale texture.

A fresh burst of tears greeted his question. He waited patiently for them to subside.

'Dave,' she said.

'He didn't! Have you split up then?' A flicker of optimism. If Ruth was single, then . . .

'No, we haven't. I don't think so. I'm not sure.'

'Why did he say it?'

'Had a meeting with my supervisor this morning.'

'You mean you got up in the *morning*?'

'Fuck off! You're as bad as him.' She half-turned, brandishing the peeler.

He backed away.

'Sorry. Go on.'

'Supervisor said I was in danger of being kicked out. I went to see Dave for a bit of moral support and comfort, and he said my supervisor was right and I should pull my socks up and stop being a lazy slob.'

'The bastard.' But Rob's heart wasn't in it. Dave had a point, really.

'Do you think so?' More woe poured from Ruth's eyes, and nose, and dripped into the vegetable water. Rob thought he might give dinner a miss tonight.

'Well, don't you?'

'No. I think he's right. I want to be better. I want to get back on track with my PhD. I want to have a lovely room and cook healthy meals and all that jazz. I just don't know how.'

'Oh.'

Rob hadn't expected to find Ruth on the road to Damascus. He had expected denial and indignation, followed by a resumption of the status quo. He supposed he ought to offer her his support.

'Do you? Do you know how?'

'Um, what does Dave think?'

'He thinks I should just somehow *know* all this organisation and domestic type stuff – like it's innate to women.'

'Sexist bastard.'

'Do you think so?'

'Yeah. I do. But he's right to say you can't carry on like this.'

'That's what I thought. So what can I *do*? Ouch!'

Her peeling had reached such a pitch of savagery that she had sliced the implement into her finger, and bright red blood gushed at an alarming rate out on to her skin.

'Shit, are you OK?' Rob darted forward and grabbed her wrist, holding her finger under the running tap.

'You see?' wailed Ruth, and the tears made an unwelcome reappearance. 'I'm useless. I can't even peel a vegetable. According to Dave that makes me a shit woman and a waste of planetary space. I hate myself!'

'Don't be silly,' scolded Rob, waiting for the blood to thin, and fade, and stop flowing. 'Have we got a first aid box?'

'In the bathroom cabinet.'

'Hold your finger there. I'll go and get you a plaster.'

He turned around in the kitchen doorway.

'Don't move,' he reiterated, pointing at her to reinforce the order.

When he came back and applied the plaster, she was looking at him in a doe-eyed kind of way, if doe eyes were red and teary.

'Never seen you like that before,' she said.

'Like what?' He fixed the plaster in place and gave her a brief smile.

'All forceful and efficient. Like Julian in the Famous Five.'

He laughed out loud.

'I always had a bit of a thing for Julian, even though he was a patronising twat,' she said. 'But I didn't like Anne. What a fucking drip. I saw myself more as George.'

'I see myself more as Dick. Sorry.'

But she had burst into laughter and he joined in with her and then, on impulse, pulled her into him for a hug.

'Oh.' That was a sigh. She was sighing. And she felt gorgeous in his arms, all soft and yielding.

'Sorry,' he said again, although he wasn't sure why.

'Don't be sorry. I needed this.'

She pulled her face away from his shoulder and looked up at him, in a kind of shy, expectant way that made his heart twitch.

'Maybe you could help me,' she said.

'Could I?'

Maybe I could kiss you. Is that what you want? Or would that be sexual assault, or abuse of male privilege, or . . . Oh, fuck it, it's too difficult. And Dave!

'Yeah.' She chewed her lip for a moment, and Rob thought he could see an inner demon trying to fight its way out. 'No,' she said eventually. 'It's a stupid idea. I'm sorry.'

'No, tell me,' he said.

She shut her eyes. 'Make me,' she whispered.

'What?'

'That tone you took before. I couldn't argue with that. You could ask me to do anything.'

Rob's eyes widened. He could use his voice to wield

power? Well, there was a thought. It had always been the case that people tended to do as he asked; he was just that kind of person. It wasn't bossiness, more a clear idea of what needed doing and the firm intention of getting it done. The idea that a girl might find it . . . Did she? Did she find it arousing? Did he turn her on when he ordered her around?

'OK,' he said firmly. 'You're going to tell me whatever this thing is.'

'Maybe not in the kitchen,' she demurred.

'Your room or mine?'

'Mine, I guess. No, it's a mess. Yours.'

Rob's room wasn't a great deal tidier, the bed unmade and a tottering pile of books adorning the centre of the floor, but it had a desk chair to sit in, and he pulled up a squashy footstool so that Ruth could crouch at his feet. This seemed to suit the dynamic admirably, and she made no protest, so he crossed his feet at the ankles, steepled his fingers and raised an eyebrow.

'Well?'

'I can't,' she said, crimson of cheek.

'You can, and you will. I won't let it drop now. Tell me what's on your mind.'

'Oh, you're going to make me,' she said, with a little tremble in her voice that owed more to pleasure than fear. 'Aren't you?' She glanced hopefully up at him.

He nodded, face perfectly straight.

'Oh God,' she fluttered, and then, sotto voce, 'Why can't Dave be like this?'

Because Dave's not the right man for you.

Her chest was heaving like nobody's business. He had an urge to grab her by the elbow and just . . . He had to shake it out of his head.

'OK,' she said. 'This is going to sound weird.'

'Weird's fine with me. Go on.'

'I want to be better at, you know, life in general. Tidier, more organised, on top of things. I've got so many bad habits I don't know where to start. I thought it might be easier if I had a, like, kind of, like, a mentor.'

'A mentor? Like a supervisor?'

'Yeah,' she said eagerly, 'except for general stuff, not my PhD. Someone to check that my room's tidy, and bills are paid, and there's decent food in the fridge and, you know, just keep me on track.'

'Keep you on track?' Rob smiled. He couldn't help it. He could see where this was going, and he liked it a lot.

'Take charge,' said Ruth, and her voice was barely there, though the eye contact certainly was.

'Take charge of you?'

'Yeah.' She swallowed and looked at the door. 'Sorry, it's a stupid idea. I know you're busy and I don't want to impose.'

She half-clambered to her feet, but he put out a hand.

'No, no, no,' he said. 'Don't move.'

She subsided back on to the beanbag.

'Give me a minute to think about this,' he said.

She sat looking at the floor while he turned the proposition over in his mind.

'What about Dave?' he said.

'What about him?'

'What about him? You're doing this for him, aren't you?'

'No. He's just the catalyst. What he said has made me think seriously about how I want to change, that's all.'

'But you want to change because you *lurve* him and you want to make him proud of you?' Rob couldn't keep a note of bitterness from his voice.

'I don't love him. I've never been in love with him. He's just . . . I dunno.'

'There?'

'Yeah. He's just there. Shit, that sounds bad.'

No, it doesn't. Give it a little more thought, just enough to persuade you to dump him.

'Not really. Since you're reorganising your life, and he's part of it, you should think about whether you want him in it. He called you a lazy slob, Ruthie. Whether you agree with him or not, that's not a very nice thing to say. Is it?'

'No, I suppose.'

'You wouldn't say a thing like that to somebody you were meant to care about, would you?'

'No.'

'Well then.'

'Oh God, this is so difficult. Do you really think I should dump him?'

'Sounds like he wants you to. If he's talking to you like that.'

'You're right. Yes. You're right. Oh, God.'

'Anyway,' said Rob, not wanting thoughts of Dave to take up any more time than was strictly necessary, 'whatever you decide, you want me to, uh, take you in hand. So to speak. Is that right?'

'Mmm.' She seemed to enjoy his turn of phrase, shutting her eyes and sighing gustily. 'In hand.'

She looked at his hands and he couldn't help following suit. He liked his hands. They were good, strong, capable but attractive. He flexed his fingers, admiring them, then felt a twinge of embarrassment at his vanity and coughed.

'I don't have any objection to that,' he said. 'But you need to make me a list of the things you want me to take charge of. You've said tidiness, finances, diet. Anything else?'

'Don't let me slack off when I say I'm going in to the university. Make me get up at nine at the latest. Um, you know, that kind of thing.'

'OK. So far, so easy. But what if you don't want to?'

'What do you mean?'

'Ruth, I know you. If you don't want to do something, you'll come up with a million excuses and reasons why it's best not to do it. I don't want to spend ages arguing with you.'

'I promise I won't argue.'

'Even if the power goes to my head and I start making totally unreasonable demands?'

She smirked. 'What kind of unreasonable demands?'

'I don't know, yet. I don't know how benign dictatorship is going to affect me. Maybe I'll turn into a monster.'

'That's a chance I'm willing to take. Let's start now. Tell me to do something. I'll do it.'

She tidied her room, changed the bedding, washed all the old cups and plates.

For two days, Ruth was a busy bee and all Rob had to do was issue gentle reminders if she left a cup on the arm of her chair or switched on the TV five minutes before she was due to leave for the library.

The other housemates seemed to notice a subtle alteration in the atmosphere, but they couldn't put their finger on it.

'Aren't you seeing Dave tonight?' asked Kalaya, applying lipstick before dashing out to a meeting.

'We're on a break,' said Ruth.

Kalaya and Lulu both whirled around.

'Since when?'

'Couple of days. Anyway, have a great night – I've got work to finish.'

She went upstairs.

'Rob, do you know what's come over her?' asked Lulu in a confidential whisper. 'She made dinner tonight and everything.'

'Are you seeing her?' asked Kalaya, always one of the sharper tools in the box.

'No,' said Rob, but he couldn't help musing on the term 'seeing'. Yes, he was seeing Ruth. He was noticing her. He was getting close to her. Was that the same thing?

'She seems very cheerful for someone with boyfriend trouble,' said Lulu.

Rob shrugged.

'Perhaps she likes trouble,' he said.

It turned out he was right about that.

At one minute to nine the next morning, he found himself knocking on her bedroom door.

'Wake up, Sleeping Beauty,' he called. 'Did you forget to set your alarm?'

Incoherent sounds filtered through the door.

'It's nine o'clock. Thought you were walking down the hill with me? I've got to leave in five minutes.'

More muttering.

He waited in the hall, jacket and scarf on. Lulu emerged from the kitchen in her dressing gown, cup of tea in hand.

'Ruthie won't be up before noon,' she said.

'She has been the last two days,' Rob contradicted her. 'You just didn't see it happen.'

'Bloody hell, she really is turning over a new leaf.'

Lulu shuffled back up the stairs, but there was no sign of Ruth.

He shouted, 'I'm going now!' No reply.

He left the house, mildly frustrated.

Two days, and already Ruth was on the slide. If she wasn't going to take this seriously, then why should he bother?

He was crotchety and pissed off all morning, then he went back to the house to work from home for the afternoon.

Ruth was in the living room, watching *Loose Women* in her dressing gown.

Rob dropped his bag on the floor, strode over and switched off the telly.

'Shit, you're back early.'

Ruth put down the yogurt she'd been eating, in dismay.

'You aren't taking this seriously, Ruth,' Rob said. 'You aren't taking *me* seriously.'

'I am,' she said. 'Just feeling a bit off today, that's all.'

'Should I call the doctor?'

'No, just a bit of a headache.'

'Headache, yeah, right. I've heard it all before, Ruth. You had a permanent headache for an entire bloody term. Don't lie to me. Why didn't you go in this morning?'

She looked genuinely intimidated. He fought the impulse to soften, to be gentler, to offer her a weasel way out.

She wants help. She needs it. Don't bottle out.

'I just felt tired.'

'Felt like festering in bed till midday. Am I right?'

Her shoulders dropped and she nodded.

'It's not good enough, is it?'

She shook her head.

'Sorry. I've let you down.'

'No, you've let yourself down. And I've let you down, too. I should've gone in there and made you get up.'

She looked up, and Rob thought he saw awe in her expression.

'You should've,' she breathed.

'You made a good start, and you *can* do this, but you need more motivation. I need to take stronger measures.'

'Do you?' She crossed her legs. He saw her squeeze her thighs together. His mouth went dry.

'Well, don't you think so?'

'Yes.'

'So, what do you suggest?'

Ruth's face tightened with alarm. He could see that she didn't want to take responsibility for this, but that was tough luck, because she would be made to. She was going to be the author of her own discipline.

He folded his arms and glowered down at her.

'What do you think?' she stuttered. 'If I don't . . . You should . . . There should be a consequence.'

It was very hard not to smile, but he managed it somehow.

'A consequence,' he repeated. 'Yes.'

She flinched, but held his eye.

'What sort of consequence?' she asked.

'Well,' said Rob. 'Not a pat on the back, obviously. What would work for you, Ruth? What would keep you on the straight and narrow? My disapproval doesn't seem to be quite enough.'

'I don't like being in trouble with you,' she said.

'But you still won't do as you're told. Come on. I want suggestions.'

'I can't say it.'

Now it was going to be easy. Now all he had to do was apply the pressure. Already the first stirrings of a victory celebration tickled his loins. She was that kind of girl. Just that kind of girl he'd always dreamt of running across.

'You can say it. You will say it.'

He moved close to her, in front of her, and crouched at her eye level.

'Come on, Ruthie. What should I do with you?'

She shifted and looked at the ceiling. Her fluffy dressing gown brushed against his knees. What was she wearing underneath? Pyjamas, loose and a bit faded, perfect lazingwear.

'I don't know, maybe . . .'

'Maybe . . . ?'

'You could . . .'

'I could?'

'I can't!'

'Ruthie.'

He took her hands in his.

'Look at me.'

Reluctant as she was, she couldn't disobey him and she turned perturbed eyes to him. He could see she was chewing the inside of her cheek. He drank in the signs of delicious conflict, her desires struggling with her pride, and then let them settle before turning the screw again.

'Tell me what you need,' he whispered.

'I want you to tell me,' she said with a pout.

He shook his head.

'Has to come from you. Otherwise you can say I forced it on you and you didn't mean it, didn't really want it. I'm not laying myself open to that. Do you understand? Much as I'd like to just . . .' He squeezed her fingers, and a smile flickered uncertainly on her lips.

'Would you?'

'God, yes.'

'I hope you're thinking what I'm thinking because otherwise I'm going to have quit uni, leave this town, leave the country, but here goes.'

She screwed up her face in anguish and Rob put her fingers to his lips; the suspense was almost unbearable.

'Would you spank me?'

The words came out in a rush, almost a blur, so that Rob wasn't quite sure he'd heard what she said, or just what he wanted her to say.

She tugged at her fingers, trying to get them out of his hands, obviously desperate to run and hide, now the unspeakable was spoken.

'Still, keep still,' he said, smiling broadly now. 'It's OK. You haven't shocked me. I think you've been very brave. Well done, Ruthie. I'm proud of you.'

She gathered her breath. 'You are?'

'That must have been hard for you to say.'

'It was.'

'Did you mean it?'

She nodded.

'I want to be better. I think it'll help me.'

'I think so, too. So, look, are the others out all afternoon, do you know?'

She clenched her fists in Rob's hands, her fingernails digging into him.

'Now?' she mewled.

'I think we should start as we mean to go on, don't you? But I don't want to be disturbed. So, do you know what they're doing?'

'Lulu's spending the night at Rick's. Don't know about Kalaya, but she did say something about working tonight.'

'At Sainsbury's?'

'I guess.'

'OK, well, I think that leaves us pretty clear.'

Ruth gave an alluring little shiver and shut her eyes.

Rob stood, pulling her up with him and held her hands close to his chest.

'If you'd gone to the library,' he said to the crown of her head, 'you wouldn't be in this situation, would you?'

'No.' She shook her head, which she'd hung low, gazing at the threadbare carpet.

'You're going to learn what happens when you slack off. Take off your dressing gown.'

He dropped her hands and watched them go to the belt of her robe, fumbling with the knot before shrugging the garment off. When she stood in just slippers and faded pyjamas with a picture of a yawning owl on the top half, he made her wait for his next move. This was partly to increase her nervousness, and partly because he wasn't sure what it should be. He settled on an introductory lecture.

'So, Ruth, I want you to tell me again why you're here.'

'I didn't go to the library.'

'You didn't do what you should have done.'

'No.'

'Why not?'

'Because, um, I didn't feel like it.'

'You couldn't be bothered.'

'No.'

'You're going to be bothered now. Very bothered. Hot and bothered. You understand what's going to happen to you now?'

She looked up, her mouth in a twist.

'Sort of,' she offered.

'Sort of? What does that mean? What do you think I'm going to do to you?'

'You said you'd—'

'I didn't say I'd do anything. You asked me to do something to you, and I'm going to do it. Don't you remember?'

This was too good to be true, a script from a masturbation fantasy. He'd never thought he'd find himself here like this, saying these words, to a willing girl with the decency to play reluctant.

'I do,' she admitted. 'Are you going to?'

'When you've asked me nicely.'

'Oh God, Rob,' she wailed. 'You're horrible.'

He took her chin in his hand and made her look at him again while he said the magic words. 'It's for your own good. Isn't it?'

'Yeah,' she said sulkily. 'I suppose.'

'I'm waiting. What do you deserve?'

She stamped her slippered feet and tried to yank her head away from his grip, but in the end she had to say it.

'A spanking.'

'That's right. So ask me for it, nicely.'

'You aren't going to give up on this, are you?'

'No.'

She sighed.

'Oh, for God's sake. Go on then. Spank me. Do your worst. I'm ready for it.'

'You call that asking nicely?'

'Yes, as a matter of fact, I do.'

'Ooh, you're brave, madam. Very brave. Very reckless. You seem to have challenged me. Well, I was going to go easy on you this first time, but I think I might just have changed my mind.'

He sat down on the sofa and patted his thighs.

'Come on then. Let's be having you.'

She hesitated and he put out a hand.

'Don't make me have to put you here myself.'

That seemed to do the trick and she folded herself gingerly and with a hint of a giggle over his jean-clad lap.

'Is something funny?'

'No, just, this is weird. Surreal. I can't believe I'm doing this.'

Rob had to concur, though he didn't voice the thought.

He concentrated, instead, on what it was like to have a young woman put herself over his knee. She couldn't quite anchor herself at first and her weight was all on one side until he put his hand on the small of her back and eased her gently into the right position. She knelt on the sofa with her bottom up high and her face against a cushion. Her stomach pressed into his thighs, and she would undoubtedly be aware of the hardening that was taking place inside his jeans. But that couldn't be helped.

The loosely elasticated waist of her pyjamas slid to the very top of her bottom, just barely above the start of her cleft. The thin cotton left little to the imagination: the full curves with their central split were well exposed to his eye. The material was white with pale pink polka dots. He wondered if he would be able to see anything of the colour of her skin through it. He would certainly feel the heat.

He put one palm on the most rounded part of her cheeks and rubbed at them, holding her around her waist with his other arm. Would she kick? Would she struggle? Would she cry? What if she cried? What the hell would he do then?

'Are you ready?' he asked, patting her bottom.

'No,' she said rudely, and the pats turned into a resounding smack.

Oh, the sound of it, and the way she jolted forwards as if he'd shot her.

'What was that?'

'Yes,' she admitted, meekly. 'Ready.'

'Good. Now this is for lazing in your bed all morning. I hope it was worth it.'

He began to lay on the strokes, taking it easy at first, anxious about really hurting her. She barely moved and made no sound, letting the room fill with the crisp reports until a low sigh came out of her.

'Does that hurt?' asked Rob, genuinely unsure.

'Not really,' she said. 'But it feels lovely.'

That wasn't the idea! He needed to make her feel this, make it count.

'Thank you for your honesty,' he said, and put a lot more into the next smack, which made her gasp and kick a little. This was more like it.

After a few more of these, exclamations of sincere discomfort began to pour from her and she squirmed mightily beneath his firm hold, never quite able to escape.

'Oh, it hurts,' she cried, perhaps twenty strokes in.

'Good,' he said, carrying on, moving his hand down her quivering arc, settling into a pattern that started at the high point of her bottom and ended at mid-thigh, then climbed back up again.

At fortyish, she tried to slip a hand of her own between his palm and the target, but he caught it and tucked it out of harm's way, spanking on while she cursed and hissed and kicked a cushion on to the floor.

'It's meant to hurt, Ruth,' he said. 'That's what makes it a deterrent.'

'I didn't know it would hurt this much,' she wailed. 'Please!'

He had spanked her about sixty times now. One minute. It didn't seem very long. Was it enough?

He paused and placed his palm on her cheeks. Warmth radiated through the cotton, but he couldn't be sure if it came from his own hand which, when he held it to his face again, was deep pink in colour and stinging mildly.

He let her huff and puff and settle herself while he considered his next move.

'Are you learning your lesson, Ruth?'

'I've learned it, honestly, I won't slack off again.'

'I'm not sure.'

'I mean it.' She wriggled in a way that rubbed tantalisingly against his erection. 'I really do.'

Minx, he thought. Is this really an elaborate seduction? Is she playing me for a mug? Not that I wouldn't like that.

'I need to see what I've done,' he said, the words coming out almost from nowhere, because his head felt as light as a bubble. 'I need to pull down your pyjamas.'

She made no protest, but lifted her bum higher as if in invitation.

Oh, you dirty little angel, I can do what I want with you, can I?

'I see,' he said, and he drew the light fabric over her luscious bottom. It was an all-over pale rose shade, nothing like the fiercely stained backsides he sometimes looked at on the internet. Call this a spanking? And she was doing this subtle hip-writhing thing that made his cock throb. She was doing it on purpose. She parted her thighs just a tiny, tiny bit, but it was enough to give her away.

'You're not very red,' he managed to say.

'But it's so sore,' she purred, rolling her hips more blatantly now. 'You're so hard on me.' She giggled.

'Ruth, are you trying to get me to fuck you?' he asked. 'Because, because, I'd like to, actually, if you want to know the truth, but this is meant to be a punishment. It's meant to make you think about your responsibilities.'

She stopped writhing and flopped back over his thighs, burying her head in the cushion.

He took one long, deep breath, tried to ignore his

insistently stiffening cock, and smacked her bare bottom. She made a muffled squeal into the cushion but there was no attempt at resistance. He watched her bottom turn a glowing bright scarlet under the incessant fall of his hand, never letting up until it burned and her expression of cushion-stifled woe had become a continuous wail.

'Right,' he said. 'Nearly done now. Hold tight because this is really going to sting.'

He reached down for one of her slippers, which she had kicked right off her foot in the course of her labours. The sole was of a knobbly material, a kind of rubbery plastic that Rob couldn't identify. But it looked as if it might hurt, and that was the main thing.

'Ten strokes with the slipper,' he said. 'And then it's over. For today.'

The first stroke made her scream and arch her back and kick like fury.

Aha, this was worth remembering.

He laid six and then she begged for mercy, which he thought he ought to give, remembering too late something he had read on the internet about safewords. They should really have sorted that out beforehand. But then, perhaps she would have assumed that this was a sexual thing.

But it was a sexual thing, wasn't it?

But it wasn't meant to be?

Oh God, he was past trying to analyse it.

He put the slipper down and rubbed her beautifully hot bottom.

'Oh, is that it?' she panted, pushing against his palm.

'Um, well, you did say . . .'

'And you said ten.'

'I know I did, but . . .'

'You're going to let me off? Let me get away with it?'

The mildly goading tone of her voice had him snatching up the slipper again.

'You aren't getting away with anything while I'm in charge,' he vowed.

She seemed to regret her self-sabotaging backchat when he smacked the slipper back down on her helpless behind.

'Oh no!' she shrieked.

'Don't,' he advised through gritted teeth, 'try to play me, Ruth.'

The last three strokes were full-bodied and burning with righteous indignation.

Ruth made a sobbing noise but she wasn't actually crying; no tears dampened the cushion.

He wondered, turning the slipper over in his hands, how much she could actually take. How much more? What would be her real limit? And, above all, would he ever find out?

He admired the crimson stain of her cheeks, brushing his hand over them. Ruth had gone limp over his lap, as if all her bad habits had drained out of her, leaving only a shell.

'Are you OK?' he asked after a minute or so of silent stroking and shoulder rubbing.

She snuffled and nodded against the cushion.

'Talk to me, Ruth. I need to know you really are OK.'

'I'm fine. Oh God. I don't know. I don't know how I am.'

Rob thought perhaps he ought to pull her pyjamas back up for her, but he didn't want to lose sight of the glorious results of his labours so soon. If he helped her off his lap, his erection would be quite uncomfortably visible too. But doing nothing didn't seem to be an option, so he put his arm around her waist and nudged her up into a kneeling position beside him on the sofa.

He kept his arm around her waist and let her rest her head in the hollow of his shoulder.

'Is this penitence?' he whispered. 'Or have I gone too far?'

'No, oh, Rob, you're so sweet.'

'Sweet? After what I just did to you?' He was almost offended.

'You did it because you care,' she said. She nuzzled her head against him.

What should he do? Was he still supposed to be disappointed in her or was the punishment now over and the air clear for, well, for other things?

'Yes, I did it because I care,' he said. 'Because I want you to be happy with who you are. Do you think it might work? Was it what you thought it would be?'

'I didn't expect it to hurt so bloody much.'

He laughed.

'I think it's meant to,' he said.

He put a hand up to her hair and stroked it.

'I did it because I care,' he said hesitantly. 'A lot.'

She looked up at him, still blushing at the eye contact. He noticed that she had made no attempt to pull up her pyjamas, and her sore bottom rested on her heels.

'Do you?' she said.

'I should probably make you get your books out now and get to work.'

'But you aren't going to?'

'I'd rather . . . Do you think it would be completely wrong if, if we—'

The sentence remained unfinished or, if it was finished, it was done by the pressure of lips upon each other rather than the use of speech.

Ruth climbed on to his lap again, straddling him this time,

pushing against his erection so that he couldn't control himself and the kiss became heavy and rough, reflecting his desires. Both his hands gripped her buttocks, fingers dimpling the hot flesh, kneading it while he thrust his tongue into Ruth's soft, pliant mouth, warning her what she could expect. Somehow, during the course of this intense kissing, Ruth's pyjamas made an inexorable progress downwards, ending on the floor.

Rob moved one hand up her top to grab and caress her breasts. Her nipples were hard and resistant to his pinching fingers. He groaned into her mouth and broke the kiss in order to nip and suck at her neck.

'Let's go to bed, Rob,' she urged. 'What if the others come back?'

It was a sound suggestion. Rob and Ruth spent the rest of the afternoon in Ruth's made bed in her tidy room, fucking as if it might go out of fashion. They pitched and tossed and plunged and thrust until dusk fell, then they ate something, then they went back to bed.

Ruth couldn't seem to get enough of him; she recovered from one bout only to scoot down the bed and take his detumescent cock in her mouth to revive it for another. He seemed to empty himself only to refill again immediately, ready for more. He had her underneath him, above him, beside him, on all fours, in every imaginable configuration of limbs. He had her until her skin shone like pearls and her hair was slick at the roots. He had her until her stubble burn threatened to bleed, as much on her thighs as her face. He made her come five times, or it might have been six, and every time she thanked him sweetly, which made him feel like a king.

The last time, her cries of ecstatic torment coincided with a ring of the doorbell.

'Oh God,' he muttered, lying entangled in Ruth, kissing

her all around her mouth while it sighed out its last few seconds of bliss.

'Leave it.' The words were hard won, as all her breath seemed spent.

He left it. But the ringing became more insistent, accompanied by knocking. Rob wished he hadn't left the bedroom light on.

Eventually the letterbox was raised and a familiar voice boomed around the downstairs hall.

'Ruthie, it's me. I know you're there. Let us in, eh?'

'Shit. Dave!' She sat straight up, looking wildly around for clothes, hairbrushes, anything.

'Stay there,' said Rob, putting one leg out of bed, making calculations at a rapid pace.

'Don't let him in! He'll know!'

'Well, shouldn't he?' Rob, on his feet now, ran a hand through drenched hair and gave Ruth a penetrating stare.

'Are you going to tell him?'

'I think you should. Don't you?'

'Oh God, I don't want to.'

'Ruth, you can't string him along. I'm not going to lie either.'

'I don't want to string him along, just, bloody hell, I'm knackered and I want to go to sleep.'

Rob pulled the duvet off the bed and threw on his jeans and top.

'You can't shirk your responsibilities,' he said severely. 'I thought we'd dealt with that?'

Ruth drew in a sharp breath and bit her lip, instantly chastened.

Rob smiled at the effect he had on her, then went to get the door.

'Oh, you're in,' said Dave, eyeing him up and down with undisguised suspicion.

Rob supposed he must look very much like a man who had spent the last few hours shagging. Perhaps this would be enough for Dave to put two and two together.

'Ruth's upstairs,' he said.

Dave had nothing more to say to him, and he charged up the stairs, calling Ruth's name.

Rob, bracing himself for impact, wandered into the kitchen to put the kettle on. The lino was cold on his bare feet and all the sweat was cooling, making him shiver. Tea, then bath, he thought. Then bed. He shut his eyes and leant back on the counter, thinking of all the pleasures of the afternoon and evening.

Above his head, the thunder of footsteps. He didn't think Dave had ever shown a tendency to violence, but perhaps he should go and check.

By the time he'd made his tea, raised voices filtered down the stairs. It must be pretty obvious what Ruth had been up to all day. The rumpled sheets, the binned condoms, the smell of sex in the air.

He wandered upstairs, choice phrases whistling past his ears.

'. . . couldn't keep your knickers on for five minutes . . .'

'. . . on a break, Dave!'

'. . . took advantage of you . . .'

'. . . more of a man than you'll ever be . . .'

Oh, that last one was good. He felt a certain welling in his chest.

He knocked and opened the door.

'Are you OK?'

Dave made the opening moves of a launch in his direction, but seemed to think better of it and held his ground.

'You bastard,' he snarled instead. 'You fucked my girl.'

'She's not your girl,' said Rob. 'Are you, Ruthie?'

Ruthie shook her head, lips pressed together, looking cautiously from one man to the other.

'So that's sorted,' continued Rob. 'There's not much point your hanging around, is there? Perhaps you should go now.'

'Who the fuck are you to tell me what to do?' Dave was enraged, but Rob had been accurate in his assessment of the other man's tendency towards violence. After a furious standing of ground for a few moments, Dave stomped out.

Rob followed him to the door.

'Look, I'm sorry, I didn't realise you thought you and Ruth were still on.'

'We weren't.' Dave shrugged and almost smiled. 'I came here to finish it for good. Just something about seeing her so obviously, you know . . .'

'Yeah, I know. It's for the best though.'

Dave snorted and made his exit.

'And that's the story of how you came out as kinky?'

Allyson sat back and crossed her legs.

'You always remember your first time,' said Rob, with a smile.

'It's a nice story,' conceded Allyson. 'You didn't live happily ever after, though?'

'I'm sorry?'

'Well, you and Ruth. You ain't still together, I presume, unless she's very relaxed about you seeing other people.'

'No, we split about two years ago. She got a place at an American university. Ivy League, as it goes.'

'So you did her a world of good, then. She stuck at the studies.'

'Oh, yes, she certainly did. It was hard going at first

though. I made things worse rather than better by, uh, getting together with her. All she wanted to do was go to bed with me and, rather unhelpfully, that was all I wanted to do, too.'

'Oh dearie me,' said Allyson, with a yawn and a glance at the clock.

'I was pretty strong-willed, though, and I didn't let it throw our careers off course. She needed a lot of chivvying along though. A lot of quite painful chivvying along.'

'You were the chivvier-in-chief.'

'Yes. I like a bit of chivvying, actually. Especially when it involves the striking of female bottoms. But you knew that.'

'I think I did, Robert, yes. So Ruthie goes to the States and leaves you all on your lonesome. That must have been a wrench. You didn't think of coming to my club for a bit of solace?'

'I didn't know about your club. I made a profile for one of those kinky dating sites. Met up with a few girls, had a bit of fun but no real connection, until Lucy. And now you see me here, all up to date and ready to play.'

'Baptism of fire,' said Allyson. 'You and Richard seem to get along all right.'

Richard looked up from his phone, on which he seemed to be surfing the internet.

'Why wouldn't we?' he said. 'Like-minded souls and all that.'

'Sorry, Richard, are we boring you?' Allyson looked pointedly at the phone.

He had the good grace to look embarrassed as he put it away.

'Broadband speed's awful here, anyway,' he muttered.

'What about you, Rich?' she asked, leaning forward. 'I mean, I know you quite well, but I bet Blake and Rob don't know how you got into all this. Care to give us a bedtime story?'

'You'd probably tell it better than I would,' said Richard modestly, trying to deflect attention by going to the kitchen for another bottle of wine.

'Oh, I don't think so,' said Allyson, once he was back in the room. 'I don't think so at all.'

'I'd be very interested to hear it,' said Blake, and Rob nodded agreement.

Richard yawned and looked at the stairs for a moment, but he knew there was no escape.

'OK,' he said. 'It was like this.'

One Hot Summer

It was getting on for ten years ago now.

I was heading for forty, my marriage had just ended because of the hours I was working, and those same hours meant I wasn't meeting anyone new, unless they worked at the bank. And the women at the bank work just as hard as I do, so . . .

Anyway. I had a holiday coming up and I took the full two weeks. Couldn't wait to get out of London, to be honest. In August it's like a sealed vacuum flask full of exhaust fumes and dust, as I'm sure you all well know.

I'd had an invitation from my cousin to spend some time at his country house. Not a giant Downton Abbey kind of place but a modest, Georgian, six-bedroomed former vicarage with a bit of land attached, in a nice village in Dorset. It sounded like just the literal breath of fresh air I needed.

Mind you, if I was serious about needing fresh air, I was going to have to stay away from Peregrine. He's a chain-smoker. He'd promised he'd only light up in the garden, though, so I wasn't too worried.

Got there, Saturday afternoon, glorious day it was, only

to find he'd invited other company. It didn't put me out, really, but I could have done with a bit of warning. There they all were on the lawn out the front, drinking already: they'd been to the pub for lunch and were carrying on. Peregrine always lived that kind of lifestyle. He's a theatre critic, I think you'd all have heard of him, so it's Press Nights, First Nights, Last Nights, champagne nights all the way. Knows tons of famous actors, moves in bohemian circles. Not like me. I know there's a fair amount of drug abuse and high living in banking, but I've always steered clear. Seen too many good people get lost in a blizzard of coke. My half of the family are down-to-earth Yorkshire people and I've inherited their thrift and their sound good sense. Peregrine's side, not so much.

But I ought to get back to what was going on that Saturday afternoon in a sleepy Dorset village. Peregrine had invited a theatre director and his boyfriend, a journalist from his paper and a strange woman with a massive peroxide hair-do. He introduced her as a London dominatrix, and I must admit, I was impressed. She looked every inch the part, even if she was wearing a linen trouser suit and not a PVC all-in-one. It wasn't just her appearance that interested me either. In my lonely months since the divorce, I'd spent a fair bit of free time looking at BDSM porn on the web. I had a feeling I might have seen her in something. I didn't mention it though.

I grabbed myself a drink, and sat down with them, and joined in the chat. It all seemed like an ordinary sort of afternoon summer party at first but, after a while, I started to notice things, little things that were just slightly off-key.

The theatre director snogged his boyfriend at one point, and when he did, he held his neck really tightly, so tightly

I felt a bit uncomfortable for him. But he didn't complain. The journalist, when he spoke to the domme – her name was Sofia, I think you know her, Al – had this weird manner about him, overly deferential, and he was all sweaty and bug-eyed, as if he was getting off on it. Especially when she was downright rude to him.

At one point, she put down her drink and told him to go inside and wait for her. He trotted off like a schoolboy who's just been given five quid for sweets.

Peregrine was presiding over all this like a lord. Once the domme had gone inside, and the theatre director and boyfriend were rolling under the hedge, I asked him who the hell these people were.

'I've been thinking for a while, Richard, that you need to make some new friends,' he said, sparking one up again, off the end of the last one. 'I thought you'd like to join the party.'

'What kind of a party is this, though? I'm getting a kind of vibe off it but I'm not sure if I'm reading the situation right.'

'Do you remember the night I came to your place for dinner?'

I did. It had been a good night, far too much had been drunk and we'd both woken up on the living room sofas.

'I had a bit of snoop while you were making that phone call to your colleague in Brussels. I found your secret stash of magazines.'

'For fuck's sake, Perry!'

'Oh, hush, and don't call me that, you know it makes me sound like a third-division basketball player. You can call me anything you like, up to and including 'you bastard', but please don't call me Perry.'

'Sorry, I'm sure.'

'Anyway, what particularly interested me about your

magazines was how very similar they are to *my* magazines. If you catch my drift.'

I caught his drift. You'll know the magazines, I'm sure. *Corrective Measures*, *Cheeks*, *The St Trinian*.

'As it happens,' he said, 'I've written a few stories for them. Readers' confessions kind of thing. All made up, of course, and it barely pays, but I enjoy my work. Maybe you've read them?'

'I tend to mostly get them for the pictures.'

He looked a little bit disappointed, then he perked up a bit.

'You need the pictures because there's a void in your life,' he said. 'A void in the form of a shapely female posterior.'

'About sums it up,' I said.

'So you and Amanda?'

'No. I never broached the subject. Meant to, many times, but when it came down to it, ah, you know. I was tired or she was tired or . . . She wouldn't have been into it anyway.'

I got distracted then by a noise coming from one of the upstairs rooms of the house. All the windows were open because of the heat. The noise was a smack, smack, smack in strict rhythm. The fourth or fifth time there was a little cry as well, a man's voice.

'Sofia's good at her job,' said Peregrine. 'She ought to get Julian to write her a review for the paper. But somehow I doubt he will. Anyway, have you finished with that drink? There's somebody I'd like to introduce to you.'

Well, I was feeling a little as if I'd gone over the rainbow, to be honest. Here I was, expecting a relaxing country retreat, and I seemed to have landed smack bang in the middle of a kinky sex party. But I was curious, and I wanted to see more, so I followed Peregrine into the house. I'm pretty sure the director – I wish I could tell you his name but I'm sworn to secrecy – was getting sucked off by his boyfriend by then, right under the hawthorn. I didn't think it'd be good manners to look, though, so I didn't.

Peregrine took me into the main downstairs room; a living room, or drawing room, if you want to call it that. Big, though, with bay windows, lots of sofas and antiques and all the Peregrine stuff. Not to my taste, really, I'm more of a minimalist, but if you like that type of thing . . . Anyway. I wasn't paying a lot of attention to the furniture, I'll admit, because something else had caught my eye straight away.

In the corner, there was a woman, a young woman, with her back to us.

It was pretty easy to see that she had a great figure, curving in and out in all the right places – even with clothes on, that much would have been obvious. But she was only wearing a corset thing – basque, is it? – with stockings and suspenders. No knickers. She had her back to us so I got a bird's eye view of her luscious bum. A gorgeous one it was, really full and round. She had her hair up in a clip on top of her head, but if it'd been down it would probably have reached down that low. The stockings were fishnets and she was wearing stiletto heels, too. She had her hands on her head.

I thought it was a bit strange that she didn't turn around or do anything when she heard us come into the room. She must have been terribly embarrassed to be bare-bottomed like that in front of two men, one a complete stranger.

Peregrine was still rambling on about the house, and the village, and what the neighbours were like. He didn't even mention her until he'd finished this anecdote about the retired army major down the road, and how he was trying to take over the parish council.

There was a bit of a natural break then, and all I could think of to do was clear my throat and look pointedly over at the, well, elephant in the corner sounds a bit rude. Maybe elegant in the corner? Heh. No. Sorry. But you know what I mean. She was right there, drawing every little bit of my available attention, but nobody had mentioned her.

'You'll be wondering, Richard,' he said, in that fantastic old-school accent of his, 'from which auction house I acquired our delightful new addition to the furniture?'

All I could do was nod. That arse. I couldn't take my eyes off it.

'If she turned around, you'd recognise her,' he said.

She moved then, a little tremor of the shoulders and I heard her draw in a breath, but she didn't say a word, or turn around.

'That's got the wind up her. She's terrified she'll end up in the papers. But you're a discreet man, aren't you, Richard? I've already told her you're a cousin of mine. And you're far too rich to bother with blackmail or bribery. Honestly, anyone would think I'd yanked you off the street. If I were you, I'd take offence.'

'Oh, no, it's fine,' I said. I was far too intrigued to play along with Peregrine's little game. I wanted to know who she was.

'I won't divulge her identity just yet,' said Peregrine. I could have slapped him, though it wouldn't have given me the pleasure getting my hands on that backside in the corner could have. 'But suffice to say that she is one of our esteemed friend Sofia's submissives, brought down here for the weekend with a very specific purpose in mind.'

'Sofia's submissives?'

'Yes, she and Sofia have a kind of relationship, I suppose.

Sofia has clients and she has submissives. Her submissives are her lovers. She has four just now, I gather.'

'Are they all women?'

'No. One of them is Raf, whom you met earlier with our friend the director. She's bisexual. Bi-sadistic. She doesn't care if the bottoms she whips are hairy or smooth. In fact, I introduced our little friend here to Sofia at a backstage party. They are both indebted to me.'

'You're quite the fixer on the S&M scene.'

He didn't disagree with me.

'So, er . . .'

I looked over at the girl, as pointedly as I could.

'Ah, yes, as I was saying. This little piece teamed up with Sofia and they've been happily in lust for a few months now. Sofia's a marvellous trainer – she's taught our friend well – but now she feels she's ready to move to another level of submission.'

'Another level?'

I felt a bit stupid, just echoing Peregrine, but I hadn't the slightest idea what he was on about.

'Sofia is a generous woman. She has a lot of toys, but she's always happy to share them with her friends. Raf and this naughty little miss are to be this weekend's common playthings. Raf's done it before, but this one hasn't. It's her first time. A very special day for her. The day she learns what it truly means to belong to Sofia.'

All of this was accompanied by smacks and moans from upstairs, which added to the strange ambience of the place. It was as if power play and erotic discipline were in the air. I was well and truly hooked.

'What does it mean? What sort of sharing?'

'Anything and everything. Her arse is ours. And so is the rest of her. But not until Sofia gives us the nod – terrible manners to just set to with somebody else's sub unless they've allowed it.'

'I see,' I said. I won't deny, I was pretty excited by now. It was looking as if I might get to join in this party. That perfect peach of a bottom was going to feel the weight of my hand, and I was going to make sure I matched up to the more experienced players.

The moaning and smacking stopped, and stiletto heels clicked down the stairs towards us. I saw the girl in the corner straighten and compose herself into optimum position.

'Hello, boys,' said Sofia, entering purposefully. 'Sorry you had to hear that. Julian's been a very silly boy and he had to be chastised. He's in the same position up there that a certain person is modelling so nicely down here. Has she been behaving herself?'

'She's been exceptionally good,' said Peregrine, and I nodded along.

'Well, that makes a change. I hope she's resolved to turn over a new leaf and work on her unquestioning obedience. She still finds that difficult, you know, Peregrine, even after all these months of training.'

I wondered how she felt, standing there, listening to all of this, being spoken about as if she wasn't in the room.

'Nobody could train her better, darling,' said Peregrine. 'You know you're the crème de la crème. The cream of the crop, one might say.'

Sofia laughed, loudly. 'Yes, one might. Especially this one. Very well. I think she's had long enough to reflect on her misdeeds. Richard, I understand you're new to the delights of discipline?'

'Well, yes, that's right. I've thought about it often but I've never—'

'What a treat you have in store. I think perhaps you should deliver the warm-up and Peregrine can follow up with the more advanced implements. I haven't quite decided what we should use on her. Peregrine, do you have any thoughts?'

'It needs to be a strong lesson, of course.' Peregrine mused on this for a bit. 'I'd say a touch of the strap, some strokes with a wooden paddle, and all rounded off with twelve good strokes of the rattan cane. We should intersperse each session with some additional punishment, too, perhaps a little humiliation or some sexual service.'

'Yes, I'm with you. Four hard spankings with fun for us in between. You can do the caning, then. I'll do the others.'

'Splendid.'

It was as if they'd decided who was going to prepare which course for a pot-luck supper, they were so clinical and decisive about it. I felt a little sorry for the girl as the punishment sounded very harsh, the sort I liked to read about but doubted any girl could really take. But perhaps they could. And I was going to warm her up!

I was nervous, perhaps more nervous than she was, especially when Sofia sat herself down on the sofa and said, 'She's all yours, Richard.'

What was I going to do with her? Getting her over my knee was the obvious choice, so I sat down on a straight-backed chair, eighteenth century or whatever, I expect, and tried to get comfortable. I was already hard, though, which I was embarrassed about – you are, aren't you, your first time? I'm well over it now, of course.

'All right,' I said. 'You've done your corner time and now you need to be punished. Come here.'

She turned round and I had to bite my lip so as not to stare too hard. If I tell you who she was, do you swear you won't tell? Allyson already knows, of course. Yes? OK. It was Celia Britt. Yes, *the* Celia Britt. God, yes, she was fantastic in that last *Cat Girl*, I know, I saw it three times. So, there I was, face to face with one of the hottest properties in film, about to give her a good spanking. Does life get much better than that? Let me know if it does.

You'll have seen her in her underwear, of course, in that movie, but she's even rounder and curvier and bouncier in the flesh. Gorgeous skin, not a blemish on her. Not yet, anyway. And she had her eyes down, all coy and meek, and her hands clasped over her you-know-what. All right, I know. We're all grown-ups here, Allyson's right. She had her hands clasped over her pussy. That's the bit I hadn't seen before, so I asked her to put her hands by her sides. She was shaved almost bare except – I don't know how she did it, must have used a stencil or something – she had the word 'TOY' in capitals in pubic hair on there. Yeah, I thought, that must have taken ages to do.

Once I was through with my stunned mullet impersonation, I found my inner top and smacked my thigh.

'Over my knee with you,' I said.

'Don't you want to give her a bit of a lecture first?' asked Sofia. 'I always do.'

'Well, I would, but I've no idea what she's meant to have done.'

'Oh, yes, good point. Just tell her she's a slut, she likes that.'

'OK.' I turned my full attention back to Celia. 'I've heard some tales about you, young lady,' I said, trying to channel old schoolteachers I'd been impressed by. 'Not very nice tales. I've heard that your behaviour is loose and you put it about with all the boys, and the girls too. Is that true?'

'Yes, sir,' she said, very softly. God, it was weird to hear that famous voice, talking to me, calling me sir. It was a head-fuck, in the best possible way.

'It is?' I was having to try very hard to sound outraged because this was pretty good news to me. 'You admit that you're a slut?'

'Yes, sir,' she said again.

'Say it, then. Say "I am a slut".'

She obliged. The way she said 'slut', kind of relishing it, putting her teeth and tongue into it, got me even harder.

'And what do sluts deserve?'

She was curling her fingers up into fists and her face was bright red. She didn't want to say it but I wasn't going to let her off the hook.

'Tell me, little slut. What do you deserve?'

'A spanking, sir.'

'That's right. And that's what you're going to get. So put yourself over my knee and we'll see about making a start on that.'

I could see Sofia and Peregrine from the corner of my eye and I think they approved. I wanted to do a good job. I wanted them to think well of me. This round, ripe bottom over my lap was going to be thoroughly and properly reddened, and nobody was going to call my handiwork into question.

She seemed to know the drill, and I didn't have to adjust her very much. She held her hands in front of her, clasped – I guess this was what Sofia always made her do. Her legs were pressed together, straight down to the floor. Even so, I could see the little swollen pink lips of her pussy peeking through. They were glistening a bit. She was as up for this as I was.

I got this surge of . . . I don't know. Confidence? Power?

I felt like a king. I knew, right in my blood, that I was going to be good at this.

I didn't smack too hard at first. I didn't know how much she could take and I was worried I might break her. I kept slowing down just before my palm made contact. I tried to make it look harder than it was because I didn't want Sofia thinking I was some kind of soft touch, but you couldn't fool her. Besides, I wasn't getting a squeak out of Celia, not as much as a wriggle.

'Bottoms are well padded,' said Sofia. 'They can take heavy impact. You have to be harder on her, Richard. I don't want to tell you what to do.'

Peregrine laughed at that.

'OK, I do want to tell you what to do, but feel free to ignore me. You're the top here. Your rules. I just think she's getting away with it right now.'

That did it. I cracked down, hard, and Celia did a sort of little jump and puffed out a breath. No more Mr Nice Guy. I kept up the pressure after that and was pleased with myself when she started to flex her ankles and gasp. Her skin went pink, then darker and, soon enough, every smack brought a little 'oo' sound with it.

I was flying. My God. It was amazing. I was finally doing something I'd never thought I'd do and I knew, right then and there, that this couldn't be the last time. The way her skin heated up and flattened under my hand then bounced back, it was the sexiest thing ever. Well, you'll know that, of course. I wanted to go on and on, but once her bum was rosy red all over I noticed that my own palm was stinging and thought she was probably warmed up now, as they'd said.

'That'll do for starters,' I said. I rubbed my hand all over her arse – it was better than a roaring fire. The glisten on her pussy lips was still there, and more of it too. She was getting her breath back and the little so-and-so rubbed herself against me, as if to tell me she knew I was hard and what was I going to do about it?

I nearly did something about it then and there, but Sofia and Peregrine finished applauding, and I knew Sofia was going to speak.

'You've done a wonderful job, Richard, absolutely terrific. She's very well warmed now. Take a look at her pussy. What do you see?'

'She's wet.'

Celia stopped squirming on me straight away and tensed up. Did she know what was coming?

'Of course she is. Because Celia always gets very wet after a spanking. Don't you, Celia?'

'Yes, ma'am.'

'Why is that?'

'Because I'm a dirty slut, ma'am.'

'Good. Our gentleman friends need to know this about you. They're going to see your sluttiness at very close quarters soon. Richard, why don't you finger her for a bit, if you like? She's not allowed to come, of course, so it makes a nice little rounding-off of part one of her punishment. Tease her.'

Celia gave a little sigh, halfway between ecstasy and despair.

'Spread your legs, girl. Wide. Show the gents everything you've got. Aww, you're doing so well. Your first time in front of strangers and you're being such an obedient little trollop. I'm proud of you.'

The way she mixed sternness with kindness was intriguing to me. Celia needed encouragement, of course, to take this very bold step forward, but she seemed to be enjoying it. This became very clear to me when I put my hand down between her thighs and pressed my fingers into her pussy lips.

She held herself perfectly still and taut. I suppose if she'd allowed herself to relax she might have had the forbidden orgasm.

It kept going through my head that I had Celia Britt over my knee, with my fingers exactly where half the men in England would like to put them. If so-and-so could see me now, I thought. It didn't seem quite real. I wanted to whip out my phone and get a picture, just so I'd know for sure it'd really happened.

But that would be looking a gift horse in the mouth. Just then, I was quite happy to keep looking at my gift sub and her lovely red bum. She was really wet down there, and her clit was swollen. I thought if I talked to her, it would make things even more difficult for her. Could I be that cruel?

Come on. You know me.

I kept saying things like, 'I saw you in that last movie you did. When you kissed your opposite number, did he know that you like a strange man's hand down your knickers? Perhaps he'd had his there already. I bet he has. I bet he was feeling you up all the way through – they just cut it so we could only see your heads. But the whole crew could see what he was doing to you further down – taking down your knickers and rubbing your pussy, sticking his fingers up inside you.'

She could hardly bear it. She was gritting her teeth to begin with, then I saw her put a finger sideways in her mouth and bite down on it.

'I bet all your directors know how to get a good performance out of you. Take you over their knees and give you a good spanking before you go on set. Do you do all your scenes with a warm bottom, Celia? Is that the secret of your success?'

'Please.'

She was so close. I could feel her body surrendering, little knots unwinding one by one.

'OK,' said Sofia.

I knew she meant my time was up, but I wilfully ignored her. She was going to have to spell it out.

'Slut, you're going to have to get on your knees and thank the kind gentleman for warming you up. Chop chop.' She clapped her hands and I finally took my fingers from that lovely, soft, wet place and let her go.

Sofia looked at me as if she couldn't work me out. 'You're sure you haven't done this before?'

I'd surprised myself with how easily I'd taken to it, so all I could do was shrug and put up my hands.

Meanwhile, Miss Britt had got herself on her knees in front of me and seemed to me making a move towards my waistband.

'What's this?' I asked Sofia.

'We've discussed how a slut thanks a gentleman,' she said. 'Haven't we, slut?'

Celia nodded. She had her fingers on my fly.

'How's that then?' I asked. Mind you, I had an idea, and I liked it a lot.

'Tell him, slut.'

'A slut thanks a gentleman by drinking his seed,' she said.

'Well, thanks for telling me. I'm new to all this, you see.'

I might have felt a bit shy or embarrassed about having my prick out in front of perfect strangers, both of them women, but if I did, I got over it pretty quickly.

My last reservations were long gone by the time she bent

her head and took me into her mouth. Ah, God, that girl could suck. I was surprised, actually, and I said as much to Sofia.

'I've had her practise every night this week on different sized dildos,' she said.

The thought of this, combined with the sight of her bright red lips wrapped around my cock and the gorgeous, deep, wet warmth, and everything that had gone before made me lose control of myself a bit. I came much too quickly, a bit disappointing, really. I wanted to keep her at it for a good ten minutes. In the end I only managed about two.

She sucked it all out of me and swallowed it down.

'You're a marvel,' said Sofia, coming to stand behind her and then massaging her shoulder blades. 'Your first blow job in front of other people and you aced it, slut. I'm very proud of you. He didn't stand a chance against my perfect little slut.'

She flashed me quite an evil smile, and I felt all that shyness and embarrassment cover me. It took its time, but it got there in the end. I zipped up sharpish and resigned myself to spending the rest of the scene in the role of observer.

'Nobody holds a candle to Sofia when it comes to training subs,' said Peregrine, who'd been watching the whole thing as if he were at a play.

'Now then, madam,' said Sofia, clapping her hands again. 'You're well warmed up and it's time to get serious. Up with you.'

She stood up. Her lipstick was smeared and her thighs were gleaming with juices. I was semi-hard again by the time Sofia had marched her to a carved wooden chest and made her bend over it with her palms flat on the top.

She was left there for as long as it took for the other two to nip outside for a smoke break. I thought I should talk to her, but I didn't know what to say, so I just sat there and watched her. There was still a lot of colour in her rear cheeks. I wondered how hard Sofia was going to spank her, and for how long.

Just before the others came in, I blurted, 'Are you OK?'

And she said, 'Don't worry.' And then I couldn't think of anything else, so we just waited for Sofia and Peregrine to come back in.

Sofia was holding a leather strap, a good, thick one with a handle at one end. She went straight over to Celia and made her sniff it.

'Your old friend, slut, come to play with you,' she said. 'Aren't you pleased to see him?'

'Yes, ma'am.'

'So show him. Give him a kiss.'

She kissed the strap. I was hard again by then.

'And a lick for luck.'

She ran her tongue along the rough edge of it. Sofia pushed it into her mouth a bit, gagging her, then pulled it out and with some kind of fancy flicking movement, snapped it straight down on Celia's poor bum.

'He burns, doesn't he? I'm going to give you thirty, slut. Push that bottom right up for me, legs wide so the gentlemen can see everything, please.'

Celia moaned, but she did as she was told.

Sofia knew her stuff. She laid on that strap good and hard and, what with her being the kind soul that she is, she used it as an opportunity to give me a masterclass. Mistressclass. Whatever you want to call it.

'See how I make sure I cover every part of her bottom and thighs, Richard,' she said. 'I like to start in the middle – never go much higher, it can cause damage – and lay a new stripe underneath, all the way down, until I get to about mid-thigh.'

She was suiting actions to her words. Long red stripes went down Celia's bum, one by one, like rungs of a ladder. She was obviously used to it: I think she knew what to expect and that helped her through the pain. I've made a note of that, actually. If I want to be really mean to a sub, I buck her expectations. They hate that. They really do.

Celia was very well behaved – uncannily well behaved, I thought at the time, but I've seen other girls who can take a good strapping like that since. Of course, our Lucy isn't one of them. She's a squealer and I still have to tie her hands when I use the cane. I like a reaction, myself. Feel like I'm getting somewhere. But Sofia likes them to work hard at their submission and suppress their natural responses, and that's her prerogative as a domme.

Celia's bottom was getting pretty dark red by the time Sofia got to the final ten.

'The reason I like to go down to the thighs,' said Sofia, whipping away, 'is because it means you can embarrass your sub by making her wear a short skirt or hotpants to the pub later on. If there's still a nice reddish tinge to her skin, you'll find that it keeps her squirming all night. People assume it's sunburn, of course. Or do they? Personally, I think they're well aware that a certain young lady's just had a strap soundly applied to her bottom and thighs, but they're too polite to comment. Don't you, slut?'

'Yes, ma'am.' She finally cracked on that stroke – about twenty-seven or twenty-eight, I think – and made a little 'ah' of discomfort.

Sofia made the last strokes so hard my eyes watered a bit and then she put the strap back down on top of the chest, under Celia's nose.

'Kiss him again. Doesn't he feel warm, now he's had a good play with your naughty bottom?'

She patted Celia's burning cheeks and had a quick rummage between her thighs.

'Soaking again,' she said, sucking in a breath. 'Well, I think I'm ready for my vote of thanks, slut.'

Celia dropped to her knees and Sofia leaned against the chest, gripping the edge. Celia pulled down Sofia's trousers to the knees – she wasn't wearing knickers underneath – and set about licking her without further ado.

I didn't dare look at Peregrine. I'd imagine he was as hot and bothered by it as I was. Celia got really stuck in, lapping and sucking and pushing her face right up between Sofia's thighs, as if she wanted to fuck her with it.

Sofia started pulling her hair after a few minutes, making her do what she wanted.

'Peregrine, darling,' she said, as if this were the most normal thing in the world. 'Go up to my room and fetch the large butt plug from my bedside drawer, would you? And the lube, of course.'

Celia moaned again, but Sofia obviously liked that, because she made her carry on moaning all the way through the rest of the feast.

'Mm,' said Sofia. 'Think your bottom's sore now? That's nothing, slut, nothing at all. By the time we're finished with you, you won't be sitting down for days. That's it. Push it. Eat it. Cover your face with it.'

Sofia came with a grunt just as Peregrine returned – walking a little stiffly – with the big rubber plug.

'Gorgeous,' panted Sofia. 'Bend her over, Peregrine, would you, and plug her? I'll go and fetch the paddle.'

Celia looked a little alarmed to be left to the tender

mercies of Peregrine while her domme left the room, but she obeyed without question when he ordered her to bend over his lap.

I envied him, having her squirming about on his rock-hard crotch with her crimson bum nicely available to him.

'You've been plugged before, I take it, madam?' said Peregrine, uncapping the lube bottle.

'Yes, sir.'

'How often does Sofia plug you?'

'A couple of times a week, sir, on average. Always during or after a punishment session. She knows I find it uncomfortable.'

'Good. So you should.'

He parted her cheeks, exposing the little brown hole. I leaned over for a good look.

'Have you ever worn one in public?'

'Yes, sir.'

'Oh, you must tell me about that.'

He let a few drops of the lubricant fall from the bottle on to her pucker. She quivered and tensed.

'Please,' she blurted. 'I don't mean to be difficult, but could this wait until Ma'am is back in the room?'

'Of course,' he said. 'I'm sorry. I should have thought. But you can still tell me that story, can't you?'

'She made me wear it while I was filming a scene in my last movie,' she said. 'You'll have to look out for it, it's released in a couple of months. I play a Russian princess. You'll understand why I look especially stiff in one particular scene. Luckily, stiffness was pretty much part of the role.'

Peregrine laughed and patted her bottom approvingly.

Stiffness was pretty much part of my role by now and it was a big relief when Sofia came back with both the paddle and young Julian. He was wearing a harness and collar and Sofia was pulling him on a leash while he crawled after her. He had a butt plug in too, one with a nice horsehair tail. She had him kneel up with his hands out like paws and his tongue out until further notice.

'Oh, are we ready?' said Sofia, coming to stand over Celia and supervise the insertion.

'We were waiting for you,' said Peregrine.

'I wouldn't want to miss it. You've done the lube already?'

'Not properly. I'll just . . .' He started massaging around her anus with a slippery finger.

She was very good, very self-controlled. I think Sofia helped a lot, putting a hand on her neck and soothing her, telling her how well she was doing and to remember her relaxation techniques. I'd have been far less calm with a strange man's finger up my bum, believe me. But I'm not submissive.

Anyway, he got the plug in, very slowly, and I couldn't take my eyes off the way she stretched to take it. I was cringing on her behalf – it just looked impossible. But he got it in there in the end and patted her poor red bottom with its black oval marker stuck there between her cheeks.

I really wanted to know how it felt, so I asked her.

'Very uncomfortable, sir,' she said. 'It feels very big and intrusive.'

'Doesn't it?' said Sofia. 'And it's going to make your paddling so much more interesting. I hope you're ready for the paddle, slut, because I'm going to give it to you right there, over Peregrine's knee. Ten strokes. Are you ready? Hold her wrists, Peregrine. She won't need it, but I like to see it. Lovely.'

I think it was the most erotic thing I've ever seen in my life. Poor Celia, upended over Peregrine's lap, butt plug in, getting paddled by Sofia while everyone watched. She didn't take the paddle as well as the strap; she yelled out loud with every stroke, and kicked a bit too. It was obviously painful and I felt a bit guilty for wishing Sofia would give her more than ten. But not that guilty.

Especially when Sofia hauled her up and told her what was coming next.

'Better give that bum a rest before the cane,' she said. 'We don't want it getting too numb and not feeling every iota of its bite, do we? Let's have an interlude. Here, you can sit between my legs.'

Sofia sat down and spread her legs. Celia sat between them, perched on the edge of the sofa. She had to bend slowly to seat herself because of the plug and she bit her lip a bit on making contact with the faded chintz.

'Good.' Sofia held her in position with both hands on her breasts. She started to pinch and roll her nipples from behind. 'Now open your legs, slut. Rover!'

This was addressed to Julian.

'Come and lick her. A good, thorough licking. But remember, slut, you're not to come.'

Peregrine and I were treated to the display of Julian eating Celia with unholy relish while Sofia carried on teasing and tormenting her nipples. Celia's face was a picture – she could hardly bear it. If I could have captured that expression and framed it . . . Ah, God, give me a minute . . .

Well, the poor girl came, didn't she? I felt sorry for her. How was she meant not to? I think the fact that Peregrine and I were watching her so intently, taking the odd sip from our drinks now and then, was what did for her. She kept looking at us from underneath her nearly closed eyelids and getting even more into it.

As soon as she started to come, Sofia smacked her breasts hard and said, 'Bad girl. Rover, leave off. Go to your corner, pup.'

Julian, tail literally between his legs, crawled off out of sight.

'Chastity belt for you after another punishment tomorrow morning,' said Sofia grimly. 'Now get to the middle of the room, bend and touch your toes. Peregrine is caning you and he doesn't go easy.'

She was right. Peregrine was a master of his instrument. Even before the cane had made any contact with Celia's backside, I was impressed. The way he swished it and made it snap the air was like some kind of arcane performance art. I made up my mind to ask him where he learnt it, and if he could teach me.

Twelve strokes. You know how much I love watching the welts rise, the white line turn dark, making my mark on my girl's skin. Watching Peregrine cane Celia, I knew myself and I knew what I was. There couldn't be any turning back now. This was what I wanted, and I wasn't going to settle for anything else.

She suffered so beautifully. I fell a little bit in love with her when she took that whipping. I wanted to touch her and hold her and comfort her, but at the same time I wanted to tell her she deserved it and she'd get more if she didn't behave herself. She got tears in her eyes around the ninth stroke and I was so jealous of Peregrine I had this mad moment of thinking I'd get up and snatch the cane off him and finish her off myself.

But he got to do it. Besides, I'd probably have done it all wrong, not being an expert in those days, and injured her.

He got to hold her and kiss her and tell her everything was all right now.

And he got the traditional thank you, of course. Her luscious mouth around another man's cock now, easy and difficult to watch at the same time.

There were tears on her cheeks while she sucked him. He asked her if she wanted to stop but she shook her head.

After he'd filled her mouth and she'd swallowed, Sofia gave her a long hug and kiss and then the pair of them disappeared up to the bedroom.

That left me and Peregrine.

It was a bit awkward, I must say. The experience we'd just shared, well! Intense wasn't the word. Plus I was painfully hard and had no idea what to do about it, apart from cross my legs and think of the fiscal cliff.

'So,' said Peregrine, making with the whisky again. 'Do you think it's for you?'

'What? All the kinky stuff?'

'Yes. You seemed to enjoy yourself.'

'I did. Yes. I think this is my, uh, niche. Very much so.'

'Excellent. Another partner in sex crime for me.'

'Well, I'd stop short of crime.'

'Figure of speech, Richard, figure of speech.' You know how he talks. All jaded and royal. 'You can thank me whenever you like.'

'Thanks! Obviously. I'm very glad you invited me here this weekend. Very.'

'My pleasure. You'll have to come to my club when you're back in town.'

We chatted for a while, about the scene and things he'd done, but it didn't do much to calm down my raging erection and I had to excuse myself in the end and take a medicinal shower.

Poor old Julian was still in his corner when I came back down.

Supper was interesting. It was a warm evening and we got

a table out in the back garden and ate there. The film director
and his boyfriend cooked – out of this world, the food was.
Everyone was dressed for dinner, you know, cocktails at seven,
dinner at eight, kind of thing. Peregrine's a stickler for all
that. I expected Celia to be shy and embarrassed about what
we'd done with and to her that afternoon, but she couldn't
have been more different. Life and soul of the party, full of
stories, most of which might land me in court if I repeated
them. No, Al, I won't be persuaded. No.

And she was a flirt! Bloody hell, she flirted with me outrageously. I thought Sofia was going to read the riot act, but
she was fine with it. Once we'd done liqueurs and Peregrine
had started chain-smoking again, Sofia suggested Celia and I
take an evening walk through the village.

'Go on,' she said. 'Such a gorgeous night. The sunset's
going to be incredible. Take a walk down to the ruins, along
the river.'

Celia seemed up for it, so I went along with the idea.

I was still a bit starstruck, to be honest, and everyone we
passed gawped – a few came up and asked for autographs – so
the conversation was a bit smalltalky at first.

'Sofia's right, it's a perfect evening for a walk.'

'Sofia's always right.'

'Yeah, she seems like that type.'

(Autograph hunter.)

'She's a sweetie under that tough domme exterior.'

'Is she? I can't imagine it.'

'I landed on my feet with her. I've heard some horror
stories . . .'

(Cameraphone snapper.)

'But you've never had a bad experience? How long have
you been doing this?'

'Physically doing it? A couple of years. In my head – forever.'

'Yeah, same here with the head thing. I didn't think I'd ever—'

A group of teenage girls sitting on a five-barred gate shouted lines of dialogue from Celia's most famous film.

'Take no notice,' I said to her.

'Oh, I don't mind. Precious little else for them to do around here. Lovely as it is.'

We were down by the river now. It was quiet, a few dog-walkers, but the more intrusive types hadn't followed us, thank goodness.

She reached for my hand and I took it.

'How's your bum?' I asked. It just sort of came out. It was on my mind, I suppose.

She laughed, anyway, so I hadn't offended her.

'Very sore,' she said. 'Did you notice I was right on the edge of my seat at supper?'

'I did.' I'd enjoyed noticing it. 'How long does it take to, you know, die down?'

'Oh, it'll be all right by tomorrow night, I daresay. Nothing left but stripes and the odd bruise. Just as well I'm not doing any bikini shoots, all the same.'

'I suppose you have to think about all that. Recovery time.'

'I have to schedule my play times very carefully. Luckily, Sofia's understanding.'

'That's just as well.' I can't stop thinking about her bottom, neatly striped and probably still throbbing. 'You're not still wearing that plug, I take it?'

'No, God, no. Half an hour of that one is my maximum.'

'I'd love to look at those stripes again.'

She stopped and gave me this odd look, sort of fearful and

excited. Then she looked around the river bank, which was empty now.

'Is that an order?' she said in a low voice.

'Is it? No, I don't think so. I was just saying . . .'

'The thing is, Richard, sir, Sofia's rule for the weekend is that I have to obey everything I'm asked to do. Everything. Unless it's completely awful, of course, then I can safeword. My safeword is "cut", by the way.'

'Oh, I see.' I thought I could see where this was heading, but it seemed a bit too good to be true. 'And you're, uh, fine with this, are you?'

'It depends who's doing the ordering. Julian's been trying to wind me up all day, telling me to fetch this and carry that. Even made me flog him. Silly little twonk. He's so jealous of the attention I get from Sofia. I like you, though. I loved the way you were with me, earlier. When I was over your knee.'

I got a bat of the famous lashes. It did the trick. Whatever she wanted me to do to her, I was more than game.

I looked along the towpath. Still empty, but there was no guarantee that it would stay that way. No proof against telephoto lenses either. But perhaps that turned her on.

'Aren't you afraid of getting caught? You're famous. Anyone could be following us.'

She smiled and half-closed her eyes.

'I know,' she said, as if on the verge of orgasm already.

'All right,' I said, pushing her into the undergrowth by her shoulders. 'But it'll have to be quick.'

'Whatever you say, sir.'

I had her on the grass, her on all fours, me kneeling behind her. The little devil had brought condoms with her in her purse: she had this planned. Her bum was still red all over and the cane marks had hardened, the way they do. I kept pressing my thumbs into them while I had her and it made her wild.

'Tell me what I am, tell me what I am,' she kept saying. She liked to be called names. I ran out of ideas in the end and had to run through them all again. I was new to it all, and I have to admit I felt very awkward calling her a whore and all that. I wasn't quite comfortable with it. But she obviously got off on it, so who was I to deny her?

When she was getting close, she said something else.

She said, 'The front page of the paper . . .'

I thought I knew what she was getting at, so I carried on.

'You'll be on it,' I said, still banging away. 'Like this. On your hands and knees with your well-whipped arse in the air, getting fucked by a man you don't know. In full colour, for everyone in the world to see.'

This was what did it for her, and she came with her fists stuffed in her mouth, quietly but hard. I'd held on for as long as I could. It was a relief to get it all out.

She had grass stains on her dress, which she was delighted with. She said she wanted to get papped looking like this – shagged out and exhausted. I wasn't so sure about that. I didn't really want to find myself in the Daily Mail sidebar of shame, though, thinking about it, banking's so macho it'd probably make me some kind of hero in the City.

I wanted to hold her and talk to her after, but she just wanted to show herself off in her post-coital state and she made a run for it along the towpath.

I guess I knew what that made me. The plaything of an idle hour. Ah well. I'm not one to complain. If beautiful movie stars want to use me as some kind of stud dom, I suppose I can live with it.

So, yeah, that was my first experience of the kinky side of life. My mind was blown, I don't mind admitting. The weekend just sort of went on like that, really. By the time I went back to London, I knew seven types of bondage knot and the best place to shove peeled ginger. And that's how you see me now.

Allyson put down her empty glass.

'That Peregrine's a devil,' she said. 'My best customer, though. So, are you still in touch with her? Celia Britt?'

Richard shook his head. 'She's pretty much permanently in Hollywood these days. We had dinner once, when she was filming in town, but that was a couple of years ago now.'

'Shame. You'd make a lovely couple.'

'I'm happy as I am, thanks. Lucy's quite a find.'

Rob concurred, and Blake looked wistful.

'Course, we all know your story, Blakey,' said Allyson, ruffling his hair. 'You turned up at the Geisha Garden on a stag night and the rest was history.'

'It's you we're all curious about,' said Rob.

'Me?'

'Well, I can only speak for myself but . . .'

'Yeah,' added Richard. 'How did you get into all this?'

'Well, I run the club, don't I?'

'But how did that come about?'

'You know me, Rich. I don't talk about myself. Too much I can't say or go into.'

'Woman of mystery.'

'That's me.'

'But were you always aware of your, uh, inclinations?' Rob wanted to know. 'Or did it gradually dawn on you?'

'What, being a domme, you mean? I did it for cash to begin with. Found out pretty quickly that I had a taste for it, though I wasn't so keen on the men. As you know, I ain't that way inclined. I'd always fantasise that the hairy bloke I was whipping was a lovely, soft, round girl. Then I met a few people, in the course of my work and, what with one thing and another, I ended up fronting the club.'

'A bit of this, a bit of that,' said Rob with a jokey sparring action. 'Ducking and diving.'

'Don't joke,' said Allyson, and the atmosphere went from relaxed to guarded in the time it took for her to snap the words out. 'It's all very funny for you, posh college boy, slumming it with the likes of me. But I could tell you stories that'd turn that lovely hair of yours white. I've seen it all. I wish I hadn't. But there ain't nothing I can do about it now.'

'You run a club,' said Richard, in an attempt to soothe.

'Yeah, I run a club. I don't get my hands dirty. But I know what goes on. Don't ask me to talk about it.'

'I didn't mean to.'

Rob grimaced at Richard, who remained tight-lipped.

'OK, well, it's getting late anyway,' said Blake. 'I might call it a night.'

'Wonder if Lucy's still awake,' said Richard, looking at the ceiling.

'I hope so,' said Rob. 'All this story telling has got me a bit frisky.'

'TMI,' drawled Allyson, but she made no move, her hand still closed around her empty glass.

'No such thing as TMI here this weekend,' said Blake, watching the other men climb the staircase.

'I'm going to check on Emma,' said Allyson, standing up, but before she could follow Richard and Rob, the newly installed landline rang.

'What the fuck?'

She went to pick it up, and recognised the voice on the line instantly.

'Why have you switched off your phone?'

'I haven't. Reception's shit down here.'

'You can't be out of range, Al. You can't do that.'

'What's up?'

'You've got to get back here. And bring that bitch of yours with you. She's got some questions to answer.'

It All Comes Down To Love

'I don't understand. What did he actually say?'

Emma couldn't get comfortable in the driver's seat, she tried resting most of her weight on one hip, but then the seatbelt was across her neck. Nothing worked. Nothing. worked and she didn't want to be here, in this car, heading for London and the unknown.

'He said jack shit,' muttered Allyson. 'Just to get our arses down to London.'

'He specifically wanted me to come?'

'Yeah. He said, "Bring your bitch."'

'He's still as charming as ever then.'

'Don't joke about McKenna. He's no laughing matter. I can't think what he wants to see us about. Everything's been sweet for so long.'

'Yeah.' Emma thought about this. Sweetness. The easy life. Why couldn't it always be that way?

In a police station in London, Poppy Livesey sat on a moulded orange plastic chair drinking tea from a machine.

The man beside her put his hand on her thigh.

'You're doing the right thing,' he said, but he said 'ze right sing', because he found the 'th' sound difficult to pronounce.

'You never said anything would happen,' she said woodenly. 'You said it was research.'

'These people aren't good people. I only got involved for your sake, Poppy. I wanted you away from them. You aren't made for that life.'

'How do you know what I'm made for? You've used me, that's all. I was a means to an end. And it was a good job. Good money.'

'Dirty money.'

'Easy money. Men like to spank me; I like to be spanked. Where's the harm in that?'

'It's a front for other things, Poppy.' He said her name oddly, the stress on the second syllable. For some reason, that melted her.

'You think I didn't know that? It's none of my business. I feel bad for Allyson and the girls.'

'Allyson is a pimp, nothing more. She keeps very bad company.'

'She's been good to me.'

'I can be good to you.'

She turned and stared at Bruno.

'You've sold me out.'

'But for love.'

'Love?'

She put down the tea before it spilled and stalked out on to the concourse in front of the police station, needing air, even if was black, exhaust-fumed, central London air.

How could that stupid man claim to love her, after one dodgy hook-up during which he'd used her as a snout? She should slap his stupid, attractive French face.

But somehow she couldn't. The L word had deactivated her slapping hand.

If he loved her perhaps he'd take her to Paris.

If he loved her perhaps he'd marry her.

If he loved her perhaps she might love him back one day.

But was that good enough? Perhaps. It wasn't as if she had that much to keep her here. Horrible family, horrible past and she'd already dropped out of her university course. Now she was going to lose her job into the bargain, and then her flat and then . . .

She turned and walked back to where a disconsolate Bruno slumped in his chair, looking as if he could use three days of solid sleep.

'I've got nothing in my life,' she said to him. 'So if you want to love me, then I suppose it's OK.'

He put out his hand and she took it.

She sat beside him and he held her while they waited for something for happen.

'I'm going to pull over,' said Emma as the sign for a motorway service station loomed ahead. 'Go to the services.'

'You need a wee?'

'No. I might have something to tell you, though.'

Allyson gave her the sharpest of looks.

'You know what this is about?'

'I don't know. But there's something I've kept quiet. I was protecting someone. Perhaps I shouldn't have.'

Emma drove up to the car park and found the most obscure corner space available.

'Emma,' Allyson said, taking her cigarettes out of the glove compartment. 'You're going to break my heart, aren't you?'

'Your heart?' Emma looked amused at the idea of such a thing existing.

'I do have one, you know. And it ain't made of stone. So, what's this dark and deadly secret, then?'

Emma drew a deep breath.

'You should have fired Poppy. After that thing with the French cop.'

Allyson lit her cigarette and took a deep drag.

'You told me you'd sorted it.'

'I think she may have stayed in touch with him.'

'Informant?'

'There was more to it than I told you. There was kind of a romance type of thing between them. I didn't think he'd let her go just like that, but I gave her the benefit of the doubt and assumed she'd steer clear. I think I might have been wrong about that.'

She tried to gauge Allyson's reaction, but none was forthcoming for quite some time.

'You might be right,' she said eventually. 'You think this French bloke has been feeding information to our local plods, ever since?'

'Yes. And Poppy has been around a lot, hasn't she? Sort of always nearby when private conversations are going on?'

'Little bitch.'

'I suppose he turned her head.'

'I'll turn more than her head for her.'

'Al.' Emma watched her grind out her cigarette and put her own hand on Allyson's forearm. 'What are we going to do?'

'Get us coffees from the caff. We need to think. And I need to clear my head. Too much vino earlier.'

'Just as well I didn't have any.'

'Is it?'

Allyson took another cigarette from the pack, watching as Emma headed up to the dimly lit service area where only the coffee shop was still open at this hour.

She had a way of moving, Emma did, that she'd never seen on another girl. A sort of confidence, almost bravura, and an absolute glorying in her big, swaying bottom. It still made Allyson's mouth water, even now, even with all that was going on. She always wore tight skirts that clung to her curves, or skinnier-than-skinny jeans. The bouncing balls inside the thin fabric demanded attention.

And she'd never met a girl more avid for spankings. 'Miss Hungrybum' had been her nickname for Emma at one time. She never seemed to use it any more though. Why was that? These days it was all 'love' and 'sweetheart'. Or just Emma.

'You love her, you silly cow. Admit it,' she muttered to herself, blowing out smoke.

That day Emma had walked into the club, that was a great day.

Allyson was holding an open audition, in the early days of the Geisha Garden. She had no idea what she would get when she advertised, so she was finding the process entertaining, if not particularly helpful. She'd been running it for a month or so. When McKenna had asked her, she'd practically spat out her cig.

'Spanking club? Are you serious?'

'Deadly. It's big, Al. Kink is big. Has to go underground because people are judgemental like that, still.'

'Yeah, like they're judgemental about your little sidelines, can't think why.'

'Don't be smart. That's different. This shouldn't be illegal. It's just people enjoying themselves. Come on, you've got clients coming out of your ears. You know how popular this stuff is.'

'So you want me to whack people's backsides as, like, some kind of act?'

'No, it's not going to be like that. It's going to be girls getting spanked.'

She sat up. 'Now you're talking.'

'Submissive men can find a domme in the Yellow Pages, pretty much. But it's not so easy for the men who like to dish it out. Sure there's Fetlife and all that, but I gather a willing bottom is still pretty hard to find, and there's all the messaging and trying to impress the sub and meeting up and not fancying each other. It's a hassle, Al. Plenty of guys don't have time for that. So, I thought, a nice private club where girls with gorgeous bums are on call whenever. Do you get my drift?'

'That could work,' she said thoughtfully.

'So are you in?'

'Yeah. Yeah, go on then. But I get to pick the girls.'

'Carte blanche, Al. Carte fucking blanche.'

She'd scribbled her tastes all over that carte blanche. She'd started up with four attractive, submissive girls she knew from the scene already, but the concept had proved an immediate hit – appropriately enough – and she needed more, a dozen at least.

So there she was, looking at a big group of all kinds, types, shapes and sizes of women. A couple of men had chanced their arm, too, but she'd taken their numbers and said she'd ask the big boss about setting up a gay night or two sometime.

Those who were left were an interesting variety. There were the usual wannabe actresses who showed up for everything. There were a number of emo-looking young women, pierced and tattooed and looking for a passage through university. There were older women too, and representatives of a galaxy of nationalities. But Allyson wasn't looking for girls who could dance or sing. She didn't even care that much about pretty faces.

She needed good bottoms, and that was the bottom line.

'OK, ladies,' she said. 'This might be the weirdest audition or interview or whatever of all time, but I'm only going to ask you to do one thing for me right now. I want you to turn your backs to me and drop your trousers, skirts, whatever you're wearing. I need a good look at your arses. Do you think you can do that for me?'

There was a great deal of nervous laughing, and chattering, and shrillness, but eventually all of the women – some thirty or so – lined up on the stage and revealed their bottoms.

Any that were too flat or too saggy were sent away. Small was fine, big was fine, but firmness and roundness were non-negotiable.

Of the twenty that remained, Allyson asked each about their experience in BDSM and made her selections on that basis.

Now that she had her twelve, she sat them down to go through terms, conditions, expectations, wages and so on.

She was halfway through her spiel when a breathless woman appeared at the door.

'Oh God, am I too late? The tube broke down just outside Kilburn. Seriously, am I too late?'

Allyson looked at her, unsmiling, and said, ''Fraid so.'

'Shit,' said the girl. Then she turned around to leave.

That bum, in its tight, tight skirt. It seemed to quiver without even being touched.

'Hang on a sec,' said Allyson. 'Come here.'

She sashayed over – actual sashaying, which Allyson had

never seen before. She was Betty Boop and Bettie Page in a devastating merger.

'What's your name?'

'Emma Frayne.'

'And how long have you lived in London, Emma Frayne?'

'All my life.'

'So you know what the tubes are like.'

She shrugged, peeking out from under her dark fringe with just the perfect blend of defiance and meekness.

'Come on. You know. Don't you?'

'Yes, but—' She made no further attempt to excuse herself.

'So you could have set off a bit earlier. There's plenty of coffee places nearby, where you can get a drink and read the paper, if you're too early. You're just irresponsible, that's all.'

'I'm not!'

'Admit it. Say, "Yes, ma'am, I'm irresponsible."'

The other girls hung on this little scene like breathless limpets.

A change came over Emma's eyes, from genuine wariness to something like relief. *She knows what this is.*

'Yes, ma'am,' she said in a mousy little voice. 'I'm irresponsible.'

'And what do irresponsible girls deserve?'

Emma swallowed. The room was full of people. There were bouncers as well, and bar staff, preparing for the late-afternoon opening.

'They deserve to be spanked, ma'am.'

'That's right, they do. I'd say bend over but that skirt's so tight, you'd probably split the seams.'

'It has a lot of stretch in it, ma'am.'

'Does it now? All the same, perhaps you'd better take it off.'

Emma stared, and looked quickly around at the dozen pairs of saucer eyes surrounding her.

'They've all done it,' Allyson reassured her. 'You'd have seen it if you'd got here on time. Quite a sight it was, too.'

Emma put her fingers on her red plastic belt and rested them there for a moment of indecision before unbuckling with determination and dropping it to the floor.

'No, pick it up and give it here,' ordered Allyson, holding out her hand.

Emma handed over the belt, which Allyson stroked absently, watching the unzipping that followed.

The skirt had to be eased slowly and carefully over Emma's hips and down her thighs. Allyson noted with pleasure the triangle of leopard print satin revealed, plus the black suspender straps that held up lace-topped sheer stockings. Thousands of percentage points better than some of the grubby, cotton granny pants she'd seen this afternoon.

'Good,' she said, once Emma had stepped out of the skirt and stood in silk pussy-bow blouse, high heels and underwear. 'Now, turn around.'

She was wearing a thong – she had little option given the tightness of her skirt. Allyson held in a breath, her gaze roving slowly over the twin white globes, not wanting to rush this visual treat. Firm as peaches, round as snooker balls, pale as moons. Oh, what she could do to them!

'Now, Emma, I'm going to ask you to bend over with your hands flat on the stage. Can you do that for me?'

The other twelve girls, sitting on the stage, whispered and rustled, thrilled. Emma was going to get spanked, and she would have to face them while it happened.

Emma obeyed without question.

Allyson, looking at her lowered spine and her thrust-out

buttocks, was excited beyond words. This perfect girl could have walked out or demanded to know if the job was still available. Instead, she had offered herself up, without demur, for a public spanking. She was a dream come true.

'Tell me, Emma,' said Allyson, once the power of speech had returned. 'Have you been spanked before?'

'Yes, ma'am, lots of times.'

Allyson stepped up behind her. Her hands were attracted like magnets to Emma's rump but she kept them clenched at her sides until the time came.

'Who spanks you usually?'

'Boyfriends. Girlfriends. Everyone. Somehow everyone always wants to spank me.'

'Because you're a bad girl?'

'Yes, ma'am.'

'You have boyfriends and girlfriends?'

'Lots of both, ma'am.'

'So you're a bit of a slut, would you say?'

'Everyone says so, ma'am.'

'Fuck me.' Allyson couldn't help herself. She was so swollen and hot with arousal she thought her face must be neon-pink. 'You little whore.' But the words were a caress, and Emma wiggled her bottom as if delighted to hear it.

'Oh, I don't charge,' said Emma. 'I just love fucking.'

'You're going to get it,' said Allyson, and she laid the first smack hard on Emma's right cheek. It wobbled in exactly the way Allyson had expected it to, and it picked up pink traces of her palm straight away.

She spanked hard and put her arm into it, but Emma demonstrated nothing but pleasure, her moans low and throaty, her bottom pushed out to beg for more.

'You need it,' Allyson said as she worked on, watching the

colour grow and deepen. 'You need it every day. I'll have you in my office, bent over the desk, every day before you go out there for the men.'

'Yes,' hissed Emma. 'Yes.'

'Look at her, girls,' grunted Allyson. 'Look at her, taking it in front of everyone. She loves it. She fucking loves it. Don't you?'

'Yes, ma'am, ohhh, yes.'

Allyson carried on until her palm stung and then she finished off with a few smart strokes of the doubled-over plastic belt.

Emma's legs were starting to buckle, but she still hadn't let out a single cry of pain by the time her bottom was bright red in its entirety.

'You're quite something,' panted Allyson. 'Get into my office and stand in the corner. The rest of you, go home. I'll see some of you tomorrow.'

Allyson paused to get her head back together and pour herself a measure of whisky. The barman, she noticed, had an erection.

'Great show,' he commented.

'You can keep your mitts off and all,' she said sharply. 'That girl ain't for the likes of you.'

'She's something special.'

'Yeah. She is.'

Emma was in the corner and had taken the liberty of putting her hands on her head to complete the effect. Her beautiful bottom glowed out into the room like a beacon.

'My lucky thirteen,' said Allyson softly, shutting the door and putting down her glass. 'You ain't easily fazed, are you, sweetheart?'

'No, ma'am.'

'So tell me about yourself.'

'Shall I stay in the corner?'

'No, come out. Come and sit down. If you can.'

Emma's roguish grin combined beautifully with the two spots of colour on her cheeks as she came out of the corner to sit on the opposite side of Allyson's desk.

'Not much to tell,' she said. Allyson noted that she sat down without any trouble at all. She was an old hand at this, it seemed.

'Go on, though. I'm interested.'

'I'm just a pretty ordinary girl from Kilburn. Convent-educated. Not especially clever. Got into drama and theatre at school, made it into RADA, did well there, but the money was a problem. It's just me and mum, see, and she works as a cleaner. I decided to take a more unconventional route. I've been doing burlesque and I've made a few spanking movies over the past year.'

'Who with? I'll have to check them out.'

'Burning Blush.'

'Ah, yeah, I've heard of them. So you want to be a star, do you?'

'I don't care about that. I care about acting.'

'Right. And were you acting, just then?'

Emma held Allyson's eyes.

She knows I want her. She knows she could run rings round me. Careful here, girl. Allyson resisted the nervous desire to light a cigarette. She wanted her breath to be fresh for Emma, when they kissed.

'No,' said Emma. 'I wasn't acting out there.'

'Right. Because, you know, I don't know many girls who would've done that. Even the girls who work here. I don't think many of them would've just gone over to that stage, took off their skirt and bent over in front of everyone, for a total stranger. That's pretty special, Emma. Are you sure you hadn't put yourself in role, inside your head?'

Emma shook her head. 'I don't think so. I do this kind of thing all the time. I'm kinky. I love it. I love an audience too.'

'We must know people in common.'

'D'you know Sofia von Keppel? Severe Sofia, they call her.'

'The pro-domme? Yeah. We're good mates. I can't believe our paths haven't crossed before, Emma.'

She shrugged.

'London's a big place. I've just split with Sofia, as it goes. Amicable. I'm looking for something more exclusive at this time in my life. Fed up with being one of a stable of submissives.'

Of all the spanking clubs in all the world . . .

'Are you gay? Or bi?'

'I'm a bit of everything, Allyson.'

You're a bit of everything I've ever wanted.

Allyson cleared her throat. 'So. I'm just putting this out there, you can take it or leave it . . .' She stopped. How was she going to phrase this? 'First of all, the job's yours. Obviously. I wanted twelve, but, like I said, you're my lucky thirteen.'

'That's great. I love the idea of this place. It was one of your customers that mentioned the ad to me, as it goes. Peregrine Sands?'

'Oh, Mr Sands, yes. He's got an eye for a good performance.'

'He keeps promising he'll have a word with some of his director mates for me, but nothing's come up yet.'

'Well, when the big spanking musical gets written . . .'

They laughed and Allyson's heart surged.

'I don't know him that well,' Emma confessed. 'Just met

him at a fetish party the other week. I got a caning and some career advice. Not bad.'

'It turned me on,' blurted Allyson, no longer able to maintain the brittle chit-chat. 'What I did to you. I'm usually able to detach but you had an effect on me.'

Emma bit her lip and for an agonising moment Allyson thought she was going to get up and leave.

'I thought I ought to be honest with you from the start,' gabbled Allyson, filling the gap. 'I don't want to be like some creepy boss trying to use their power to get you into bed. I don't want to be like that. So I'm telling you upfront. That's all. You don't have to say or do anything about it. But if you ever . . .'

She broke off, desperate for something to do with her hands, opened and shut the drawer, picked up the cigarette packet and then dropped it again.

'It turned me on, too,' said Emma quietly.

'Yeah?'

Allyson slammed the drawer shut for a final time and leant forward.

'Of course. I mean, I'm a sub, aren't I? But there was more to it than that. You're such a natural. And you're – oh God, don't take this the wrong way – but after Sofia, you're a breath of fresh air, because you aren't this polished, icy beauty type of person. You're a little bit rough around the edges. You're real.'

Allyson wasn't sure whether to laugh or cry. *Rough around the edges!* But Emma was right, of course. Allyson would never win any beauty contests, nor was she one for pouring herself into skintight latex. But she had the attitude and she had the imagination and, when it came down to it, that was what mattered.

'Come out for dinner with me,' she said. 'It can lead somewhere or it can lead nowhere. It's up to you. But if you want to give it a go . . .'

'I think I do. Thanks. Is tonight good for you?'

'It'll have to be late.'

'Late's good.'

'Midnight in Chinatown?'

'You romantic, you.'

The midnight rendezvous in Chinatown went well. They laughed so much the other diners constantly looked over at them and then, oh glory, there was footsie under the table, something Allyson had never before experienced.

When Emma went to pour her third glass of wine, Allyson put her hand over the glass and shook her head.

'You're keeping a clear head, my girl,' she said.

'Oh? And what for?'

'What do you think?'

'I can't imagine, ma'am. Why don't you take me outside and tell me there?'

Allyson couldn't pay the bill fast enough.

Outside, on the wet street, she took Emma into a side alley where they kissed, menthol and nicotine and soy sauce and chilli, until the rain drove them to seek shelter.

In Allyson's Soho flat, they spent the night discovering each other, granting pleasure, sometimes pain, using nothing more than their hands and mouths, until the sun came up.

'I'm your bitch, if you want me,' said Emma.

Allyson had never heard anything more romantic.

'I want to own you,' she said. 'I'll rent you to the customers, but at the end of the day you're mine.'

'Oh yes,' said Emma, shutting her eyes in rapture. 'Rent me out. Pimp me. Use me like your whore. I'm yours.'

It seemed too good to be true and, in those early days, Allyson could never quite shake a fear that it was all an act by a girl on the make.

But, no matter what exalted company she bared her bottom for, she always came back to Allyson, and her heart was open to nobody else.

After getting spanked at the club she'd go up to Allyson's flat and put on her harness and wait, sometimes for hours, until her mistress was free.

Then there would be such nights, of strap-ons and dildos, of butt plugs and buzzers, and clamps and paddles, of lubricants and gels, and massage oils and everything. Most of all, their two bodies, working together, complementing each other, and inside them, their two hearts, beating in rhythm.

She loved Emma and she was as sure as she could be that Emma loved her. Sometimes she feared that Peregrine would have that oft-mentioned word with one of his friends and her love would be taken from her and put in an altogether brighter spotlight. But Peregrine either lied about it, or failed to convince the directors, and Emma stayed at the club.

Perhaps, if it weren't for her, Emma would have had her big break.

Perhaps, after all, her love was a selfish one.

And now here they were, parked up outside this tatty service station, contemplating ruin. Allyson knew she would be invited to take the fall for McKenna and the Mr Bigs behind him. She was looking at a good stretch in Holloway, without doubt. And there would be punishment for Emma, too – and not the kind she liked. The kind that would spoil her pretty face and leave her no career alternative but to prostitute herself in one of McKenna's brothels.

'OK, Em,' she said, taking her paper cup of coffee as her lover climbed back into the car. 'This is what's going to happen. I'm going to make a call or two from the payphone up by the services. You're going to take this car, turn it around and go back to the cottage. I'm going to ask Richard if he can help you. They won't come looking for you, you're small fry. Richard can get you a place in a different town, a new name, all of that.'

'What? No. I'm coming with you.'

'No you ain't, sweetheart. Not a chance. I've got to go and face the music, but I'll be all right. I'll be out in a couple of years.'

'Al, don't! We don't even know that it's this!'

'We can't risk it. I can't let you risk it. You've done nothing to deserve trouble. I have.'

'I should have told you.' A tear was in the corner of Emma's eye. Allyson leant over and kissed it away.

'You weren't to know. Now, look, are you going to do as I say?'

'I can't let you . . .'

'Emma.' There was a tense silence, broken only by their hiss as they simultaneously burnt their tongues on the blistering coffee. 'I'm going to call Richard now,' she said. 'On the payphone so they can't trace it. Stay here.'

She couldn't look at Emma's face. She walked to the phone, jingling her purse, with her eyes fixed hard on the telecoms company logo. Stay calm. She had to stay calm.

Richard was trying his best to keep the noise down, but the bed was creaky and the cottage so small that he didn't doubt some of Lucy's little wails and moans were filtering through the walls and doors to where Emma, Blake and Allyson lay beyond.

This was going to be the noisiest part of all. He put his hands on her shoulders from behind and lifted her from her bent angle, removing her mouth from Rob's cock, to his fellow dom's gasped disappointment.

The dismay was to be short-lived, however.

Richard put his hand over Lucy's mouth and spoke softly into her ear.

'Get on him. Get his hard cock inside you.'

He nudged Lucy into the right position, the pair of them straddling Rob's thighs, then he held the back of her neck and watched Rob's thick stalk disappear up inside his lover's tight sheath. What a sight that was to see. Her round bottom cheeks, pink from a session with a suede flogger, pushed out towards Richard, hinting at pleasures to be had.

Lucy's sighs were effectively muffled by his big palm pushed against her face until she was fully impaled and Rob reached up to fondle her breasts, his eyes glazed with lust.

Threesome sex was not, after all, as awkward or uncomfortable as Richard had always assumed it might be. After a few initial misunderstandings, he and Rob had established a partnership, working together to dominate Lucy in the ways she most wanted. It wasn't like having a rival. It was a bit like watching a porn film and participating in it at the same time. He didn't feel threatened by Rob and, although he knew Rob still felt a little threatened by him, the prickliness was fading now.

He took his hand from Lucy's mouth, trusting her to behave herself now, and held her hips firmly while she rode Rob, making sure she didn't slack.

'What do you think of that rule, Rob?' Richard whispered. 'That rule about Emma not being allowed to come? Do you think we should give that a try some time?'

'No,' whimpered Lucy, grinding away.

Rob put his hand between Lucy's thighs and began to rub at her clitoris.

'She'd never make it,' he said. 'She'd fail that test straight away.'

'I think you're right,' said Richard. 'She doesn't realise, does she, that her orgasm doesn't belong to her. It belongs to us. She gets it when we feel she deserves it. Don't you think?'

'Might be fun to try sometime,' gasped Rob, redder in the face now and damper on the brow.

'Maybe not tonight,' conceded Richard. He tightened his hold on her hips. 'Hope you're not too close. You've got a long way to go yet.'

He let go of her then and pushed her spine downwards so that she lay almost flat on Rob's chest, altering the angle at which he was fucking her.

Now Rob had hold of Lucy's hips and Richard was free to lubricate between her bottom cheeks, which had become temptingly available in a rudely displayed invitation.

'Oh God,' gasped Lucy. She knew what was coming.

Richard smiled and pushed his fingers further.

It had become an unspoken competition between himself and Rob: who would get the front door and who the back? Somehow, taking her anally seemed to score more kudos points, though neither had ever discussed it. But they jockeyed for this position every time and the one who lost was always obscurely resentful.

Tonight, I win, thought Richard, mentally totting up the number of times he had been the victor in their double penetration game. He made it four to Rob's three. *Got to keep on top*.

'What's the matter, Lucy?' asked Richard, thrusting two

fingers in and out of her. 'You must have been expecting this. You know perfectly well that when we three get together your arse is going to get filled at some point. Don't you?' He jabbed and she wriggled violently.

'Yes, sir,' she admitted.

'You'd be disappointed if it wasn't. Wouldn't you.'

She made an incoherent sound, perhaps hoping that it would stand in for this humiliating confession.

Richard shook his head. Surely she knew him better than that.

'Wouldn't you?' he repeated, holding his fingers all the way in and twisting them.

'Yes, sir,' she said hurriedly, breathlessly, the words mutating into a moan. Rob must be rubbing up against her g-spot. Richard needed to get inside her before she lost control of herself.

'Still, Lucy,' he commanded.

It was Rob who obeyed the order, though, holding her in place so that Richard could start inserting his long, stiff rod into her compact passage.

Lucy had had this so many times, and yet she never seemed to get used to it. There was always that moment, not quite all the way in, when she insisted it was never going to fit and she couldn't take it. It had almost become ritual and, for Richard, it made this ceremony all the sweeter.

Tonight was no exception.

'Oh God, I can't,' she panted. 'I just can't. Please!'

'You know you can.'

He held her by her round breasts and eased himself all the way up, the tight fit making his head swim with pleasure.

'There,' said Rob. 'I know he's in now. I can feel it, too. You're exactly where you belong now, Luce. Exactly.'

Richard took up the theme. 'This is your place in the world. Between your masters, filled with their cocks. Wherever else you might go, you always know that you aren't where you belong until you're here. It's true, isn't it?'

'Yes, sir.'

'Take a moment to enjoy being in your special place.'

All three of them held their positions. Richard didn't know what the other two were feeling, but he knew that the rest of life was anticlimactic compared to being here, snug in Lucy's rear, held close in her hot clutches.

They began to move very slowly, experimentally, tiny twitches. Richard ground his hips, Rob did likewise. Lucy, on the receiving end of both their efforts, snuffled and whimpered.

They kept up this economy of motion for as long as they could, using their hands and mouths to increase her stimulation, sometimes clashing, two hands on the same breast, both mouths on her neck simultaneously.

Richard would start the thrusting, then Rob would try to complement it, so that as one pushed forward, the other pulled back. This was not easy to achieve or sustain, though, and the rhythm often faltered. Not that it seemed to worry Lucy, who was kicking her feet and pummelling the mattress, so very close to her orgasm now.

'Oh, I'm going to . . . I'm going to . . .'

Richard sped up then and started to make his thrusts big and punishing. Lucy buried her head in Rob's shoulder, jerking between them as if trying to escape, but of course, that was out of the question.

He kept going as she yelped and twisted beneath him. She always came so hard like this, as if her very essence was being ripped from her. Perhaps it was.

Once she was limp and spent, he and Rob moved to their savage endgame. Who would be last to come? Nobody wanted to finish first.

Richard had to concede. It was much easier to hold off in Rob's position – the only drawback of winning his rear occupancy. He held Lucy by the neck and poured himself into her, swearing as he emptied. Then he had to wait for Rob, enjoying the sensation of his softening inside the dark recess, deliberately not looking at his rival's face. He didn't need to see it.

Afterwards, they lay Lucy on her back and held her and kissed her all over. She was always a little faint after these occasions, and in need of reassurance that she was treasured and adored for her permissiveness, and not reviled.

Richard understood that what they did together took her to a dark and secret centre of herself and afterwards she was shatterably vulnerable. He took his time with her, as did Rob, showing her how grateful they both were for the licenses she granted them.

'Thanks for coming,' he said, when she had been kissed and loved back into herself.

'I wasn't sure at first,' she said. 'I'm still not sure I'd want to go as far as Emma goes. But it's so interesting. People do these things so differently, and yet the world calls them all the same thing. Perverts, freaks, kinky weirdoes.'

'The world.' Rob kissed her nipple. 'You know what we think of that.'

'You're my world,' she said seriously. 'The two of you. I don't want to live anywhere else.'

The phone shrilled out downstairs, making all three of them jump.

'What the fuck?' said Rob. 'That's the second time tonight.'

They lay drowsing, listening to Blake's indistinct voice.

'Rich,' he called.

Richard sat up.

'Oh, for God's sake,' he muttered, running a hand through his hair. 'Who is it?' he called.

'Allyson.'

'Allyson? But she's—'

'I heard the door go earlier,' said Lucy. 'But hadn't she been drinking? She can't have driven anywhere. Maybe she went for a midnight walk and got lost?'

Richard grunted his dismissal of these ideas, pulled on his dressing gown and went to the phone.

'Where is she?' he asked Blake, who handed him the receiver.

'Don't know. She only wants to talk to you.'

Blake, bad-tempered at being woken, threw himself back on the camp bed.

'Allyson, what the fuck's going on? We're trying to sleep here.'

'Never mind that. Something's happened and I need your help.'

'What? Where are you?'

'You don't need to know that. I want you to promise me something. It's important. I don't want to blackmail you, but I know and you know . . .'

'Allyson, Jesus! What is this?'

'I want you to promise you'll take care of Emma.'

'Take care of her? Why? Where are you going?'

'Probably to prison. You'll see. But I don't want to talk about that. Promise me.'

'OK, I promise. Take care of her how?'

'You know people. I want you to find a place for her.

Somewhere out of the country. Maybe a new passport, identity, that kind of thing. Get her to safety. Can you do that for me?'

'I don't know. I can try, I suppose.'

'You've got to. It's important. If I can't save Emma, then . . .'

He heard her gasp for breath. Tough-as-old-boots Allyson, the only woman he'd ever been afraid of, was on the verge of tears.

His stomach lurched. Something bad was happening here.

'Please, Richard,' she whispered. 'It's all I care about. Please look after her for me.'

'Of course. I will. Of course.'

'Thanks. You're a mate. I owe you one, OK? She'll be with you soon; she's driving back to the cottage in my car. Try and get her out of the UK as quickly as you can, right?'

'OK. I'll make some calls.'

'See you in a few years then.'

'Al!'

But she'd hung up.

Peregrine Sands was enjoying some late-night drama, but he was nowhere near a theatre.

Instead, Callie Reddish was bound, hand and foot, to an interesting cross-shaped apparatus he'd ordered from a fetish furniture catalogue. It made a splendid addition to his apartment, he decided, especially when an attractive naked woman was lashed to it with leather ties, having her shapely bottom flogged by her other boyfriend. Leo never put quite enough finesse into the operation for Peregrine's tastes. He was enthusiastic, but amateur. Just as he was as an actor.

'No, Leo, you need to hold it differently.'

Peregrine stepped up, took the whip from Leo's hand and demonstrated a grip that facilitated stronger, more compact lashings.

He laid ten such on Callie's reddening rear, enjoying her little mewls of pain.

'Ah, I get you,' said Leo. 'Give us the whip again.'

'Better.' Peregrine watched, stroking his chin, as Leo tried hard to hold back and flog with a little more elegance.

'How much do you think she should get?'

'How much do you want to give?'

'I don't know.'

Peregrine sighed. Leo wasn't his ablest pupil. He tolerated the young man for Callie's sake really: she had this silly fondness for him. She also kept dropping hints that she wanted menage sex, but Peregrine had no wish to share a bed with the fellow.

'Do you want me to finish off?'

Leo handed Peregrine the whip again.

Peregrine thrashed Callie until she was incoherent, then laid a few upward flicks on her pussy, just for an encore.

'If you want to fuck her, Leo, take her to the spare bedroom. The bed's made up. You can call a cab from here once you've finished.'

Peregrine poured himself a brandy and sat down with a book, pretending not to watch Leo release Callie from her bonds and carry her out of the room.

It was hard work, being stylishly heartless, sometimes. Harder work trying to read with moans of ecstasy drifting into your ears. Leo could at least have shut the door. But no. Even that was too daunting a challenge for the great lummox.

The moans of ecstasy mingled with something else after a

while. It took Peregrine a few moments to identify the gentle beeping of his phone.

He looked at the clock. It was after midnight. Usually only lovers called at such times.

Feeling optimistic, even though he would have to postpone whomever it was for Callie, he picked up the call.

Cousin Richard? Odd.

'Sweet coz,' he said, putting the phone to his ear. 'What is amiss?'

'We've got a situation on our hands.'

'Do we indeed? At this time of night the only situation I want on my hands is a brunette one with a firm pair of buttocks.'

'Well, that pretty much describes her, actually.'

'Oh?' Peregrine shifted in his seat, holding the phone closer to his ear. 'Do tell.'

'Emma Frayne from the Geisha Garden.'

'A personal favourite of mine. What about her?'

'Allyson's been busted over something, I'm not sure what, and Emma needs to go into hiding. I can sort out plane tickets, paperwork and all that, but I don't know where to send her. I don't know anyone much overseas. I thought you might.'

'Why on earth? Has the club been raided? Is she going to name names?'

'Al wouldn't do that.'

'There isn't an awful lot Allyson Bruce wouldn't do, Richard,' he said sharply. 'I've known her longer than you have. She's a pragmatist, loyal to her own skin.'

'She loves Emma, genuinely loves her. If you help her, she'll keep your name out of it.'

'Well, there might be something in that. Leave it with me, Richard. I'll make some calls.'

'Thanks. But we'll need an answer by the morning. She can't stay here longer than tonight. We all have to clear out of here as soon as we can.'

'What a marvellous screenplay this would make.'

'Yes, Peregrine. Goodnight.'

'Right.'

Allyson climbed back into the car and looked through the windscreen for a long time, her hands cupped round the cardboard coffee cup, before speaking again.

'Did you call Richard?' asked Emma.

'Yeah. Told him to expect you back. He's going to take care of you.'

'What does that mean? Take care of me?'

Allyson shrugged. 'He's all right, is Rich. He'll think of something. Hey, don't look so . . .'

She put down the coffee, placed a hand on Emma's thigh and squeezed it tight.

'I want to come with you.'

'You can't.'

'When will I see you again?'

'I don't know. One fine day. Somewhere over the rainbow. Oh, love, don't cry.'

'I don't want you to go. Come with me. We can both make a run for it. Thelma and Louise.'

'You're an old romantic, Em, aren't you? No, sweetheart. They won't come after you but they'd come after me. I ain't got nowhere to hide from McKenna, except prison, and I'll take that. Prison's not that bad.'

'You've been there before?'

'Yeah, didn't I ever tell you? Problem child, I was. Spent a lot of my teens in and out of the slammer. Girls don't go as bad as me without a bit of help from their criminal friends. I didn't just wake up one day and think, I know, I'll get involved in organised crime. By the time you realise what you've let yourself in for, you're already in it up to your neck.'

'Is it really too late?'

'Believe me, darling, if I could turn back the clock . . . But there's no use thinking like that. I am what I am. I ain't proud of myself. But I'm proud of you, and of having a girl like you. I know I'm going to prison and the one thing that'll make it bearable for me is if I know you're all right. So be all right, Em. For me.'

'I love you,' she whispered, tears raining from her eyes.

'I know. I love you too.'

The coffee was kicked over in the course of the kiss that followed, soaking the passenger footwell.

When Allyson left the car again, her shoes were wet and squelchy.

'Go,' she said, gesturing violently towards the access road to the motorway.

Emma wound down the window.

'I don't know if I can,' she said desperately.

'Listen, girl.' Allyson leant in at the window and spoke firmly and deliberately. 'Next time I see you – and there will be a next time, and it'll be sooner than you think – I'm going to take your knickers down and give you the spanking of your life. So think about that. Think about it every night, darling. I know I will. Now go, or I'll drag you in the coffee shop and do it right there.'

She stepped back and watched Emma wind the window back up.

The car remained stationary for a few moments more, then the engine revved and Emma reversed out of the parking space. She didn't look back at Allyson again.

Allyson watched the tail lights until they turned the final corner and their glow faded to nothing. Then she returned to the telephone box, looking up McKenna's number on her mobile as she trudged.

Two Years Later

'Have you read it?'

Richard, trying to concentrate on leaving the freeway at the correct exit, didn't reply for a minute or two.

'No, I haven't.'

'So what's it about?'

'I'll give you three guesses.'

'It can't be a porn movie! Are you saying it's got spanking in it?' Lucy almost bounced in her seat.

'It's not a porn movie. At least, he says it's not. He says it's a, what was it, modern and sophisticated take on an age-old fascination.'

'It's a spanking movie.'

'Yeah. I think it is. With a lot of witty dialogue in between and a bittersweet love story and all that but, basically, a spanking movie.'

'Got to hand it to Peregrine,' said Rob reverently, looking up from the sat nav receiver. 'He's the don. Left here, I think, Rich.'

'Wow, oh my God, look, the Hollywood sign!'

Lucy was beside herself with excitement now. As if she hadn't been Tiggerish enough for the last twelve hours. Both Richard and Rob had had to warn her repeatedly to let them read their book or watch their in-flight movie in peace. While Richard waited at the baggage carousel, Rob had taken her into a disabled lavatory and given her half a minute's worth of disciplinary attention with her knickers down and hands on the seat.

People milling outside had almost certainly heard them, but that just made Lucy feel smug, watching the suitcases ride by, knowing that the whispers opposite were about her and her bottom.

'Which studio did you say it was, Richard?'

'Maximo.'

'OK, that one is two blocks up and . . . I'm not sure if that's a one way street . . . No, I think it's fine.'

'Oh my God, look, that's where they film *Jimmy, Jo & Co.* The outside of the coffee shop, I mean!'

Lucy's shriek was the last straw for Richard, already nervous at driving this enormous car along these unfamiliar street layouts.

'As soon as we get to the car park . . .' he said.

'Parking lot, it's called a parking lot here, that's what they call a car park.'

'And here it is,' said Rob, pointing ahead.

They were waved through by security after spending some time establishing their names, and the legitimacy of their guest status, and Richard found a spot as close to the studio buildings as he could get.

As soon as the engine was off, the two men turned to look at the woman in the back seat.

She was already diving for the door, but was puzzled by its failure to open.

'Child lock,' said Richard grimly. 'Since you're behaving like one.'

That got her attention.

She drew in a quick breath and looked from one man to the other.

'What?'

'You've already had one warning,' said Rob. 'At the airport. You knew Richard needed to concentrate on his driving, and I had to keep my mind on the sat nav.'

'GPS, they call it here . . .' Her voice trailed off. 'I'm just excited,' she pleaded.

'You know what we put in our hand luggage just in case,' said Richard.

'Oh, I haven't been that bad.'

'I don't know. What do you think, Rob?'

'I think, regrettably, none of our warnings have been heeded, so . . .'

'I think I agree.'

'Not here!' Lucy looked out of the windows, craning her neck for signs of other humans whose presence might save her. The lot was deserted.

'Why not? Nobody can see. Get into position, now.'

Richard brooked no argument and Lucy, with a huff and clenching of her fists, turned around so that she was kneeling on the floor with her stomach resting on the leather back seat.

'Cheek each, Rob?'

'Don't mind if I do.'

'Bare bottom, please, Lucy.'

The spanking was no more than a quick flurry, Richard smacking at one cheek while Rob took the other, and it stopped after a minute or so. Lucy's bottom was already satisfactorily scarlet.

'Now then,' said Rob, unbuckling his canvas satchel and removing a couple of items from it. 'Hold your cheeks apart, Luce.'

'Oh, must I?'

'You asked for it.' He coated the large butt plug in a layer of some kind of embrocation, applicable by a twist-up stick. It smelled piney and sinus-clearing and Lucy would know exactly what effect to expect: her little whimper of dismay signalled as much.

Rob made no concessions to Lucy's fuss and pushed the plug quickly and firmly into its target, twisting it into position and patting her rear once it was seated.

He smiled at Richard and together they waited for the first moans of discomfort.

'It burns,' she whined, as if this experience was new to her, which it was not, by any means.

'That's the idea,' said Rob lightly. 'Now perhaps we can expect some better behaviour from you, hmm?'

'I can't go in there wearing this.'

'Of course you can,' soothed Richard. 'Nobody will see it. Unless you want to keep your knickers and skirt pulled down like that.'

She reached around and hurriedly pulled her panties tight over her plugged bottom, following with the skirt that she now considered much too short. She should have worn trousers, damn it. But then perhaps people would be able to see the little flange of the plug making an impression in the fabric. Maybe it was best this way.

It was awkward to walk with such a large presence in her behind and she had a slightly bow-legged gait as she allowed herself to be borne along between Richard and Rob, on one arm of each. Plus the coating stung and burned to buggery and made her want to squirm, and clench, and unclench all at once.

The worst side-effect of all still hadn't come into full effect, though. But it would. Before too long, her knickers would be soaking wet with her own juices and she would be desperate for a good, hard ride.

And how likely was that, in the middle of a big film studio set?

They showed their day passes to the security guard, walked into a huge hangar, and wandered around for a while until they stumbled upon the centre of activities.

'Look,' said Lucy, although in a much subdued tone. 'There's Peregrine.'

And so he was, immaculate as ever in the finest tailoring, modified for the California heat, deep in conference with a bearded guy in a baseball cap.

'He's the director,' said Richard. 'He did *Zombie Dawn*.'

'Oh, I loved that,' said Lucy, clamping her thighs together. The heat had made its inevitable way between them.

'Did you? Load of crap,' sniffed Rob.

'Don't say that to him,' cautioned Richard.

'Of course I won't.'

Peregrine looked up and saw them. There was no enthusiastic wave or hastening up to greet them, but he nodded and gave a slightly imperious toss of his head, beckoning them over.

Lucy felt every eye on her, from the leading actors to the best boy grip, and burned with shame, sure that each one of them knew she was plugged and gagging for sex. Richard and Rob strode confidently, making her speed up to an uncomfortable pace so that she shuffled along with tiny, fast steps.

'Richard,' proclaimed Peregrine. 'How wonderful to see you. And Robert, of course. And not forgetting Lucy. I hope you've been behaving yourself, young lady.'

His stern expression made her squirm all the more. He knew. He had to know.

'Fat chance,' laughed Richard.

'I hope you're keeping her well in hand.'

'Oh yes.' Richard smiled rakishly, causing Peregrine to unbend too.

'So this is Hollywood,' he said. 'And you're welcome to it.'

'Aren't you enjoying it?'

'No. Can't smoke a fucking cigarette anywhere. But apart from that, I suppose it's not the worst place.'

'Not the worst place?' Rob was bemused. 'You've fallen on your feet.'

'Into a septic tank, dear boy. Anyway, it's marvellous to see you all. We've just one more scene to shoot, then we can go back to my hacienda. Do find yourselves a seat. Must dash: something I need to tell our esteemed director.'

Lucy found a vacant chair against the back wall and lowered herself painstakingly into it, grateful that Peregrine wasn't witness. He would certainly guess immediately what was afoot. Richard and Rob watched avidly enough, though, the gits.

She fidgeted and fought to keep her breath from erupting into gasps for the next ten minutes while her lovers sat on either side of her, each holding one of her hands.

'Where's Miss Britt's PA?' someone shouted, causing Lucy to look over in the direction of the query.

Celia Britt, as glacially beautiful in the flesh as on film, was having her face powdered and her lipstick reapplied at the side of the set.

'Mimi?' bellowed the questioner again.

'Oh, there she is!' Lucy exclaimed, seeing Emma flit across the studio towards the star of the show.

She entered into an urgent-looking conversation with Celia before nodding her head and running back the other way.

'Emma!' called out Lucy, wanting to take back her mistake straight away.

'For fuck's sake,' growled Richard, while Rob tutted loudly.

But Emma had heard her and looked over, pale as milk and haunted of eye, until she saw who had called her.

'Sorry,' muttered Lucy, squirming violently. The menthol coating of the plug was moving into its most diabolical phase.

'You will be,' said Rob, then he stood and held out a hand to Emma.

'Please don't call me that,' she said, hurrying over.

'I'm so sorry,' said Lucy, almost in tears now – partly from the thought of having to get up and then sit down again, if she was honest with herself.

'She'll be punished for it, don't worry,' said Richard, standing himself and folding the former Geisha Girl into a heartfelt embrace. 'It's great to see you, love.'

'And you,' said Emma. 'Really great.'

'I hope Peregrine and Celia have been looking after you.'

'Oh yes. Celia's been wonderful. And Peregrine's been Peregrine.'

'As you'd expect,' chuckled Richard. 'I've got a note for you, from Allyson.'

He took an envelope from his breast pocket and passed it into Emma's hand.

She stepped out of his arms and turned her back to read the message.

Lucy noticed how her elbows shook and jerked around, her shoulder blades severely knitted.

'Thanks,' said Emma, turning back. 'Thanks so much. So she thinks she might be up for parole, next year. That'll change the whole scene again. She can't come here, can she?'

'Love will find a way,' said Richard.

~~Emma smiled away the anxious frown.~~

'Yeah,' she said. 'Oh, right, they're shooting the final scene on the sheet now. Should be ready to pack up very soon.'

The group hushed and watched as Celia Britt walked into the set. She was wearing a very sexy nipped-in and flared-out fifties-style skirt suit with sky-high heels and the set was an office, with a well-known actor sitting behind the desk.

They couldn't hear the dialogue very well from where they sat, but they were well positioned to watch Celia bend herself over the desk while the actor walked around to her rear.

His hand fell, over and over, on the tight seat of her skirt.

Lucy kept expecting the director to call 'cut' – especially when Celia began to utter some rather genuine-sounding yelps – but he didn't.

'Celia and Tack are together in real life,' whispered Emma. 'It makes the chemistry really hot in their scenes.'

Lucy didn't doubt it. This was doing absolutely nothing to stem the flow in her panties. That was what they called them here. Panties.

She crossed her legs, shifting that damnable plug into an even more uncomfortable position, but at least the coating was starting to wear off now.

All the same, if she didn't get to come very, very soon, she was going to go crazy.

She nudged Rob.

'Will you take me to the bathroom?' she whispered.

'Bathroom?'

'That's what they call it here. The bathroom. Weird, because there's no bath in it, but . . .'

'I know that. Why do you want me to take . . . oO. Come on then.'

Richard didn't look as if he approved, but Lucy was past caring. She was already due a punishment – he could do his worst.

In a stall of the really rather splendid Ladies' – pink marble fittings, with a tray of selected perfumes by the door – Lucy lifted her skirt and let Rob lift her, until she was wedged between him and the wall.

The sex was necessarily fast and frantic, but Lucy felt a bone-deep relief with each hard thrust Rob made inside her.

She felt him nudge the plug every time he plunged in, and the sinful sensation of double penetration sent her quickly and giddily to the brink of orgasm.

Which was where Rob particularly liked to keep her.

He stopped moving and stood, pinning her tight, quite still.

'Noooo,' she moaned, thrashing about against him.

'Not yet,' he whispered. 'Naughty girl.'

'Please let me come. Please.'

'Patience.' His hands, which were holding her at the meeting of buttock and thigh, pulled her bottom cheeks wider. She had to clench on to the plug, suddenly fearing that it might fly out. Not that that was likely to happen. The reminder of its presence made her feel small and humble and utterly submissive.

She knew this was what Rob was waiting for, and she prepared herself for the resumption of the engagement.

'Now you can come,' he said.

He drove into her hard and she needed little more of this treatment before she was seeing stars.

Satisfied, a little bruised and dripping with something other than her own juices now, Lucy put her panties back on and spritzed herself with a heady Versace scent before kissing Rob deeply and returning to the set.

Emma and Richard, both perfectly aware of what had just been done to her, gave her knowing looks. Emma's eyes widened when she noticed the difficulty Lucy had in sitting back down.

'You're wearing a plug,' she accused.

'She is,' confirmed Richard.

'You lucky cow,' said Emma wistfully. 'Is it a punishment?'

'Yes.' Richard again.

Lucy both loved and hated how he never spared her an iota of shame or humiliation.

'Aren't you seeing anyone? You know, here?' she asked.

'Nothing serious. I don't like to get involved. Peregrine's been scratching the itch since he arrived, but that's just a friendship, as you know.' She sighed. 'I do miss having someone who wants *my* submission, rather than just *some* submission.'

The director called 'Cut' and Celia, who by now was out of her pencil skirt and jacket with Tack between her thighs pretending to fuck her, stood up and said, 'If my bum looks big in that shot I won't be happy.'

'It looks great, Celia, real cute and petite,' Tack assured her.

But she was already off set, picking up her bag and marching towards the dressing rooms.

Peregrine drifted over, linen jacket slung over his shoulder.

'That's it for today. We'll just wait for Tack and Celia and then I'll lead the way to my not-so-humble abode.'

Peregrine was right about his abode being not-so-humble.

As Richard, Lucy and Rob followed his car up the driveway, each one exclaimed at the perfect setting and the giant swimming pool.

'Pool party!' cried Lucy.

'I think she's getting overexcited again,' said Rob, and she calmed herself instantly.

By the time they'd parked in the carport and transferred their luggage to their guest room, the others were outside by the pool, enjoying cocktails.

A bikini-clad Emma was in the water, doing laps with Tack, while Celia and Peregrine lounged on recliners, chatting about the movie.

Lucy, still plugged and feeling messy, sweaty and sex-stained in her little skater skirt and poplin top, was almost too embarrassed to join them.

Richard and Rob bore her on, though, bringing her to stand in front of Peregrine while they took the two spare recliners.

'Cocktail, gentlemen? What's your poison?'

Lucy, ignored for the moment while Peregrine pottered over to his mobile cabinet, could do nothing more than stand there, feeling the languid gaze of Celia upon her.

'Long time no see, Richard,' she said.

'Too long,' he replied. 'You're looking great, as ever.'

Lucy pressed her lips together, trying to bite back a stab of jealousy. It was in the past. Richard was with her now. He'd said so dozens of times. And Celia had Tack, the *Hot Property* magazine's Stud of the Year.

It was all good, she said to herself, all good.

'Aren't you coming in?' Tack shouted.

'Can't risk sunburn, darling.'

'Jeez, Ceel, you're smothered in factor three thousand there. C'mon. Give that butt a workout.'

Celia sighed, shrugged off her kaftan and walked to the pool.

Lucy was fascinated to observe a few tiny pinprick bruises

at the exposed edge of her buttocks – Celia Britt had been recently spanked. Paddled, most likely. She recognised the effects. There was no make-up required for her onscreen spanking.

She made a move for the vacated sunlounger, but Richard held up his hand.

'No,' he said, and it was all he had to say.

She sighed with exasperation and tossed her hair, but she obeyed all the same.

Only when Peregrine had returned, with bespoke cocktails for her two lovers, was she permitted the luxury of notice.

'Well, young lady,' said Peregrine, reclining once more and putting out his cigarette. 'You're looking rather sheepish. Do I gather that there has been some misbehaviour?'

'She was driving us mad on the plane,' said Rob. 'Wouldn't give us a moment's peace.'

'Hm, not ideal on a twelve-hour flight,' said Peregrine. 'But I think there's been some recent punishment, unless I'm very much mistaken and no longer recognise the walk of the plugged.'

'You're quite right,' said Richard, enjoying Lucy's florid embarrassment. 'In fact, I think it's time that was removed.'

He sat up and patted his thigh.

Lucy knew this might happen. They had discussed the idea of her first public scene taking place in the US, where she would benefit from the safety of her relative anonymity. The moment seemed to have come awfully soon, though.

She glanced over at the pool. The three swimmers were happily oblivious.

Peregrine's broad smile, on the other hand, made her terribly nervous. But Richard was still patting his thigh and wouldn't stand for hesitation.

She draped herself over his lap, directing her eyes to the ground. At least she didn't have to watch him watching her . . .

Richard made a meal of raising her skirt and lowering her knickers, drawing Peregrine's interested attention to the semen stain on the gusset.

'Filthy little minx,' murmured Peregrine. 'I can imagine she needs plenty of correction.'

'Plenty,' said Richard, resting his fingertips lightly against her vulva for a moment before tracing the path to the plug.

This was always a stomach-churning moment, but Richard was especially cruel today, taking his time, tugging it little by little instead of his usual swift, eyewatering but clean motion.

Her muscles rebelled, wanting to cling to the dratted thing. She moaned with discomfort and the gentlemen laughed.

'It had a heated rub stuff on it,' said Rob. 'Warmed her up, I think. Always makes her madly horny too. That's why she was so desperate for a jump on set.'

'I must get some of that. A kind of joint or muscle rub, is it?'

'Yeah.'

'I daresay Emma would enjoy it. We've been exploring the pleasures of figging recently. Do you ever fig Lucy?'

'All the time,' said Richard.

Finally, it was out. Ah, the relief.

But the relief didn't last long.

'Where shall I?' Richard held up the removed plug.

'Oh, I'll call the maid. Consuela!'

Lucy lay, bare bottom up, face on fire, as Peregrine's maid approached the scene.

'Put that in some soapy water, would you? It's been in this bad girl's bottom, so I wouldn't touch anything other than the handle. Thank you so much.'

The maid said nothing, not even a yes or no. She must be familiar with this kind of thing, Lucy supposed, but all the same . . .

Richard's hand travelled all over her back and shoulder blades, then lowered her skirt so that it covered her bottom once more.

He bent to speak into her ear.

'Are you OK?'

'Think so,' she said, not really knowing the answer.

'Let's go to our room, shall we?'

'Don't you want to—'

'There's plenty of time, Luce. We've got two weeks. Let's not gallop into anything you aren't ready for.'

In their room, with its panoramic view of the hills and its ensuite magnificence, Lucy reflected, not for the first time, how lucky she was to have two doms who so perfectly understood her limits. They knew the difference between a clench of aroused dread and a clench of genuine fear, meekness born of joyful submission, or tension. It was a gift she had no intention of relinquishing, ever.

Lying between Richard and Rob, kissing one then the other while they stroked and massaged every inch of her, she felt the impossibility of ever giving either of them up.

Outside, Tack had chased Celia to the edge of the pool, over the side of which she was now bent, with her bikini bottoms pulled to her knees.

She shrieked and flipped from side to side as Tack smacked at her wet bottom, sending fine spray up into the air with each stroke.

'Think what you got on set was a real spanking, huh? Think again,' he said. 'You're getting it good now.'

Peregrine watched with a distant smile, sipping intermittently from his cocktail. Emma came out of the pool and joined him on the neighbouring sunlounger, observing proceedings just as keenly.

'Do you ever get jealous?' she asked him.

'Jealous? Why?'

'All these lovebirds all around. Celia and Tack. Richard and his menage. What happened to Callie?'

'She and Leo decided they wanted to be exclusive. It's part of the reason I'm here. Didn't want to bump into her every three minutes. You know how small a world the London theatre is.'

'Well, only from the point of view of a person who failed lots of auditions.'

'I thought you'd make it one day, you know.'

'Thanks. I know. So did I.'

She sighed.

'And now, here you are in Hollywood, the perfect place to make a name for yourself, and you can't even try.'

'I've thought about it. Thought about risking it. But it's not safe. Not with McKenna and his crew still at large.'

'It's a tragedy, Emma. Someone should write it.'

'Maybe you could.'

'Maybe I will. It's not a bad idea, actually. How Emma Frayne's beautiful bottom ruined her prospects.'

Tack had now removed Celia's bikini completely and was thrusting into her with a wet slap-slap-slap no less noisy than the spanking.

Emma laughed.

'I think there's more to the story than my arse.'

'I find it quite hard to see past it, personally.'

'Yeah, well, you're a pervert.'

'Guilty. Speaking of perverts, what did Allyson have to say?'

'Allyson.'

Emma looked shocked for a moment, and pale beneath her compulsory LA golden sheen.

'Yes,' persisted Peregrine. 'She sent you a note. I saw Richard give it to you.'

Emma reached over to her beach bag and fished out the folded paper. She handed it to Peregrine without a word.

He read it swiftly, then handed it back.

'She loves you,' he said, lighting a cigarette.

'I know.'

'Do you still love her?'

'I do. I lose sight of it sometimes and think I'm over her, but then something happens, like this, and I know she'd only have to crook her finger. But how can we be together, Peregrine? I'm here now. She won't be able to leave the UK when she gets out, and I don't really want to go back, not now.'

He took a long drag, his eyes still fixed on the rutting couple on the poolside.

'Love finds a way,' he said. 'But there's no need to worry about it now. It's still at least a year off. And didn't she say she hoped I was taking care of you? You know what she means by that.'

'She knows me too well to expect me to live like a nun.'

'She loves you too much.'

'Don't you think it's weird, though, Perry?'

'Don't call me that,' he almost spat.

'Sorry. I mean, that she's fine with us being kinky together. She must trust us a lot.'

'She trusts you. She knows me. She knows I'll never settle down. I suppose I'm the safest option. If she doesn't let you get spanked and the rest by me, you might find someone else, and then that dangerous thing could happen. Love.'

'You'd never fall in love with me, I suppose?'

'I'd never fall in love.'

'You must have done, once.'

'Once was enough.'

He looked away sharply, as if fascinated by the diminishing contents of his glass.

'I'm sorry for you.'

'Don't be. Be sorry for yourself. I'm going to cane you for calling me Perry. Go and stand in the corner of the living room and wait for me there.'

'That's not fair!'

'I know. But it'll take your mind off things, won't it?'

'And yours.'

'Perhaps. Go on, then.'

He sent her on her way with a cracking smack to her rear, loud enough to interrupt Tack in his enthusiastic fucking and make him stare, astonished, towards them.

'Carry on,' said Peregrine with a wave of his hand, and he did.

Love was a strange thing.

This thought occurred to Poppy, standing on the balcony of her Parisian apartment – the one that obstinately refused to look over the Eiffel Tower or the Seine or anything picturesque or charming. Even when it wasn't what you thought it might be, it was the best thing imaginable.

For Peregrine, it was too complex and too dangerous to allow. Its theatrical representation was as close as he wanted to get.

For Emma, it meant this half-life, this standing in a corner waiting to be thrashed by a man she liked but didn't love. Doing it for *her*, making him her avatar.

For Richard, Rob and Lucy it meant happiness, no more, no less.

And for Allyson, in her cell, it was pure torture and yet it was the only thing to get her through the indifferent food, and the boredom, and the endless bickering and jockeying for position and the loneliness, the godawful loneliness. Somewhere at the end of it all was love, and it had to be enough. It just had to be.

Acknowledgements

I have many people to thank for their hard work and support in the writing of this book. First of all, Gillian, Emily, Hannah and all of the team at Black Lace, plus the imprint itself for being decent enough to rise from its ashes. Many thanks also to all of the wonderful Black Lace authors who have offered advice and inspiration – particular thanks must go to Charlotte Stein and Portia Da Costa, but there are many others who have earned gratitude simply by writing the books that spurred me into action in the first place. Finally, all the friends and family who might not want to be named in an erotic book, but who know who they are.